AF066223

DEGRADE

Also by Mark Lingane

Para-Noir-mal Detectives
Beyond Belief
Sucker
Das Metro

Tesla Evolution
(MG/YA Science Fiction)
Tesla
Decay
Faraday
Fusion

Tesla Expansion
Degrade

Hadron Damnation
(Science Fiction)
Fault/lines
Blink
Fa//en

Short Stories
NT-5
The Second Story Girl
Floored
The Rose, the Night, and the Mirror
Note to Self
Of Ghosts and Broken Promises

Available in paperback and ebook formats

TESLA EXPANSION, BOOK 1

DEGRADE

MARK LINGANE

Degrade
Mark Lingane

Copyright © Mark Lingane 2019
First published in Australia by Insync Holdings Pty Ltd
PO Box 526, The Gap, Queensland, Australia 4061
ABN: 74 087 648 600

The right of Mark Lingane to be identified as the Author of the Work has been asserted in accordance with the Copyright, Designs and Patents Act 1988.

This book is a work of fiction. Any similarities to actual persons, living or dead, is purely coincidental, although you may want to check out the Tesla Evolution. This edition is also written in English (Australian).

All rights reserved. No part of this publication may be reproduced, stored in a retrieval system, or transmitted in any form or by any means, electronic, mechanical, photocopying, recording or otherwise, without the prior written permission of the publisher. Some paragraphs of this work use information gathered from Wikipedia under the Creative Commons Deed.

Book cover design by Insync Books
Content set in Garamond.
Cover image by Grandfailure

Cataloguing-in-Publication (CiP) entry:
A catalogue record for this book is available from the
National Library of Australia.

to the dreamers

In Praise of Degrade:

The prose in Lingane's often claustrophobic novel is tightly woven, highly descriptive, and evocative ... the author excels at crafting a vivid sense of atmosphere with characters (both human and creaturely), esoteric enough to linger in the minds of readers.
                                            - *The BookLife Prize in Fiction*

Inyerface, banging action.
... there's much more to enjoy about Degrade. The first is the world it envisages - post apocalyptic, dry, stark, violent. It's realised with harsh and evocative prose on a desolate landscape. And the attention to detail is wonderful, from the huge mechanised cities through the desert monsters to the cyborgs and the strange, stuttering variety of English they speak.

And there's the large cast of characters, all lively and vivid and three dimensional. I found myself drawn most to Arid, the boy with a good heart and a lingo all his own, who finds himself in the middle of an intricate - and violent - chess match but whose good sense and ability to self reflect sees him through. Then there's the intricate plotting - no straightforward goodies and baddies in this book, and the fearless mixing of styles from dystopian to speculative to steampunk, and the unflinching battle scenes, and the wonderful chases and the odd moment of profundity punctuating them all. 4 stars.
                                                              - *theBookBag*

The descriptive passages are rich and visceral ... and the prose is tightly polished.

Blending elements of sci-fi and fantasy with dystopian horror and suspense, Mark Lingane has struck upon something special with Degrade, which bodes well for the rest of this riveting new saga. 4 stars.
                                                                    - *SPR*

[PART 1]

[1]

QUEEN BEA SHIELDED her eyes against the unrelenting sun, clasping a wrench in her oil-stained hand. From the observation deck atop the command station between the enormous venting stacks, she watched the outlines of the distant rigs circling in their individual skirmishes. Outright war on the western plains, when it finally came, would be short and violent. A cacophony of unstructured savagery. Their only chance of avoiding a bloodbath lay with the council meeting in a week.

In defiance of her position and the unwritten rig-leader grooming rules, her black-and-grey hair was a tangled nest piled on top of her head. She existed in a mechanic's overalls, with her face often painted with sweat lines trickling soot down her face. The striped pattern had the effect of placing her face behind bars or, from her point of view, everyone she saw in a cage.

She'd never worried about survival in her youth. The rig, Lady Moonshine, was the biggest megaRig out on the west coast; twenty-five towering metres of rust-coloured steel and fire that no one dared challenge. Once, trade had been good. Times had been good. The Moonshine mined and processed an unmatched amount of ore, allowing it the luxury of a static location. Everyone came to the Lady Moonshine, and thriving communities assembled around its base. Until the flood came and washed them away. A hundred thousand people dead in five minutes. With a population already decimated in the Reckoning a thousand years before, it was a loss the region couldn't take.

The Moonshine had survived because its gas-exploration drill secured it to the rock. Everything else had been lost. Trade dried up, and the mad-genius engineers modified the rig to be mobile, with towering tank tracks to drag it around the countryside. Life used to be about the ore and trade; now it centred on survival, both political and physical.

The territories reigned by selfish and frightened family heads formed mechGang alliances, shifting and breaking as quickly as the sands when opportunity and greed shook hands. Nothing was forever out west. Moving the Moonshine became a necessity, although it dug at every fibre of the queen's predilection of strength through stability. Up close, the rig's mammoth size generally dwarfed and discouraged attackers, and although robust, it reacted slowly in the occasional skirmish, resulting in dents and metal scars. Lady Moonshine was built for production at the rate of a crawl.

Then something new changed the world. A quantum happened. Dread crawled out from the east on little more than whispers, and terrified the smaller rigs into treaties, which integrated to form mechCities. In their newfound conjunction, might made them ruthless. The mechCities' crews and general population numbered in the high hundreds, outstripping the three hundred-odd in the Moonshine, with rumours of one rig, the Hawkesbury, carrying thousands and being able to self-repair with the excess steel it produced.

But life moved on, and combat was today's reality. The Moonshine had new features that set it apart from the other rigs. With the uncertainty of living where the rivers ran dry, Bea had confidence they'd outlast all the others.

Except ...

There was news that someone was attempting to initiate the Omen. It was a horrific weapon. Bea would know; she'd ordered it to be built. But the Geigers, the mad scientists and friends who had designed it, became turncoats and ran away with the instructions after they finished fabrication. Because of who she became, on reflection Bea considered the abandonment had been a Good Thing. The world was a safer place. Everyone had recognised the significance of the Good Thing and memorialised it in law: Peace Alliance Declaration 157, or PAD-157 for short, and added several other clauses about how to respect one another. Everyone hated it. It was going to be Bea's challenge and responsibility to bring the heads together, settle their differences, remind them of the PAD, and form an alliance. Easy, if she had about ten years. It was a pity she only had a week.

The air hung heavy, drenched in humidity and soaking up every sound. The eeriness reminded her of the quiet morning prior to the tsunami; an ominous feeling of danger pervaded the light mist and put everyone on edge. Hence the threat of impending war. It hardly seemed worth the sacrifice for what amounted to little more than epic expanses of wasteland.

In front of her, an ancient CAT-MD6310 rotated on the spot and sounded its attack sirens to challenge for the territory. Deep below the other rig was an enormous aquifer; the winner would gain the lease entitlement and drilling rights.

The two rigs turned to face each other for a megaRig confrontation, dirt thrown wide as the caterpillar tracks tore at the dry ground, bringing the opponent's name into view: DESTROYER. The central drill lifted and prepared for a spear attack on the Lady Moonshine. Bea counted half a dozen drillers operating the primary weapon—more than usual, and a drill bigger than expected. The suspended habitats pocked the subframe, allowing fifty to a hundred to live on the rig. Bea shook her head. The other rig's commander was irresponsible, leaving so many unprotected. The confrontation was pointless, and a lot of people were going to die. Only one rig would walk away.

The Moonshine was powerful, but the spindly Destroyer moved quickly. Would this be her final fight? It was the question she asked herself before every confrontation. Bea's eyes darted to the right. A dust storm approached; it was still miles away but they moved quickly these days, and dangerous things lived inside them.

She reached for her communications tube and threw a marble into the opening. The rattling echoed for several seconds, haunting in its solitude, before she heard the cursed response from the command deck.

'Control, prepare for battle.'

The storage tanks released a steady flow of gas over the igniters, producing an intense billowing flame. A pall of black smoke was ejected from the nozzles and drifted toward the other rig.

The Moonshine's feed conveyors, positioned on either side of the drills and rock cracker, twisted up and over the caterpillar tracks, whipping the battered scoops around the conveyor on rattling chains. The noise became deafening, forcing Bea to turn her head to lessen the brutality.

The Destroyer burst through the black cloud and speared its massive drill at the heart of the Moonshine. As the rigs collided, the Moonshine's scoops smashed into the frame of the Destroyer and gouged deep tracks in the fading yellow metal. Sparks fountained as they ground together.

The air filled with the intense screaming of tearing metal, combined with the roar of the engines, blocking out all other sounds.

The rock cracker speared out, but Control misjudged the angle and it buried itself in the ground, missing the Destroyer by metres. The retractor pulled back, but the cracker remained fastened, anchoring the Moonshine in place.

The enemy moved in; its prey was now unable to escape. The other rig's stabilisers locked down into the ground and its drill bit tore into the Moonshine's red facia. Rope bridges were launched between the two, and soldiers from the Destroyer streamed across, searching for entry points. The drill ripped an opening in the

Moonshine's protective plate steel and drove toward the engine's water supply. The soldiers forced their way through and jumped at the Moonshine's defenders. They clashed, using a combination of power tools and shields. Blades slashed into skin and blood sprayed out over the walls.

One of the Moonshine's crew, a huge bare-chested man hefted a heavy-duty power saw and rammed it against the Destroyer's spinning drill bit. The saw blade shattered, shearing off into the surrounding metal. Steam billowed out from the incisions, searing invaders and defenders alike.

Queen Bea watched the altercation unfold below and counted the number of attackers. There were enough on board. She grabbed the tube and shouted, 'Fire!'

Projectile Division One released the harpoon. The tip caught fire as it launched through the Moonshine's roaring furnaces and sailed across the gap, leaving a trail of dark smoke in the air. It pierced the enemy rig's subframe and sliced into its pressurised fuel chamber. The gas erupted, rocking the Destroyer to the right. The subframe buckled, sagging the rig to the side, twisting in on itself. The escaping gas shrieked out from the punctured chamber, the flames boiling into an intense fireball that consumed the rig. People were jumping free, some not surviving the fall. A fire defence team crawled over the subframe, spraying foam and carbon dioxide to restrict the burn.

A siren boomed out from the Destroyer's command deck and the rig wrenched itself free, tearing away part of its body in the process. It toppled to one side, catching its balance as a stabiliser stabbed into the sand. The rig's caterpillar tracks bit into the sand, and the Destroyer limped away as fast as its charred and shaking remains could tolerate.

The command tube whistled. Bea picked up the receiver and listened, then glanced over at the retreating rig.

'Stab it in the heart and burn it to the ground,' she replied.

Arid Geiger pumped the lever fastened to the floor, and the drill bit plunged into the ground. His head smacked against the cockpit wall as the dowser kicked to the side. After so many years, he still struggled to judge the first bite. Or maybe the ground was becoming harder, drying out after the endless summers. The groundwater table was certainly dropping. The sound of the drill resonated through the metal as it bore downward, occasionally slowing as it hit harder rock. He sunk the rig's long legs into the soil and locked it into position.

For the first time in five years—forced by a necessity to survive—on the anniversary he wasn't laying a wreath for his parents. It didn't put him in the best of moods.

Scanning the area, he didn't have a great feeling about the site; not dread, but doubt over its viability as a deep aquifer. The colours and the lay of the land didn't add up. The information from Revvy had been questionable, and Arid's instincts also said otherwise. Revvy had been less than reliable over the previous months, being short with him on most issues. Maybe he should have gone to her stupid Bachelor and Spinsters Ball. Her new favourite band, No Bearing, had travelled from over east, gotten special dispensation to come over at the Belt, which should have been enough of a warning. Never trust anyone from over east. Maybe he shouldn't have let her kiss him.

Arid also harboured a kernel of jealousy. She had a clan, a bunch of Moonshine escapees headed up by a guy called Cameron, who was building up a reputation in the off-grid communities. The "clan" allowed Revvy the luxury of an education of sorts, although she seemed to hate it and lamented loudly how excruciatingly boring it was. Here he was, every day, having to work to survive in an antiquated hand-me-down with intermittent air conditioning, living by his wits—a lone warrior carving out a dangerous and exciting existence. Living the dream. And Arid hated it.

The dowser had belonged to his parents, inherited after their demise. He had spent what he could recall of his life in this rig;

it was all he had known. There was so much he didn't know about his parents. The memories relied on smiles and silly hand games.

Five years. He wasn't even a teenager when it had happened. Even then he'd had a feeling the sand wasn't safe, something about the colours, a tingling in his hands. When they'd jumped down from the rig, the ground rose and swelled as the stick crawler swarm drowned them in a whirlpool of flashing talons. The screams still rang in his ears.

But that was drilling: it was a risk. The continual beats as the bore dug through the rock attracted the crawlers. If they were near, they were going to find you. A trace of water and it was inevitable. He still questioned why his parents had stopped at such a bad spot, as though they were given bad information, had been set up.

The rig was devoid of memories. The only other item left to him from his parents was a small grey rectangular pendant covered in thin black lines. It had two red lights on either end that flashed when he touched them simultaneously. It had no use or value except sentimentality.

The dowser's cabin shook as the drill cranked into the rock and came to a juddering halt. The pillow from his bed, positioned under the roof, slipped and fell on his head, forcing his hair over his eyes. He angrily brushed the offending strands aside. He didn't worry about the unruly mess living on top of his head. His black hair never received more than a non-strenuous shake in the morning. He ran his fingers through the sweaty tangle, pushing his curly fringe upwards.

His beat-up rig, reliance on observation and instinct, and dishevelled lifestyle separated him from the other diviners. For a start, he lived on his own.

Many relied on historical data stored like gold within family archives. He didn't have that.

And some—those with native blood—were simply gifted, working with nothing more than string and sticks. He didn't have that.

Some brought in specialist equipment built down in the battery by crazed criminal artisans. He didn't have that.

What he did have was a unique way of looking at the world. He could see it in the shape of the land, the mix of the soils, a mathematical grid overlaying the terrain in a statistical understanding of the elements making the formation and colours; the tone of the drill as it cut through the ground added another dimension to his knowledge of everything that lived on it. The mathematical perspective put off the other diviners and left him out of their collectives. Just like his parents.

The compass spun wildly in the glass dome. Odd. Arid tapped the top, but the magnetised sphere continued to swing. Every year the compass shifted. The magnetic lines were realigning, and he wondered if that was normal. If he went to school he'd know that kind of thing. He cursed Revvy.

Twang.

He rolled his eyes and let out an exasperated groan. The drill had detached from its motor, one of the many recurring problems with an ageing rig.

He grabbed several steel diffusers in case he needed to cut anything free. A diffuser was a handy invention his parents had left behind: a coil that, when activated, would turn any metal caught inside to rust, cutting through the thickest rods or beams. Something to do with adding extra electrons, or removing them, he didn't understand it. But it was exactly the kind of thing a diviner needed out in the middle of a desert, where power and tools were in short supply, or when your drill bit had bent and you were under attack. Or so he had found.

With the rig locked in position and immobile during the drilling process, Arid's view was limited. The expanse of red sand visible through the porthole looked still and lifeless. Grabbing a wrench, he loosened the butterfly nuts fastening the hatch and eased it down, exposing a small patch of dry earth. The heat rolled in and sweat gathered on his forehead. The whole cabin increased to an uncomfortable temperature in seconds, but still he watched and waited. The air-conditioning unit rattled as it worked to disperse the heat buildup. His odour was enhanced by the heat. The sand remained still. Too still. Now he didn't trust it; he certainly didn't want to stand on it unless necessary. And, today of all days, it was vital to remember what had happened five years ago. But food and water needed to be sourced. There were bills to pay and equipment to be repaired if he was going to provide the best data.

Water was a scarce resource fetching ridiculous sums. You couldn't waste it on things like washing. However, this did have a tendency to impact his negotiations. Even he had to admit that on particularly hot days the smell bothered him.

He pulled his sleeves up to his elbows. The patchwork of materials he wore, loosely fitted to his thin frame, were held together with a combination of tape and staples; his skills for repair didn't stretch past hitting things with heavy objects. As he peered out of the hood of his shirt, it slipped over his head, providing a sliver of shade for his eyes.

A gust of heat made him light-headed. His stomach rumbled. Fending for himself, he'd never mastered more than the rudiments of food preparation, amounting to little more than boiling starchy noodles. That, and the supplies he'd been able to forage or trade, had kept him thin. Thin enough for any old women he met to cause a fuss and force leftovers on him. Still, the minimal food kept him going.

Arid placed his legs in a canvas harness and eased down, swinging out to the ladder fastened to the rig's left leg. A pin attaching the drill to its motor had worked its way free. Luckily, it hadn't fallen out. Finding it in the sand would be, well, needle, meet haystack. In the time it would take to locate it with the metal detector, either the heat or the crawlers would get him.

He fastened his harness underneath the hatch, snapping the large hook into a maintenance point by the motor. Suspended from the rig, he swung free, enjoying the minor breeze from the movement. The moment was only ruined by the monotonous clanking of the drill against the pin on each revolution, yet another alluring sound to the crawlers. He pulled a lever on the side of the motor and the drill slipped into neutral, a low hum replacing the incessant banging. Now it was peaceful.

He whacked the head of the wrench against the pin, forcing it back into the clasp. One bash ... two, three. In.

A shadow fell across the dowser. Out here, only one thing could cast shade. Then came the sound of engines, overpowering the drone of his own motor and air conditioner. He swung out to identify the approaching noise, but the object remained out of his line of sight, blocked by the dowser's cabin. His only option was to get out of the harness. The noise grew louder, a combination of scraping metal and rig engines as whatever it was approached rapidly. Surely it had seen him. He was the only object for miles.

Arid grabbed the ladder, unclipped from the harness and descended to the sand, testing it tentatively before treading on it. A huge mechRig was approaching him, on fire and lurching uncontrollably in a zigzagging line. It emitted an enormous trail of black smoke and dust. He squinted at the identification signature on its side: DESTROYER. That had to be false advertising, considering its current state. Judging by its direction, the megaRig would come close but should avoid him.

A harpoon speared out of the clouds of dust, leaving a trail of twisting smoke and cutting straight into the boiler of the wrecked rig. Steam and scalding water sprayed out, drenching the dowser and washing away the dirt. Arid leapt to the side, diving away from the wave's trajectory.

Water on the ground. Bad news. It bubbled as a dark patch appeared.

Another megaRig appeared out of the smoke, reeling in the harpoon on a thick steel cable. It had the words LADY MOONSHINE printed down the right side of its bulk. Revvy's old home. The Destroyer teetered on its side, pulled off its axis as the second mech wrenched it backward. It swung out over him and the dowser, hundreds of tonnes of steel now a barely controllable wrecking ball. He didn't have time to get back and move the dowser, and judging by the way the Destroyer was swinging it would be unbelievably dangerous. The crippled rig swayed back in a wide arc at the length of the harpoon's cable. Arid had to do something or his craft would be smashed flat. The sun reflected off the steel cable. He grabbed a diffuser from his belt and threw it upwards. It missed. A second attempt hooked the diffuser around the cable and locked it into place.

He pressed the detonation button on his remote, and the coil went white. The cable snapped and the second mech lurched backward. The Destroyer toppled over, narrowly avoiding the dowser. Arid let out a sigh of relief. The motors of the standing megaRig roared as they fought for stability. He turned and ran toward the ladder that would take him back into the cabin.

As his hands wrapped around the bars, a high-pitched voice, shouting, cut through the cacophony. Should he go inside, or see if someone was in trouble? He should go.

There was another shout. Hesitation. Arid scanned over his shoulder.

A girl appeared flying out of the swirling smoke and landed heavily on the ground, rolling forward before jumping lightly to her feet. She wore a dark cloak, with a hood covering most of her face. He thought the outfit impractical in this heat, but the way it billowed around her as she strode briskly toward him was impressive.

She raised her finger and pointed at him. 'What do you think you're doing?' she shouted.

'I'm saving my rig.'

Arid shielded his eyes from the dust and smoke. The girl remained elusive in the clouds, moving quickly over the distance between them. Uncertainty hit him like a rock, and getting back inside the dowser's cabin became imperative. Hand over hand, he clambered up, the heat from the ladder's rungs burning his palms and fingers. Then his ankle was yanked down, wrenching his hands from the ladder. He flailed at the steel bars, but tumbled, landing face down in the sand.

The girl released her grip and towered over him.

'What are y' doing?' he shouted.

'You cut the cable. You've interfered with a rig duel. I can arrest you for that.'

He raised himself on his hands and knees. With his fingers buried in the burning sand, he felt a slight tremor. The ground shook with a deep rumble that vibrated the air. A mound grew behind them, and then exploded upwards. Sand cascaded down to reveal a mech rising from the sand. The monster towered over them as it continued to erupt. RANKIN had been scorched into the rig's side.

Arid nodded. So that's what had affected his compass: the magnetic fields emanating from the mech's traction system. He stood, clapped the sand from his hands on his trousers and stared up at the huge mech. It continued to rise until it towered above them; it was less than half the size of the Moonshine, but it was built for battle. The Moonshine halted, and he heard the sound of the gears changing as it started to move in the opposite direction.

The Rankin swung an enormous steel beam fastened to its roof and smashed it into the side of the Moonshine. The megaRig lurched to the side but remained standing. Another blow came in from the opposing side, hammering the Moonshine's frame, which bent under the impact.

'Hate t' tell y' this,' Arid said to the girl, 'but it ain't a duel. Y' been caught in a trap. That rig is a Collins Class, and it was waiting for y', and it's going to obliterate y'. And I'm outta here.'

The Rankin lurched to the side, its tracks skidding toward Arid and making him dive out of the way. The attack beam swung around, gathering momentum, and smashed into the side of the Moonshine. The force buckled the side, damaging two levels, bending the rig's engine pistons and rupturing the left-side boilers. Scalding water spewed out, spraying over the sand.

The Rankin closed the distance between the rigs, rumbling forward, its monster tracks churning up the earth.

Arid let out a squeak as he realised the Rankin was going to run directly over his dowser. He ran to the inside of the Collin's tracks and examined the suspension configuration. Coils. Maybe he could do something about that. He combined two diffusers and threw them into the rig's coils. He threw his last diffuser up onto the piston controlling the movement of the wrecking arm, getting it on his first attempt.

The diffusers ignited and incinerated. The coil snapped and the Rankin collapsed to one side, snapping a second coil. The metal fragments seared past Arid and became embedded into the rig's opposing wheel. The piston on the beam sheered in half and swung free. As the Rankin tipped, the beam swung out in an uncontrolled arc and smashed into Arid's dowser. He clutched his head, disbelieving what had happened.

Smoke billowed out from the Moonshine as the Rankin limped in a wide arc. It had been disarmed, leaving it only one action: retreat. The motors and tracks ground away, accompanied by the horrific screeching of grinding metal as the Collins Class headed east.

'You saved the Lady Moonshine,' the girl said.

'Not on purpose.' Arid gestured at the mangled remains of his rig. 'Look what it did.'

The Lady Moonshine ceased its retreat and groaned to a halt, unable to move with the piston ramming against its casing. The rhythmic banging echoed out over the desert expanse.

'Quick, follow me,' the girl ordered.

'But my dowser!'

'We don't have time.' She grabbed his arm and pulled him toward the Moonshine. 'If the Destroyer's crew gets you, you'll be crucified. It's them or us. And you just saved us.'

The decision lay before Arid. He could probably escape, come back when the battle was over and repair his rig. But he couldn't abandon his home.

His hands tingled, a familiar sensation flaring the hairs on the back of his neck. Luck had run out. He turned. Out of the sand emerged a pool of fully-grown crawlers, all at their adult size of around a metre long, with their pincers adding another half-metre.

A dozen. Not many, but enough to kill, and he had nowhere to run. Their skeletal legs clawed toward them, clicking and rattling.

    The girl pulled a pistol from her belt and fired into the pack. The bullets splattered several, but the rest came charging onward.

[2]

Mathias Byrne, senior officer of the *Hawkesbury*, felt uncomfortable in the presence of the cyborg, especially in this backwater of a town, with a workman's pub that served barely cold beer, which you needed a licence to order. It bordered on the barbaric; PAD gone mad! A cyborg would sit for minutes, not moving or making a sound, then spring to life as if turned on. But each cyborg was, at its core, a person—or had been. The experiment, often verging on the extreme with its integration of technology and people, chilled most who heard of it or saw the results. How much could be lost before you were no longer human? Was there a tipping point? Still, you had to deal with whatever representative they sent.

'Are you the leader?' Byrne asked.

'I @scott2Morryson, the current representative of the Cyborg Hive,' he replied.

'What happened to the last, er, cyborg representative?'

'Iris[1] considered his efforts bad.bad.'

A barmaid delivered a warmish beer and a glass of water to the table. Both glasses had metal straws.

---
[1] Ruler of the Cyborg Hive city.

Byrne took a sip and screwed up his face. 'Shame, I liked him. Anyway, give me a progress update.'

'We attempting to fix the Omen,' @scott2Morryson said, 'but little.little information available about it. Our investigations reveal it has an ignition. But it is missing. Without ignition, it is futile.'

'But you built it.'

'We assisted in assembling. The information was fed to us in unconnected submissions, with key components missing. Even if we built a copy, we could not make it work because there are parts that are missing or that we do not understand. The scientists known to us as the Geigers were smart.smart and deceptive. There are several projects of theirs we do not understand.'

'What's this ignition like? A key?'

'It is a small rectangular device that carries a code. Lights are placed on each end to represent a secure connection.'

'Can you make sure everything else is in working order so that once I find this key it'll work straightaway?'

'We cannot promise the desired result.'

'What if I double the fee?'

'Money doesn't work like that. We can only promise to do the best we can. Bring us the key, and we will make it work.'

'You are asking me to do a lot, considering that I'm paying you, @scott2Morryson. Where do you want me to send the money?'

The cyborg handed over a plastic card. Byrne examined it: a black card with blue rings at one end.

'PayWave,' @scott2Morryson said. 'Present it to your preferred transfer system.'

'You mean I have to *interact* with a bank?' Byrne shivered. 'Those leaches are impossible to find.'

'If you want it to be anonymous. Or use a recognised transaction point.'

'Where am I going to find one?'

'There is one outlet at Marble Bar.'

'There is? And this card works? Unlike that virtual assistant you sent. You'd ask it to play music and the lights would turn off.'

'That was a prototype.'

'Everything you build is a prototype,' Byrne said with a groan. The cyborg rose from the seat, his artificial legs lifting him in a smooth, mechanical motion. 'We will contact you.'

@scott2Morryson left the 100^2 in the bar and proceeded across the road to a hotel. In contrast to the dull box that comprised the drinking house, the hotel had the traditional wide verandas. The cyborg raised dust as his heavy feet clumped on the wooden flooring. The hotel's elderly owner watched him walk past and sit down in a corner booth that contained another cyborg. A small glass of chilled water sat in the middle of the table.

@scott2Morryson positioned himself on the opposing seat.

'Was the ping successful?' the other cyborg asked.

@scott2Morryson nodded. 'Yes, @redFive. We establish communications and reach agreement.'

@redFive pushed the glass of water across the table. @scott2Morryson gulped it down, keeping most of the water in his mouth. Vents on the side of his neck opened and he sucked in a deep breath of air.

'We charge a low fee for the amount of work required. Potentially low.low.'

'We not here for the 100's ends,' @redFive said. 'The Faraday project requires components. Send out a broadcast on dark web for body parts. We pay good.good dollar for good.good bodies.'

The girl quickly outpaced Arid. Fear fuelled him, but he struggled to distance himself from the pincers stabbing at his heels. The clouds of smoke intensified, and visibility ahead dropped to zero. The first billows of the dust storm drifted in. Then he was alone. The clicking of the crawlers rattled in his head, taking him back

---

[2] Cyborgs refer to non-cyborgs as '100 per cent', meaning that they are 100-per cent flesh. It's seen as an insult.

to the day they mauled his parents, gripping him in terror. He ran along the side of the *Lady Moonshine*, searching for an entrance. The girl must have used a ladder or trapdoor, not flown away. He hammered against the metal of the tracks with his wrench and cried out for help, hoping someone would hear.

As he charged along, a crawler sprang out ahead. He jerked to the side, and the pincer skewered through his shirt, tearing his sleeve. He smashed down with the wrench, breaking the creature's leg. It let out a strange piercing stutter, but still flailed after him with its remaining pincer as he vaulted over it. Another scuttled out from the smoke and lashed out, grazing his foot and managing to trip him up. He tumbled forward as the creature stabbed its pincers in a whirlwind, narrowly missing him as he rolled, throwing up a fountain of sand. As he came up on his feet, he took a wild swing with the wrench and swatted the crawler aside.

Arid didn't know what to do. Even if he could see where he was going, he couldn't outrun the crawlers. He couldn't fight them, and he couldn't defend against them. He'd seen them puncture steel. Death by a thousand stabs was an excruciatingly painful way to die. And he didn't want to die.

He backed against the wheels of the megaRig. A breeze rolled in and lifted the smoke, enough to reveal the horror of his situation. Crawlers streamed in from all directions. The circle of spindly legs rushed in toward him, and in moments he was pinned against the *Lady Moonshine* with no escape route. Could he charge through? Then what? You could only run for so long before the heat killed you.

Arid closed his eyes, holding the wrench in front of him with both hands.

Soft material wrapped around him, accompanied by a metallic click. A rescue harness was secured to his waist, with a thick steel cable running up to the *Moonshine*. The crawlers clattered into the side of the rig as he was winched upwards at a terrifying speed, the pincers hammering into the rig's wheels, sounding like machine-gun fire. A muscled arm wrapped around him, absorbed the momentum from the harness and threw him to the side on to a spongy surface. And then it was dark. *Breathe.* And cool. *Breathe.* He fell away from the soft material and collapsed onto the floor; the sun hit his eyes, washing out his vision.

Cold steel tingled against his back. The smell of oil permeated the air, blocking out all other odours. His eyes adjusted to the light and he made out silhouettes encircling him, then the sound of huge pistons chugging away in the background. He felt reassured by the wrench in his hands, a useful weapon if the situation turned sour.

'What happened?' he whispered.

'We pulled you out of the swarm with a rescue claw,' the man replied.

'I thought those were banned.'

'Lucky for you we have a more flexible view of the laws. What are you doing out here?'

'The mech flattened my rig.'

'You got a one-seater out here? You got guts fighting it out alone.'

Arid raised himself onto an elbow. 'I'm a diviner, ain't some thug.'

The man raised his eyebrow at the mention of the diviner. 'Interesting. I think there's someone who'll want to meet you.'

Arid could see the guards surrounding him now with a range of weapons. Angry-looking men with oversize arms, they were coated with soot and blood. The alcove built into the side of the rig was closed in on three sides, with the fourth offering a panoramic view. The wreckage of the battle could be seen, with the *Destroyer* toppled on its side and smoke pouring from the engines. The *Rankin* was a distant object, also leaving a trail of smoke.

The man who had spoken slid a heavy door across the opening, sealing them inside in the dark. He indicated for the other men to lower their guns. There was a hesitation, as though it was open for debate—or sport.

'We can't trust him, Greyson,' one guard said. 'He's an outsider.'

'He's just a kid,' Greyson replied. 'I'll see what QB says before I chuck him down with the others. You know what she's like with diviners.'

The guards glared at Arid as Greyson led the way. He steered Arid down a series of utilitarian corridors that rose through the various levels, some hotter than others as the furnaces boiled away. Faded yellow paintwork. Small doors. No windows. Metal grating in the floor allowed sight of the other levels. It felt like a prison.

Greyson's posture stiffened as they reached the tenth level. He paused at the front of a large set of double doors. Voices drifted through. One sounded familiar to Arid.

'It did what?'

'Rose up out of the sand,' said the familiar voice.

'Who was it?'

'Rankin.'

Greyson raised his hand to knock.

'Hunter! Damn him. You cannot trust that man. I wonder what he was doing so far away from the *Hawkesbury*.'

Greyson paused as he heard the name.

'I think you may be looking through rose-tinted glasses at how you treated him, Mother. And what you did to his family.'

Greyson pushed open the door without knocking and entered, followed by Arid. The room was large, with panoramic windows giving a view of the desert sands. A sentry stood beside the door. A bank of consoles positioned near the window was staffed by a handful of people wearing dark blue uniforms.

A middle-aged woman wearing stained overalls was leaning forward in an oversized chair—wide enough for three people—that faced the back wall. She appeared to have a nest on top of her head. Maps of the area covered the wall, with various red rings drawn over them. In front of her stood the hooded girl in the cloak. They both turned to look at Arid and Greyson.

The older woman went quiet. 'War has a price. Come.' She turned back to the hooded girl and indicated for her to come closer. They hugged in an affectionate way and then she waved the hooded girl away. 'Don't be late for dinner,' she called out after the disappearing figure. 'And clean up your room. You've got clothes all over the floor.'

'Stay out of my room,' the girl replied.

The older woman rolled her eyes before focusing on the guard. 'Yes, Sergeant Greyson?'

'Queen, we rescued this boy from outside. He is a diviner.'

'Where's his rig?'

'Y' destroyed it!' Arid blurted.

The queen shrugged. 'Sorry,' she replied, apparently not meaning it. 'Why is he here?' she asked Greyson.

'He was being chased by crawlers. They had him pinned down. He didn't deserve to die.'

'I'm sure you had your reasons for rescuing him,' the queen said, 'although we've left others behind.'

'You did bring up the issue of reliable data sources on water at the last town-hall meeting,' Greyson said.

The queen narrowed her eyes. 'Good diviners seem to have died out. Most we get through don't bring worthwhile data, even if they say they're good. Anyway, you're here now,' she said to Arid. 'I'm Queen Beatrice. You have heard of me?'

'No,' Arid replied.

She sat upright. 'Really? Surprising. Yet you look familiar to me. What is your name?'

'Arid.'

The queen hesitated upon hearing his name. Her eyes drifted and she bit her bottom lip, as though recalling an old memory.

'Ma'am, the *Destroyer* is incapacitated,' Greyson reported. 'What would you like to do with its crew?'

'Round up the captives and send them to work in the bellows.'

Greyson saluted and left, leaving Arid with the queen.

'How did you know how to attack the *Rankin*?' she asked him.

'I don't know. It sort of felt right.'

Queen Beatrice paused, tapping her fingers on the arm of her throne. 'But you knew the weak point. Have you seen it before?'

'Why are y' asking me this?'

'No one brings down a Collins Class by feel. Certainly not a child. It's suspicious.'

'What y' should find suspicious is how y' fell into a pretty obvious trap. They were waiting for y'.'

'You need to watch how you speak to an adult.'

'I apologise.' Arid lowered his head. She was the queen and probably deserved some respect. His parents had been particularly clear about manners.

'Anyway, you have saved the *Lady Moonshine*,' Bea said. 'I must reward you.'

The cloaked girl burst into the room from a side door. 'Mother, have you been moving my—' She halted when she spotted Arid still in the room.

He was able to observe the girl fully for the first time. Her golden hair flowed around an elegant face, partly obscuring two dazzling, large blue eyes. She smiled, her full lips parting to reveal bright white teeth, and lifted her face. The sunlight from the window caught the outline of her hair, making her glow like a halo.

'This is Ella,' the queen said, introducing the pair. 'Ella, this is Arid.'

Ella nodded at Arid. 'It's good to put a name to a face. Welcome aboard.'

'Good t' see y' again.'

'You've met before?' Bea asked.

'Outside,' the girl replied. 'I did a quick scout and ran into him.'

'Ella, I've told you about going out without security.'

'Mother, it's fine. I was hardly out five minutes. I can take care of myself.'

The door opened again, and another girl appeared. 'Mama-Bea, Ella's been using my stuff again.'

The girl was shorter and darker than Ella. Her hair blossomed out in tight spirals like a slow-motion explosion. Her round face was covered in freckles. She wore a short, bright orange dress decorated with yellow dots. She smiled at Arid, exposing uneven teeth. He didn't spend much time looking at her before returning his gaze to Ella.

'Please, I would like you to meet my other daughter,' Bea said, indicating the newcomer. 'This is Frey.'

Arid couldn't help noticing a slight dip in the queen's enthusiasm as she mentioned her second child. He thought Frey appeared to notice it, too.

'Er, hi,' she said, waving at him. Arid was transfixed by Ella, but Frey persisted, her voice taking on an annoyed tone. *'Hi!'*

'Uh, yeah, hi.'

Ella sat down on the steps at the foot of the command throne. The queen stared at Arid. He shifted uneasily as the woman hesitated.

A vibration shuddered through the floor. The rig was drilling.

The queen sat staring at him, her hand covering her mouth, her face frowning. 'Arid … it's an unusual name for these parts. I used to know …' Her sentence trailed off.

'What are y' drilling for?' he asked.

'Since we need repairs, we're taking the opportunity to drill for water. The boilers ruptured in the skirmish.'

'There ain't no water here. The aquifer's out t' the north.'

'Our maps say otherwise.'

'I'm a diviner.'

'You are but a child.'

'I'm not. I'm nearly fifteen. Gives me as right a claim on adult as any other.'

Bea laughed. 'I cannot argue, as I believed the same at your age. How joyous to wrap the world in innocent impossibilities and incomprehensible ambition.'

Arid's pendant bounced against his chest, catching the light.

Bea sat straight and withdrew a long knife from her boot. 'Come here,' she commanded in a stern voice. 'Stand before me.'

Several staff turned to look at the object of her unexpected anger.

As Arid shuffled forward, the queen raised her knife. 'Again, tell me your name,' she hissed.

'Arid.'

Her eyes ran over his body, scrutinising his clothes, face and stature. He didn't meet many people, and he felt small and vulnerable under her gaze.

'What's your *full* name?'

'Arid Geiger.'

Frey gasped. The room seemed to freeze. The others went quiet as they watched.

Bea reached out to Arid, grabbed his arm and pulled him close. He stumbled forward, glancing hesitantly between the concerned faces, and stopped a few paces in front of the queen. With her other hand, she raised the knife to his neck, tracing it down to the pendant. He trembled as the sharp edge approached, his eyes straining to watch it.

Bea lifted the necklace so the pendant swung free and hung in the air. Her face paled, caught in another moment of recollection.

Arid said, trying to keep his voice calm, 'Why are y' using a knife?'

Bea replied, 'I will not touch it, for it is possibly the most precious thing on this rig. I haven't seen this for years.' She shook her head and whispered his name repeatedly. After what felt longer than a monsoon, she lowered her knife and stared into Arid's face. She placed her finger against the corner of her eye and wiped away a tear.

'Are y' all right?' Arid asked. He felt moved by the display of emotion in such a powerful figure.

'You remind me of some people I once knew. I wasn't nice to them and I'm reminded of my regrettable behaviour.'

'Oh,' he replied. He'd never come across an adult who'd said they were sorry about something they'd done. They always seemed so certain.

'I'm not the person I once was,' Bea said. 'We all fade. But we are all allowed a chance to change for the better, to hurdle the barrier of tragedy. And we should reflect on our past errors and promise to do better. What can we offer you?'

'Can y' fix my dowser?'

'That is something I *can* fix. Guard, ensure Greyson sees to it, would you? It is a decree from me. In the meantime, Arid, you will stay as my guest. Girls, take him to a class-B chamber. I need to be alone.' She clapped her hands and the deck staff left the floor.

Frey indicated for Arid to follow her. He moved next to Ella, and all three walked down the corridor.

'Some pretty cool moves y' did out there,' he said to Ella.

She glanced over at him and smiled.

'Ella, were you out again? You know Mama-Bea hates that,' Frey warned.

'Oh, shut up, Frey. She worries about everything. She understands me.'

'What else do y' do here?' Arid asked Ella.

'Oh, this and that.'

'Sounds cool.'

'I help out with the rosters,' Frey replied, unasked. 'Mama-Bea is teaching me how to keep the soldiers happy.'

'Yeah, yeah,' he said dismissively.

'I bet she is,' Ella said with a sneer.

Frey sighed in exasperation. 'Making sure the equipment is up to standard, and the quarters are clean and in good condition. It's important, you know.'

'Dull,' Ella said, and gave Arid a wink.

'Sounds like it,' he said.

Frey said, 'Where are your parents?'

'They were killed by crawlers,' Arid replied.

'Harsh,' Ella said, shaking her head. She ran her hand down his back. Arid nearly exploded. 'Sorry to hear it. I lost my parents, too.'

'Odd, that, your parents being diviners and not knowing about stick crawlers,' Frey said to Arid.

'What are y' saying?' he growled.

'Just saying it's odd. That's all. I thought diviners knew all about the dangers of the plain.'

Arid frowned at the young girl. 'Pretty dumb thing t' say.'

Frey shook her head and walked away. 'Fine, I've got stuff to do.'

'Get some rest,' Ella said to Arid. 'I'll show you around later.'

He looked around the room they'd led him to. Small, but stocked with solid, comfortable furniture. There was food, and a tall container of water, so cold that more water ran down the outside of the glass.

'I'll look forward t' that,' he said. 'I like it here. It feels familiar.'

'I'm sure you'll be fine.' Ella turned on her heel and flashed away.

In the lowest level of the megaRig, a guard patrolled along the inner frame. Between the tank tracks sat the enormous motors that churned away, powered from the furnace on the second level. It was hot, and the constant drone of the drive chain created a claustrophobic atmosphere. The engineers had been seconded to the damaged decks, leaving the guard on duty alone. He paused at a water dispenser and poured a drink.

Most of the perimeter passage lay adjacent to the treads, but at the rear, where the wall stood next to the wide-open plains, he found a refuse outlet that had been forced open from the outside. They'd had a security breach.

The guard turned and ran to the central staircase, where he made his way up to the top level. Sweat poured off him as he took the stairs two at a time, his breath struggling in the muggy climate. He burst in the door to the command deck, startling Bea, who had been lost in thought.

'Ma'am, we have a raider.'

As the guard delivered the line, a figure dressed in black descended from the roof on a long black rope. The intruder lunged at the queen, grabbing her around the throat. Breathing heavily through a full-face mask and staring into her eyes, the assailant unsheathed a long-bladed dagger.

The queen stared back, unflinching. There was a moment of hesitation. Then, as the intruder thrust forward with the knife, the guard grabbed the attacker's arm and wrenched the dark figure away. The two tussled in a tight circle before the guard cried out. Falling to his knees, he clutched at his stomach. The assailant grabbed the rope and quickly climbed up, disappearing through a vent in the roof.

Bea ran over to the guard, who was struggling for breath. 'Quick, anyone near, I need first aid. A doctor!' she cried.

Suzie, the queen's personal assistant, appeared through the door, puffing and red-faced from her dash, her lanky arms flailing around as she moved. 'What's the prob—' She stopped mid-sentence when she saw the queen kneeling next to the bleeding guard.

'Find out who is responsible,' Bea ordered.

'Yes, ma'am. Anyone in particular you would like examined?'

'We have only one new person on the rig. Only one who has not pledged loyalty to me.'

'The one who saved us?'

'See how true that is.'

Three years ago …

Byrne and Hunter watch the children challenge each other in the arena, making sure they are visible to them all. It is believed this exercise will make them fight harder. The training area takes up the entire floor within the Hawkesbury.

Byrne says, 'Are you all right with watching children? You know, with the loss of—'

'The rage and sadness I feel can only be propagated through primal screams that merely mute the agony,' Hunter replies. 'But it does not affect my daily life. We all have our own lives to live. Our own breaths to exhale. I don't

believe I'm the only one,' he says, giving Byrne a knowing look.

Hunter rarely talks about his past. Byrne is the opposite. He even talks about things that didn't happen. Alex is here because of yet another confrontation. Careless words spoken without thought and avenged upon.

Alex doesn't understand why Hunter and Byrne are always teasing. Always pushing. Endless hateful speech digging right into the heart.

Hunter approaches. He squats next to Alex. 'Are you all right?'

Alex wipes the tears away and tries to present a stronger face. 'Why are they so mean to me?'

Hunter shrugs. 'When the queen killed all your parents, it hurt each of you in different ways. Does it make you angry?'

Alex nods.

'Do you want to do something about it?'

Alex nods again.

'To do something, you need to be a stronger person, give up many things. And train very hard. Do you think you can do that?' Hunter waits for a response. He seems to be able to wait for things indefinitely. It takes a while for a decision to be made.

Cameron, a big boy in his teens, approaches. 'You having a good cry?' he says to Alex, his voice full of nastiness.

Hunter says nothing. He gets up and walks away.

To be a stronger person, you need to do something. Do you think you can do that? It's time for Alex to show them exactly what is possible.

Cameron is older and stronger. But there is more to strength than muscle.

Alex wipes away the last tear—ever—and smiles. 'Say that again.'

Byrne watches on. Hunter joins him, brushing his fringe to the side. His colourful shirt stands out a mile in the military-themed area.

Alex kicks Cameron in the shin. Cameron doubles over and is met with an uppercut. It's weak, but unexpected and Cameron reels backward.

'Cameron is acting on your instructions?' Byrne asks Hunter, folding his arms across his chest.

'Yes.'

'I'm glad they follow orders without question. We should send more of his kind against Alex. Find the pain threshold, physically and mentally.'

Byrne watches. He smiles. The fight is a good one. Although struggling and uneven, Alex is performing well above expectations. 'Aren't you concerned about what they might do?' he asks Hunter.

Alex is on Cameron's back, but gets flipped over onto the metal flooring. The landing is brutal but brief as the young recruit kicks up into Cameron's groin, forcing him to his knees. Alex jumps up and spins, planting a solid kick into the side of the other boy's head, again knocking him to the floor.

A couple of savage and unrepentant kicks to the head and Cameron is down for the count. Alex turns and walks away. No doubt. No fear. No remorse. No looking back.

'It will be a learning experience. Send in two more of those boys. The cost of victory needs to be understood. At any cost. It's not easy and is never given freely,' Hunter says.

[3]

Arid awoke to a clattering outside his door. It was the first time he'd been in a decent bed for years—clean sheets and soft pillows—and he'd fallen asleep instantly. Now, a security guard lunged toward him. The man grabbed him by his shirt and forced him upright, then dragged him out of the room.

The guard pushed him along, gripping his shoulder and steering him through the corridors at a pace Arid found difficult to maintain in his groggy state. On the next level down, multiple cabins were jammed together to squeeze in as many people as possible. An overpowering scent of sweat and body odour permeated the air.

'What's going on?' Arid's head spun as shock overrode his tiredness.

The guard didn't respond.

He was ushered into a medium-sized, windowless room. In the centre was a long table with several people sitting behind it. A massive fan took up the entire height of the rear wall, drawing in a gentle breeze. The guard forced Arid into a seat directly across from the table.

In the middle of the table sat a tall, thin lady with long blonde hair tied back in a ponytail that sprouted from the top of her head.

He had seen her on the command deck behind the queen. She appeared angry. Her face was long, and in fact her whole appearance seemed stretched. Long hair, long face, long arms; her thin frame was fragile in its formality. Even her fingers were ungainly, dancing on loose wrists around the paperwork covering the tabletop. Apologetic and timid, she was very different to the queen, who looked as though she could take on anyone. Twice before breakfast.

Stretch-woman picked up a small pink bottle beside the paperwork. She squeezed it and pink cream oozed out, and she rubbed it into her hands, which she held up in front of her face, the scent of desert roses floated across to Arid, making his eyes water.

'Let's start,' she announced. 'We have never had an attack on the queen inside the *Lady Moonshine*. You turn up and within minutes there's an assassination attempt.'

'But it has nothing t' do with me,' Arid replied. 'I was in another room, asleep.'

'You may not have personally wielded the knife, but you may know who did. On the other hand, you may have sneaked out and attacked her yourself. You were fortunate enough to see where her command level is.'

'What are y' saying?'

'Let's see where this inquisition leads.'

Stretch-woman tapped together a series of papers then turned to the first page. The six others sitting at the table, three on either side of her, all focused their attention on him. They were sitting straight, hands clasped together and staring earnestly.

The woman continued. 'This panel has been convened at the behest of the queen to assess the possibility that the new resident was either wholly responsible or complicit in the attempted assassination of Queen Beatrice.'

'I didn't do it.'

'Hush. You will have your chance to state your case. Before we begin, you need to understand the potential offences that may be synchronised with you. On the roll, under the PAD agreements, you are implicated in an attempted assassination of a council head with the intent of attempting to destabilise the Western Alliance.'

'Wait a minute, say what?'

'Shush. You are also implicated in the attempted sabotage of the *Lady Moonshine* through the use of external third parties. Please present your evidence of innocence.'

Arid cleared his throat and stood. 'Dear members of the jury—'

'This is a tribunal, not a court of law,' the woman corrected. 'Continue.'

'Oh, um. I give to y' the evidence of my word. I did not do this.'

There was a pause as the tribunal members looked at one another.

'Do you know what the word 'evidence' means?' the woman asked.

'Um, yes.'

'Do you have something independent of your own testimony, irrefutable proof that corroborates it? For example, was your dowser a one-sleeper?'

'Er, no.'

'Are you registered as a solo vehicle with the Department of Licensing and Transportation?'

'Ah, no.'

'Do you have someone who can vouch for your whereabouts?'

'Um, no.'

'"Er. Ah. Um." You're not speaking with much confidence. When it's only your word it's difficult to prove anything. How do we know you were living out there on your own?' Stretch-woman laughed. 'How many passengers is your rig registered for?'

Sweat prickled on his forehead. He could feel the pressure building in his head. 'It ain't actually, er, registered.'

'You are running an illegal rig?'

How do you explain that you meant to do it, but with your parents being dead and the rig registered in their name, and when you do mention your name, they seem to get angry and call in the supervisor and you have to leg it before they call the Feds because they're asking all sorts of strange questions, saying things like 'duty of care', whatever that was.

'Well, what is 'illegal' anyway?' Arid asked.

'What if you crash? Insurance. If you're caught by the DLT the fines are huge. They have found a significant correlation between unregistered vehicles and wanted outlaws.'

'Not wishing t' sound argumentative, but ain't that considered a generalisation? Not everyone with an unregistered rig is a crim. There are reasons.'

'Shush. A person cannot exist out on the plains on their own. People die out there from the heat alone. And who protects you when you sleep?'

'I have—had—a secure rig. No one was getting in. I've been living out on the plains for years. It's safe if y' know where t' hide.'

'The plain is safe for no one, from the largest mechCity to the lowest outlaws living in the smallest rollers. And you didn't even see anyone else to blame.'

'Just because the crim wasn't seen doesn't mean he wasn't there. Outside is a big place.'

'Okay. You have a point. But if we look at what happened inside, you must see that we can't rule out that it wasn't you. You allege you were in your room, but there is no proof.'

'Don't y' have security or something?'

'We have operational priorities here that are higher,' Stretchwoman replied. 'We operate on trust. You were heard to say the rig felt familiar.'

Arid went quiet. It was true. There was something about the place, the smell, the layout—it did *feel* as though he'd been here before, although he had no memory of it.

The woman sighed. 'Let's get to the point. The heart of your defence relies on a witness. Do you have someone who can vouch for your location at the time of the attack?'

He lowered his head. 'No.'

'Any external witnesses? Did you see anyone at all out there?'

Arid raised his finger. He had a name. 'Ah, yes! Ella was there. She can say I was on my own.'

'You want the daughter of the queen to testify against her mother on behalf of someone she barely knows?'

'Is that bad?'

'Let's leave it at yes.'

'Ah …' Arid replied hesitantly.

The woman raised her hands to her head, her elbows forming particularly sharp angles. 'Place him in the cells. The queen will decide an applicable punishment.'

'Wait, what if someone from the other rig jumped off and boarded this one?'

'Really? Take him away.'

Before he could understand what had happened, or the implications, guards clamped onto Arid's arms and escorted him back down through the corridors. People muttered as they passed by, and he didn't know if that was good or bad. He'd been among other mech crews; many of them were prisoners, and the anger and repression could be tasted. But here it was different. They'd taken everything that was in his pockets. Even his pendant. He needed to get it back. His parents had been very particular about it.

Her report from the tribunal complete, Suzie bowed, her long frame sweeping in a lasting arc, and she departed the command deck, leaving Bea to pace the expanse. It had been hours since the attack and the following tribunal. Nothing had been proven and, potentially, no would-be assassin caught.

Bea clutched a small blue velvet box with her right hand, and her left was clenched around something else. She hadn't had long, and the assassination attempt had accelerated the timeline. She'd never felt worried about her life, never looked back on actions or consequences, but for the first time in years she'd been forced to come face-to-face with the mistakes of her past. Planning on the fly wasn't one of her strengths, but times were officially 'desperate'.

The megaRig's craftspeople had been working under a combination of fear and extreme reward. She glanced at the reproduction of Arid's pendant in her left hand, smiled at the authenticity of it and put it in her pocket. She placed both hands around the box and closed her eyes. An original item from her youth.

'Mama-Bea, you called?'

Bea turned to face Frey, her face a mixture of solemn grief and concern.

'Have a seat,' Bea said, indicating the command chair. 'You and I have a long history, and it has been rocky. I'm sorry about the early days. I didn't know better. I *wilfully* didn't know better, and that is inexcusably selfish behaviour. Although the damage is already done, I'll make it up to you somehow, although I have no idea how. I hope one day you'll find it within your heart to forgive me. I apologise for the abuse when you came into my life. I apologise for not being there when you needed help. I apologise for being me.'

'Mama-Bea, we've reached an understanding. I carry my thoughts, and you carry yours. We're civil in public. Your actions have set the consequences. You have made the relationship repeatedly obvious. Do we need more understanding?'

'You know the reasons. And you know what I've tried to do, and where I started from. But now we need to put those things aside. You must take care of this. Keep it a secret.'

Bea handed over the small box. Frey opened it. Her eyes went wide.

'You used to talk about this all the time,' Frey said. 'Isn't this really important to you?'

'Frey, *you* are important. Don't forget it. Ever. Now, there are a few things I need you to do.'

The jail wasn't a nice place; it was brutal and hot. Stretch-woman didn't seem that nice either. Maybe she was having a bad day. The windowless cell was bleak, small with a tall ceiling, and contained only a metal toilet and bench. The walls were heavily gouged with deep score marks on each surface, showing them to be the scavenged exteriors of other rigs. Arid sat on the cold metal and waited. The vibrations of the drilling continued. The pounding of the repairs echoed through the metal frame.

A scratching sound from behind the wall startled him. He moved over and placed his ear against the metal. He could hear breathing.

'Hello?' he said.

'Are you angry?' came the reply.

'Er, what?' The question surprised him.

'They have taken your liberty. You must be full of rage.'

'Not really. I'm sure it's just a mix-up. They'll sort it out.'

'They're lying about your parents. The queen knows something. You can see that.'

'My parents? No one's said anything. Well, I'm sure that once we talk again we can sort it out. Misunderstandings are easy.'

'She *lied* about your parents. Doesn't that mean anything?'

'Who is this?'

'Do you want out? The queen lies about many things. She will kill you as soon as you look at her face. To escape you must kill her. Do that and you will have many friends.'

'I ain't going t' do that.'

'You have been warned. Ask her about your parents and look into her eyes when she replies.'

'I'm going t' explain it t' the queen. She'll work it out.' There was no reply. 'Hello?'

Arid returned to the bench. The exchange had been odd. This place operated on its own rules, which seemed detached from the outside world. He couldn't understand why Stretch-woman didn't believe he could survive on his own. There were heaps of solos on the plain, mainly diviners selling the results of exploratory drilling. She was probably confused. Once he explained it, he was sure they'd understand it had been a big mistake. And once the queen had fixed his rig, he could return to his old life.

His parents. No one had mentioned them to him since their deaths, but now they seemed to be everywhere.

The door opened. Ella peered in, her face a mask of concern. Arid's face broke into a broad smile.

'Quick, you're in trouble. You need to get out,' Ella said.

'Ain't that a bad thing t' do?'

'Mother can be tricky. You shouldn't think sentimentality is an option with her. You don't become a commander on the plains by being nice. And at the moment there's a big question mark above you. Follow me.'

She led Arid out through the jail level, pausing to check down each corridor first.

'Can I ask a question?'

'Sure. Is it personal?' Ella replied.

'Er, not really. Yer mother went odd when she asked my name. Do y' know why?'

'No idea.'

He bounced along beside her, hoping they'd accidentally bump together. As she led him through the levels, it occurred to him that escaping 'from' was an improvement to being 'in' jail, but it presented a new problem. He needed somewhere to escape 'to'. Which meant off the rig, and away from Ella.

'Where can I go? Should I hide on the rig, somewhere near yer quarters?'

'I think we can find something in the quarter stores, even if it's a screamer. You'll be safer in one outside than hiding here.'

'Why are y' doing this?' Arid asked.

'You saved the *Moonshine*.'

'Oh. Not for any other reason?'

'No. Why?'

Ella ran ahead, the cloak billowing out behind her. In the close quarters of the mech, her scent cut through the foul air like a fresh breeze. It was intoxicating. His heart skipped a beat as she looked back over her shoulder at him and smiled.

But he struggled to keep up. Her speed in the narrow corridors was extraordinary. Her abilities included grabbing the rails on the stairs and sliding down them without touching the steps. A trick he tried, but he just ended up burning his hands and tumbling down to the next level. Ella paused on the second-lowest level and waited for a patrol to pass, then they quickly moved along the equipment deck, passing the drilling machinery and gas canisters, halting at the midpoint.

Drilling technicians were packing the drill away, extracting it from the ground and rotating it into the cleaning machinery. Steam spread from the seals and water dripped through the structure. A younger technician mopped furiously.

'They must be getting ready to move,' she whispered.

Right in front of him, Arid's dowser was being lowered onto a repair platform. A wire frame holding a mind-numbing array of tools caged the area. A man with thick hairy arms lowered a welder's mask over his face and fired up a welding torch. The light from the intense blue flame burnt into his eyes.

Arid paused, making false steps toward the area.

Ella grabbed his shirt and pulled him along. 'We might have a shredder or roller. Those would be cool, wouldn't they?'

The sleek black vehicles shimmered under the ceiling lights, their hunkered-down and stripped-back silhouettes presenting a menacing image.

'But my rig …'

'We need to get you to a working rig. Once out, you need to keep near. I'll let you know when it's safe to come back on. I'll work on Mother. She does change her mind, but it takes time. She's not bad. Not anymore.'

Ella spotted several workers, all covered in grease, taking a break and resting against the wall, and, more importantly, blocking the main passage. The megaRig engines wound up and the *Moonshine* shuddered. The movement of the floor had Ella and Arid swaying as the rig slowly moved forward.

'Great,' Ella grumbled. 'We'll have to find a way around.'

They took a secondary passage along the outside wall of the rig that was full of old and dusty equipment. Stepping over the junk slowed them down, but gave safe passage past the staircase up to the military barracks and a large storeroom. They peered around a corner to examine the vehicles nearest to the service platform.

'Where the hell do you think you're going?'

They spun. Frey faced the pair, with her usual angry features, her legs planted wide, and a large gun under her arm. The weapon was almost comically large, and its muzzle glowed a deep blue. A claw rotated at the end of the barrel.

Arid and Ella raised their hands.

'Frey, don't do this,' Ella pleaded. 'He hasn't done anything wrong.'

'We don't know that. It's not the rules. He's a prisoner and he's escaping. Step away from him.' Frey indicated with the barrel for her sister to move away.

Ella took a step, putting some space between her and the other two. Her eyes darted over to the nearby shelves, where small weapons were stacked. She slowly inched her way toward them.

Frey caught the movement and stepped to one side, next to the wall so she had a better view of Arid and her sister. 'Okay, let's all be cool,' she said. 'We head back and see Mama-Bea.'

'You know what she'll say, how she'll see this. Please, be sensible,' Ella said.

'Let's see who's favourite after this,' Frey sneered.

'Do you have to make everything about popularity? You could just be useful.'

Frey laughed. It was as sincere and heartfelt as an amateur politician's. 'I've had a nice little chat with Mama-Bea and had some expectations explained. I've been given an important task.'

She did seem to have a new necklace around her neck. Probably some sheriff's badge, reflecting new and important duties.

The rig shook as it picked up speed.

The gun's lighting switched from blue to red. Frey frowned and tilted the weapon to examine its firing condition. It started to vibrate, then glowed brightly. She threw it on the ground as it exploded. The blast took out the wall and floor and threw them all apart.

The wall tore open, revealing the desert outside. The sun, high in the sky, shone in, the glare momentarily blinding them. Ella leapt toward the other two as the floor buckled. Arid and Frey tumbled out with Ella's arms flailing behind them.

Arid fell. The descent seemed to last forever as the *Lady Moonshine* drove onward. Above him, Frey, wild-eyed and with her limbs spinning, followed behind. She was probably swearing. Back in the mech, Ella threw something small out after them.

He hit the ground. All went black.

From the command deck, Queen Bea and Suzie watched the two fall and then tumble to a stop in the sand.

'That was unexpected,' Bea said.

'Do you want me to send out the rollers?' Suzie replied. 'Nothing focuses the mind like being chased.'

'There are worse things out on the plains. We need to trust the process. Do you play chess?'

'I'm more of a poker player.'

'Pity. Send out a message—a reward—on the dark web. Queen's pawn to E4.'

Byrne fumed. The *Destroyer* had been lost. The 'lazy' *Moonshine* had been victorious again. He dropped his head into his hands. The win gave the queen another tenement on the aquifer, meaning she controlled over sixty per cent. No one was that good. Even the early mechs from the gangland wars, where they lived and breathed the art of Maw in the world of real steel, occasionally stumbled.

Bea had been around a long time, and there were stories about how ruthless she'd been in her younger days, often overplaying her hand, pushing equipment and people past their limits. Every fight was to the death and was never hers. Byrne would have liked to see that. To take her on at her most formidable would have been the ultimate challenge. These days she seemed sensible and unbeatable. And that was suspicious. And suspicions needed to be examined and accounted for.

Those 'experts' around him had no answers. A kind of reverence coloured conversation about Bea, as if she was aspirational rather than a demented leader from the past, who only had greed and ego as priorities. The damage she had done in the name of victory was vast. Ecological, economic, humanitarian. It had been unrelenting and without conscience.

When younger, Byrne had told the council—warned them—about Bea's hunger and they'd laughed. He'd stood alone for so long, losing so much of his past through defiance, as she had taken what she'd desired, the anger building inside him like high-pressure furnaces powering the *Hawkesbury*. So he'd made his way up the ranks with grit and talent, building the relationships and alliances, bringing together the rigs she'd decimated, and he had created the first mechCity.

Who was laughing now?

For all his effort and sacrifice in bringing this security, Byrne only asked for one thing: loyalty.

And had council given it to him?

No.

His command meant nothing to them. Bea's celebrity and reputation were more intoxicating, and fellow counsellors queued up to defend her with a mixture of awe and fear. And so he'd stood alone against the wannabe dictator, spreading the word of unity and regeneration. And it was this level of adulation that had him questioning the command around him. His own people, were they trustworthy?

He tapped the end of his pen on the list he'd drafted. He'd already drawn lines through a handful of names, people no longer part of the command. But still no traitor.

Who was left?

Inside the rig: Major Danny Latter. Major Maria Tyson. Outside: Jozee. And the one whose name couldn't be spoken. The last unmentionable name was always going to be an issue. He couldn't even write it down in case he was wrong and someone found the evidence.

But each one needed a test: who was loyal?

Byrne had always had doubts about Danny. He'd been a good foil, sorting out difficult situations with other people of questionable alliance. Muscle when you needed it. But when placed under pressure by the commander, Danny had been a bit quick to give up information, requiring overly complex backstories to obfuscate reality. Dates changed. People bribed. The commander had been suspicious, but there was nothing definite. Danny was thrown into the cells.

Maria was next. Byrne needed to send her to collect valuable information—false, of course—regarding the *Hawkesbury*'s next destination and the contract budgets. The test would be to see if she'd sell it to the enemy. It was lucrative, and better people had fallen for less.

Were there better people? Somehow, the management team, the ones he should be able to trust, were falling by the wayside, but he had found loyalty outside in the most unexpected places. Not for money or power, but a broken heart. And it gave him an inside line to the heart of a rebel network of unnoticed spies.

He was still concerned about Jozee. As a pirate, by definition she was untrustworthy and disloyal. But she was a vital cog in his machinery and lived by some sort of pirate code. She was also the only person who knew his secret. Speaking of which, he needed to get in contact with the 'secret'.

Byrne looked down at the shortening list of potential threats.

They'd been asked for loyalty. Their understanding of what that meant needed to be refined. A strong management team needed loyalty to thrive. And, of course, they all wanted to thrive. The alternative was so extreme. Time to tighten the noose.

ARID'S BODY ACHED from head to toe. All he could taste was sand. All he could smell was blood and gas. The darkness swirled as his eyes fluttered. It was probably a mistake to progress any farther, but he couldn't stay lying in the desert forever. He yelped when the first identifiable object materialised as Frey's annoyed face. It should have been a hint.

'You moron,' she said.

Blood smeared across his hand as he wiped his nose. His head pounded. He spat the sand out of his mouth. The sun approached the horizon and was cooling, but the glare was intense. He must have been out for a while.

They were alone on the plain. The *Lady Moonshine* had limped on, leaving only its wide, shallow tracks.

Arid rose shakily to his feet, and Frey pushed him over. 'Hey, how's this my fault?' he said.

'You were escaping.'

'I didn't open the cell.'

'But you followed. You could've stayed in the cell,' Frey said.

'Y' didn't need t' get involved.'

'Get involved?' she said, mimicking him. 'We all need to do

our bit when protecting the *Lady Moonshine*. It's our *duty*.'

'And y' ended up blowing a hole in it,' Arid said.

'Again, wouldn't have been a problem if you'd kept your stupid head in your stupid cell. And someone needs to keep dear sister out of trouble.'

'Ella can look after herself, from what I've seen. At least she was kind t' me.'

'She's wrapping you around her little finger. She does that to all the boys. Gets them jumping for her, leaving me on my—look, we're in trouble out here. We'd be better off using our time chasing after the *Moonshine* than talking about flippin' Ella. *Again*. Everyone talks about her all the time.'

Arid attempted another stand. Frey let him get on his feet this time. The nearby terrain offered little in the way of shelter, only a scattering of boulders that formed a rough semicircle.

'Did I see Ella throw something out after us?'

'You're still talking about her, but yes, she did and it was a gun.' Frey waved it in her hand. 'Knowing her, she probably wanted it to be for you.'

'At least she has a heart.'

'Yeah, a dark one.'

'Why are y' so mean t' her?'

'Hah. Mean? To little Miss Perfect? You don't even know her, yet you're prepared to defend her. Why is that? Is it because she's pretty?'

'Er, no. It's, er, because she was, er, considerate and funny. And she helped me escape.'

'And where did that get you?'

'Because of you.'

'I refer you to the previous comment. Stay in cell. No problems,' Frey insisted.

'Enough. It's going t' be dark soon, we need shelter.' Arid looked up at the clouds drifting in from the northwest. 'At least the temperature won't drop too low. Y' better give me the gun.'

'I'm good with it.'

'But it's a gun and you're a girl.'

'At this point in time, it's a whole lot more useful than you are. Do you even know what type it is?'

'Er, sort of. I've seen them around.'

She hefted it over, offering him the grip. 'Oh, really? Show me. Fire it.'

Arid snatched the gun out of her hands. He rotated it, examining each component, then aimed it at one of the nearby boulders and pulled the trigger. Nothing happened. In fact, so little happened it was as though it sucked in all the happenings going on around it.

'It's broken,' he said.

Frey wrapped her hand around it, keeping his fastened to the grip. 'This is a TEER-2-CF3-101 short-range pulse pistol with suppressed recoil and fast recharge. At fifty feet, it will disorientate you. At twenty feet, it will boil your internal organs.' She positioned the barrel against her chest and clasped her hand around his fingers on the trigger. 'At zero feet, it will obliterate every living thing. There won't even be blood.'

Arid tried to pull away. Her hand didn't budge. She squeezed his hand, forcing the trigger down. He closed his eyes. It clicked.

'And, unlike most dangerous things in this world,' she said, 'it has a safety catch.' She pulled the gun away from him, twisted the base of the grip, aimed up and fired. A bird squawked and fell from the sky. 'Don't assume my limitations based on your personal biases. Some of us are more than we seem. Now, be manly and barbecue that bird.'

'*You*,' Arid said, 'are psychotic.'

'Me? I'm the one finding food.'

He peered out in the direction of the dying squawks. 'Even if I can find it, I ain't sure if it'll be edible. We need t' find a place t' stay. People die at night.'

'From what?' Frey asked, sarcasm dripping from her words.

'Many things. Crawlers, mutant dinocrocs …' Arid spotted something in the distance. 'Something that glows.'

Frey couldn't make out what he could see. 'What? How do you know something glowing can kill you?'

'Because I don't know what it is. And if I don't know what it is, it's probably dangerous. It might be an outpost,' Arid said. 'We should go there.'

'Shouldn't we follow the *Lady Moonshine*?'

'At night, and with it moving faster than us? And with no supplies?'

She glared at him. 'Yes. The *Moonshine* will need to stop at some point soon for water. It will need to drill to fill the furnaces once they're repaired. And the ground's flat. Out that way,' she said, pointing toward the outpost, 'is a battlefield, with crap everywhere.'

'Well, I'm going t' the outpost.'

'Enjoy yourself. I'm going home.'

'No, *you* enjoy yourself. I'll be in a soft bed tonight while yer struggling through mud and fighting off monsters.'

Each hesitated. Travelling alone was the quickest way to die. They both knew it.

Arid sat on a large rock and folded his arms in defiance. 'I ain't following the *Moonshine*.'

'Don't you want your rig back?'

He had to be careful because she could be right. And that would be annoying. His rig was the most important item in his life. Not the most precious, but it was his home, and life without it would be like losing a leg.

But his rig had been badly damaged, so would there be any point in getting it back?

But the queen said she would fix it.

But he had been in prison.

But if he could explain his situation, the queen would be able to see that it had been a mix-up. Adults understood that kind of thing.

But following the *Moonshine* would be dangerous.

But it was his territory.

But he knew the risks, and the outpost was an unknown one,

meaning it could be *more* dangerous.

Arid sighed and lowered his head. 'All right.'

Frey smiled. 'A wise choice.'

'Yer not much of a warrior princess.'

'The second part is the important bit.'

'Y' see, that's the difference. Adults don't get caught up in all that title stuff. Y' want t' be a princess without any real understanding of what y' mean t' do.'

'Stop with the arguing! The last person I want to be stuck with right now is *you*.' She turned her back to him. 'I just want to go home.'

He suddenly stiffened, his eyes opening wide. The rock underneath him was shaking. He leapt up as it roared and shifted. A dinocroc uncoiled and rose up on its back legs before pounding its body on the ground in a declaration of combat.

Frey screamed. They both ran. First in circles, as they struggled to decide a direction, then Frey took off after the *Lady Moonshine*.

'No!' Arid shouted. 'They're faster over flat ground. This way.'

He took off over the broken battlefield toward the outpost. The dinocroc roared again and reared up on its hind legs. Frey froze underneath it, peering up with terrified eyes. Arid turned and charged back, pulling her out of the way. They tumbled into the sand as the beast powered through the place where she'd been standing. Leaping to his feet, Arid helped the stunned girl get up and they ran through ruins that littered the ground.

There had been a battle, a ferocious one, and a long time ago, judging by the state of the rusted and mangled machinery. Rollers lay broken and semi-buried; sheets of metal stuck up out of the ground. Arid was caught on a piece of metal that tore his clothing as he pulled free. He paused, examining the edge that had caught him. The area was full of sharp objects.

He charged after Frey. 'I think this is the Yandarah battleground,' he said. 'Follow me, I've got an idea.'

He ducked between the remains of two burnt-out tracks with charred engines. The giant croc crashed in front of them, forcing them back and under. They waited, concealed in the wreckage as the beast stomped by. Its ponderous legs thumped down and it snorted through its enormous nose in deep gusts that blew up loose sand. It paused, raising its head and sniffing the air.

Arid pointed to the medium distance, where a fracking unit lay on its side with the drill facing outward. 'Let's go,' he shouted.

They sprinted from the hiding spot, clambering over the dinocroc's tail. The creature twitched, and the tip of its tail caught Arid's foot, sending him tripping and tumbling.

Frey hesitated, seeing him floundering on the sand, and the dinocroc turned toward them. Again, she was mesmerised by the prehistoric relic. Then she snapped out of her trance and helped Arid back up. His first step buckled. Ankle. Pain. Bad. Frey slipped her shoulder under his arm and they hobbled away as the croc built up speed behind. They dodged around various pieces of metal as the croc gained on them, crushing the smaller objects beneath it.

The thick drill flashed past as they peeled to the left, its pointed end shining in the sun. Arid glanced over his shoulder, monitoring the location of the croc. It was time. He indicated to his right, and he and Frey quickly moved to the opposite side of the drill. The croc switched directions after them and plunged onto the point. It speared into the creature's chest and drove downward as the monster's momentum pushed it forward. It thrashed against the steel, opening up the injury and spilling its insides.

Arid and Frey huddled beneath the turmoil as the croc bucked, its movements becoming frantic until they quietened and then ceased.

After several minutes of silence, they removed their hands from their heads and peered out from their hiding spot. The head of the dinocroc greeted them, mouth open, teeth bared, tongue lolling out. Its eyes stared straight ahead.

'Is it dead?' Frey asked.

Arid limped around to the rear of the creature, impaled on the great spike. 'I think so, but I wouldn't trust it.'

Frey sat on the round casing of a dislodged wheel. The gun slipped out from the pocket in her dress.

'Y' had the gun. Why didn't y' use it?' Arid asked.

'I forgot. It'll need to time to recharge.'

'Yer not going to be much help in an emergency.'

'You know, that was a pretty scary moment and I was really scared.'

'We're outside. That is the reality. Y' need t' be scared all the time, otherwise you die.' He reinforced the point by indicating the dead dinocroc. At least he hoped it was dead. He strode back toward Frey, but his ankle gave out and he fell. He sat up and nursed it. 'And now I can't walk. This is your fault.'

'Stop being a baby,' Frey replied.

She scanned the ground and found a piece of material: a torn blue uniform. She ripped it into strips and wrapped them around Arid's ankle. A thin bar stuck out of the sand. She pulled it free and handed it to him. She stood back with her hands on her hips and inspected her work. 'There you go, bandaged foot and walking stick. You're as good as a new cyborg.'

Arid glared at her, and then eased himself up. His foot tested well, taking the weight.

'We can't go after yer stupid rig now. We have t' go t' the outpost. And if we'd gone that way in the first place I would've had a good foot.'

Frey glared at him before turning and storming off in the rough direction of the *Moonshine*.

'Wait,' he called out. 'Y' won't survive out there on yer own.'

Her shoulders hunched forward, and she continued on her way, increasing her speed.

He stepped out after her, but toppled over. Rolling over onto his back, he shouted, 'Please, I can't survive without y', either.'

Frey slowed, then stopped. She turned and scowled at him for what seemed like an age, and then stomped back. 'Fine, we bunk down here for the night, then decide tomorrow.' She swept her eyes over the surroundings. Her voice then softened. 'Is there somewhere we can stay here?'

A sweeper sat not too far away, its rear wheels elevated off the ground by a roller squashed underneath. It appeared to be in good condition, except for a shattered windscreen. Inside, the interior was relatively clear, with two skeletons up front in the drivers' seats and sand covering the floor. Cobwebs lined the corners. Ancient.

The sun bounced on the horizon and the temperature fell. A chill crept in over the plain as the winds picked up across the desert, whipping between the broken machinery.

Frey searched the area for something they could burn. She didn't return with much, just rags and some heavily varnished wood. And some old bones, which struck Arid as odd.

By the time the sun had fully set, they had established a small camp in the remains of the sweeper. A fire spluttered in the corner of the vehicle, hidden from anything attracted to heat or light. The outside temperature started its descent into negative territory, forcing them close to the embers and the hypnotic flames.

Arid felt vulnerable. He hadn't slept outside the dowser in the open for years. They were going to have to be as silent as a parent's disappointment.

Frey sat with a long bone, probably somebody's leg, beside her. It sunk in that she was thinking of it as a weapon. Still odd, though, since plenty of metal lay around them.

The quiet of the night was broken by the waking of nocturnal life. Deep howls echoing over the plains, answered by distant responses, unexplained sonic rumbles, all set against the background of the continual scuttling sound of the stick crawlers. Cold nights brought out the cold-blooded killers.

Frey pulled her knees into her chest and folded her arms across them. 'Are we safe?'

'Here? No. But we'll survive.'

'Maybe you should've barbecued the bird.'

'There's a whole giant crocodile out there y' can rip some meat off if y' want. Once y' get past all the parasites and bugs living on it.'

'Thanks. I'm not hungry.' Frey's stomach growled, and she squinted up at him. 'It's wind.'

The fire crackled, and they both stared into the flames.

'Can I ask a question?' Arid said after a while.

'If you must.'

'Yer mother went weird when she heard my name. Do y' know why?'

'From what I remember—and it was a few years back—she had some friends or something called Geiger and they betrayed her. The name is known on the *Moonshine*, and not in a good way. They were building something for my mother when they took off, for some reason. She used to get real angry when it was brought up, real dark, but eased up over time. I guess hearing the name brought it all back.'

'Betrayal's a pretty big thing. What made her soften?'

'She changed. Like she said, she's not the person she used to be.'

'Y' know what they were building?'

'Some kind of weapon. She used to talk to all of them about it for hours. It was part of a big plan to destroy the other rigs.'

'That sounds pretty bad. What did y' make of it?'

'I didn't understand it at the time. It was just words. Reverse polarity. Molecular induction. Electron manipulation. I don't understand what any of it means.'

'Hang on, y' saw them? These Geigers?'

'Yeah. I had to sit at the table while they talked.'

'Did they look like me? Could they've been my parents?' Arid asked, his voice lifting with hope.

She looked at him. 'I don't know. Could've been. It was a long time ago.'

'Come on, this is important. I've got so little information about them, anything is helpful.'

'How? Just put them out of your mind. It's worse living with a distant recollection that fades, you know, like clutching at smoke.

Forget them, move on.'

'But I've got nothing. What I did have is on the *Moonshine*.'

'Just leave it. Parents only let you down.'

'Take that back.'

'Sorry. We sound like Mama-Bea and Stephanna.'

'Who's Stephanna?'

'Mama-Bea's partner.'

'Y' mean your dad?'

'Does Stephanna sound like a dad name? No, Mama-Bea adopted me. I'd have thought not looking anything like her would be a clue.'

'Why didn't I meet, er, *her*?'

'Because Stephanna's dead. Someone poisoned her.'

'I'm sorry for y'.'

Frey shrugged. 'She wasn't that nice. I wanted out, to go and live wild on the plain, like you, but where could I go?'

'What happened?'

'They met about twelve years ago. They were rivals in some battle, Mama-Bea won, as she always needs to do.' Frey punctuated the sentence with a sigh of resignation 'And me and Stephanna were brought on board. Stephanna and Mama-Bea just clicked. Always together. Then Mama-Bea asked us to live *with* her. They moved in together and I got a pretty nice room. When Stephanna died I thought I'd take off, but Mama-Bea began to be nicer. She has a phrase about tragedy forcing you to face yourself. And she decided to be around more. To *engage*. Actually started to hug me.'

'Where was Ella?'

'She didn't come along until after Stephanna was killed. About two years ago. She was such trouble, but eventually settled down.'

'Hang on, was Stephanna yer mother? Y' said 'we'.'

'I can see you're quick. She didn't deserve that title. As I said, she wasn't that nice.'

'So y' were adopted by the queen and Stephanna together?'

'Yeah, I suppose.'

'Why would they adopt?'

'You generally need a female *and* a male to produce a child. I guess it answered some awkward questions.'

Something didn't add up. If she was Stephanna's daughter, and Stephanna was the queen's partner, why would they adopt?

Frey continued. 'They weren't great, but they were my parents, I put up with them. Mama-Bea's been making up ever since. Suzie helped a lot, picking up the pieces, being a friendly ear. Always around the place, being caring and stuff.'

'Who's Suzie?' Arid asked.

'She's the tall, lanky one.'

'She didn't seem that nice to me. At least not during my tribunal.'

'She was just protecting Mama-Bea.'

Wrapped in the relative comfort of the cocooned interior, they kept to their individual worries, leaving them unvoiced. There were so many issues they had to face. Could they chase after the *Moonshine*? The tracks might be easy enough to follow as long as it didn't rain, but they had no food or water. If it rained they would have water, but it would turn the ground to mud and bring out the wildlife.

On the other hand, they had the outpost. Unknown danger, but probably within a day's walk. But who knew what lived among the debris. Scavengers. Rebel rollers. More crocs? It was rare to find a dinocroc on its own.

Frey said, 'Why is it so noisy?'

'It's life on the plain,' Arid replied. 'Creatures come out t' feed. With the temperature drop y' get all the reptiles and insects.'

'What are the booms?'

He shrugged. The great sonic rumbles were the backdrop to his life. He barely noticed them. At night they became the sloweddown heartbeat of a missing mother. 'You've never heard them before?'

Frey shook her head. 'I've never been outside the *Moonshine* at night before. My only memories are on it.' She lay down and stared into the fire, placing her hands under her head. Eventually she closed her eyes and her breathing relaxed.

Byrne waited for the contact to arrive, his patience wearing thin. He'd been outside of his roller for only fifteen minutes and already the back of his shirt was soaked, even as the temperature dropped. Insects swarmed around him and filled the night with an orchestra of clicks and buzzes.

The sweeper came into view, bouncing over the rocky terrain that was lit up by its headlights; the rig's dented exterior nearly invisible in the night light, displayed identification of its purpose and allegiance. The brakes hissed as it slowed and stopped. The hatch on the top opened and a head appeared—a woman with short hair—and scanned the area.

Byrne waved. The head was joined by a hand that responded with a rude gesture. The side door clicked open and lowered, the gas supports groaning as it touched the sand. A figure dressed all in black appeared at the entrance but didn't venture out.

'Any updates?' Byrne asked.

'The queen chooses not to attend the meet,' Alex replied.

'Why would she do that?'

'She probably doesn't trust you.'

'But she can't know what I'm planning,' Byrne said. 'Are you telling anyone at all about the plans?'

'No.'

'You wouldn't lie to me, would you?'

'Have I ever? Why do you ask?'

'I have a feeling … it's nothing.'

'There is something you should know,' Alex said. 'Today I tried to assassinate the target.'

'Today? Why?'

'Someone new came aboard. It provided the perfect alibi.'

'But you failed?'

'This time, and I'm sorry. It won't happen again.'

'Never mind. It's not as if you've been training your whole life for it. Can you use this new person again?'

Alex paused. 'Yes, but it's complicated.'

'How so?'

'He's no longer aboard.'

'I don't follow.'

'There's an opportunity to lure the queen to the alliance meeting and blame the boy for the assassination. One of the queen's daughters fell off the *Moonshine* with the boy. Get her daughter to the meet and the queen will follow.'

'How can I do that?'

'Simple. Tell her the queen will be there. They'll all want to meet up and be happy families.'

'Which daughter is it?'

'Frey.'

'Are you sure the queen will turn up for her?'

'Of course.'

'Where is the daughter?'

Alex shrugged. 'Somewhere out there.'

'That's not helpful. Who's this new person?'

'His name is Arid Geiger.'

'Really? Any relation to—'

'I believe he could be. Claims to be a diviner. The timeline adds up. The only one who could confirm it would be the queen. His appearance may be a blessing in disguise.'

'Tell me, did he have a small rectangular object? Grey with a couple of lights on it?'

'I believe so.'

'Interesting. Get the boss.'

Alex disappeared inside then reappeared with the rig's captain, the shorthaired woman.

'Hello, Jozee,' Byrne said.

'I'm not overly inclined to speak to you,' Jozee replied. 'My hearing is being affected by lack of pay.'

'Find the kids and take them to the usual place.'

'Jozee can't go,' Alex protested. 'I need to get back to the *Moonshine*.'

'I'll take you,' Byrne said.

'Any idea where they are?' Jozee asked. 'The desert's a big place.'

Alex replied, 'I believe Frey and the boy left the *Moonshine* near the Yandarah battleground. They'll probably make their way to Tom Price.'

Jozee patted Alex on the back as the assassin disembarked. 'Good luck.'

As Alex climbed into the roller, Jozee grabbed Byrne and raised a finger to his face. 'I don't trust you or your friend. Be aware that I'm keeping a close eye on your assassin. Just letting you know I've made sure I'll see 'em coming.'

Arid woke to a dull thumping sound. Yawning and stretching, it took a moment for the sound to register through the fog in his head. He shook Frey awake. 'We need t' get going.'

'What's that noise?' she asked, as she rubbed her eyes.

The fire had long since burnt out, its charred remains providing a strong scent of smoke in the heavy morning air. You could see the humidity.

'There's a dinocroc nearby. It may be eating the other one. Either way we need t' get out of here now.'

Arid tested his ankle; it felt a lot stronger. Maybe not running-away strength, but good enough to walk with minimal assistance from the thin bar.

Frey clutched at her stomach. 'I'm so hungry.'

'We ain't going t' be eating for a while. Y' better get used t' it.'

'Thanks for the sympathy. How's your foot?'

He rolled his eyes.

As they peered around the edge of the sweeper, a new dinocroc came into view. It was slamming its tail into the ground in great ponderous strokes, throwing dust in the air. Its mouth tore into the deceased giant croc, which was now shrouded in a cloud of flies.

'Why's it doing that?' Frey asked.

Arid sighed. 'It's summoning stick crawlers.'
'What do we do?'
'Two choices. We run.'
After he said no more, Frey asked, 'What's the other one?'
He gave her a withering stare.

Two and a half years ago …
Hunter throws the rope back at Alex, who is sitting on the perforated metal floor, exhausted, fingers gripping through the floor's holes. Vibrations fill the training room as the mechCity turns to head in a new direction. The sounds of combat filter in from the training arena. The area stinks of sweat, blood and urine. Fear does that to the young.

'Do it again,' Hunter orders.

'I can't,' Alex replies. 'My arms are shaking.'

'We're not stopping until you do. Learn to embrace the pain. It's your friend in the darkness, an ally when all else fails.'

'I'm not strong enough.'

Hunter grabs Alex's collar and drags the child off the ground. 'It's only your mind that's weak. Don't your parents mean anything to you? The woman killed them, and you'll find her at the end of this damn rope. You'd get justice, you'd get revenge—if you weren't so weak.'

The man's breath repulses Alex, and it says plenty about him.

On the outside, he's neat but quirky, with his brightly coloured floral shirts, knee-length shorts and sandals. Everyone else dresses in some kind of uniform identifying where they sit within the command hierarchy. But not him.

On the inside, the man overflows with a brittle anger that explodes unpredictably. Yesterday, he'd been sympathetic to Alex's efforts and fatigue levels. Today he's an insatiable monster. Who knows what the difference is?

'Weak,' Hunter bellows.

The volume has Alex flinching away. One day. One day. When all this is over, one day, it will come tumbling down. It's a thought that will never be forgotten. 'Don't push too hard,' Alex says. 'You might not get the response you're after.'

Hunter smiles. 'Now you're talking. Show me your anger. Show me the belly of the beast.' He hands over a knife. *'Come at me.'*

The two circle each other. Alex lunges, but is trapped and thrown to the floor.

'You're going to need to be faster than that,' Hunter says.

[5]

ARID AND FREY hustled through the battlefield, breaking through spiralling columns of mist, with Frey leading the way. Arid limped as quickly as he could, using the stick for support, but it was biting into his hand. The crawlers were finding it tough to keep up over the difficult terrain, their pincers slipping on the metal surfaces. But it was only a matter of a few dozen metres and the pair would be out in the open.

Then where?

Being realistic, there wasn't anywhere. The outpost looked to be kilometres away. There was another croc on the loose and the area was swarming with crawlers.

Arid slowed as they reached the field perimeter, placing his hand on Frey's arm. 'We can't make it across with the crawlers after us. We'll be safe if we get height on something metal.'

'Like that,' Frey said, pointing to a staircase ripped out of a rig and jutting upwards.

It felt surreal climbing a detached staircase—eight steps to nowhere. Frey's knuckles turned white as she gripped the handrail. At the top, they turned and watched the activity below. Were eight steps going to be enough?

The crawlers scrabbled at the metal but failed to gain traction. The sea of insects started to swirl clockwise around the base of the stairs. As they built momentum, the bodies mounted one another, gaining height as they slowly climbed the steps.

'What's that over there?' Frey said. A trail of dust coiled to the north.

'If we're lucky, a traveller on their way t' the outpost,' Arid replied.

'And if we're not?'

'I guess we find out if they turn up.'

'Can we signal them or something?' Frey asked.

'What about yer gun? Does it have a flare mode or something?'

'Um, I don't think so.'

'Y' don't know much,' Arid said.

'At least I know how to fire it.' She examined the controls, lowered it to its minimal setting then fired it directly up into the air in a sequence. Three short. Three long. Three short.

'What was that?'

'SOS, the international distress code. The soldiers back on the *Lady Moonshine* look out for it. It's the best I could come up with.'

They watched the vehicle in the distance roll on. The crawlers continued to climb in their swirling pyramid, slowly mounting each step as the numbers built. The clicking sound became an intense death rattle as the volume increased.

The dust trail disappeared. Their hearts sank.

'I guess we're not going to be saved. Do we need to worry about the croc?' Frey asked.

'No. They sleep after a feed,' Arid explained. 'The crawlers will get to us before then.'

'At least I've got the gun.'

Arid sighed. 'That won't do anything against a thousand crawlers.'

'Not for them, for us.'

Arid put on a face. 'That's a bit dark.'

'You want to be stabbed to death? The gun can take us both

out in one shot. No pain.'

'It seems so final. I always like t' think there's a last-minute way out.'

'Between the dinocroc and crawlers, there don't seem to be any last-minute anythings. Other than extreme pain and death. And if I had a choice of one rather than a guaranteed both, I know which I would pick.'

'Well, I think it's dumb. I'm sure the adults will be out looking.'

Frey stared down at the manic creatures, her bottom lip quivering.

Arid thought about saying something. Frey was right; she was more princess than warrior, and this was an awful time to come to terms with it.

'Here's something else y' probably won't want t' know,' he continued. 'As we're up high, we'll become targets for the crows later in the day. They'll wait for us t' dehydrate and our skin t' soften so they can get a good purchase, then rip it off.'

'Is everything here out to kill us?'

'Yeah. Except for … no, everything.'

'Maybe it's best if you don't talk for a while.'

'My pleasure.'

And as the sun inched its way across the sky, the birds started to appear. Frey let out a long sigh and then played with the gun, turning it around in her hands. The birds had been closing in, drifting around in tighter circles. The first dived in at them. Arid thrust his walking stick at it, narrowly missing the bird.

Frey put her hands over her head.

'Shoot them!' Arid shouted.

Frey gasped and stood up. Bouncing through the battlefield was a sweeper rig, badly dented but mobile. She waved frantically at it.

Arid swatted away a bird, causing it to shriek. Two more came diving in at them from opposing angles, swooping past Arid's stick and aiming their talons at his clothing.

After what felt like an eternity, the sweeper came rolling through the crawlers, crushing them under its balloon-like wheels and causing the remaining creatures to scatter. The pyramid collapsed as the lower tiers disintegrated. The sweeper stopped at the base of the stairs and the top hatch opened.

The head of a woman with close-cut hair emerged. 'You all right up there?'

'Um,' was Arid's only reply.

Major Maria Tyson scratched her head. The instructions from Byrne had been confusing. She had met the contact with the contract information, a job well below her pay grade. Then she'd traipsed another hundred clicks to a blown-out town, where a shifty lady with short hair looking more butch than a blood-soaked butcher—probably a pirate—turned up offering a staggering amount of cash for the information. Enough to flee this forsaken place and start fresh over at the Belt.

Holding the illegal currency in her hands, it was hard to say no.

Maria reflected upon her decision, standing in the silence of the cracked and broken building. Why had the pirate been here? How could she have known? The story the woman had spun hardly made sense, as though read from a script. Then there had been some fuss outside and the pirate had run away.

Enough was enough. It was time to go.

There was a shifting in the shadows. A familiar silhouette emerged. She raised her hands to peer into the dark.

'Hello? Byrne, is that you?' she asked. 'You're late.'

'Major. You, I see, have followed your orders to the letter.'

'Of course. Cog in the machine and all that.'

'And I'm happy to say you're here on your own.'

'Was anyone else expected? Some pirate turned up, but I sent her on her way. The orders didn't mention her, and I found her highly suspect. Luckily she wasn't armed.'

'One can never be sure who's listening in on our communications.

So that's one point in your favour. What did the pirate say?'

Maria harrumphed. 'Some ridiculous story about some other commander offering me a reward for the exemplary work I'd been doing. It made no sense. She started to get testy, but I think one of our patrols came close and she scurried off to the hills.'

Byrne went quiet. 'Did you tell anyone about this?'

'We have a chain of command that must be recognised. You, of all people, know this and continually bring it up if someone tries to talk directly to the commander.'

'You told him, didn't you?'

'You need to be honest. What are you planning?'

Byrne sat on the remains of a crumbling wall. 'A revolution. I'm going to bring peace.'

Maria laughed. 'You, the master of mayhem?'

'I didn't say *how* I was going to do it.'

'The commander knows?'

'Is it a requirement? You feel he should?'

'Is this about your brother? It's about your brother, isn't it? Did you send the pirate? Are you testing me?'

'I test everyone,' Byrne snapped. 'Loyalty needs to be at the heart of all our actions and relationships. Without it, we never know who the enemy is.'

'But you've never been loyal to me. This test in itself is proof of that. I've never done anything wrong. I've stood by you when required, when you needed the votes of confidence in your sometimes-reckless attacks. And what have you done for me?'

'That's not the way it works.'

'I'm telling the commander. You're going too far.'

'You have a choice. Prison ...'

'Or?'

Byrne fired his pistol. Maria stood for a moment, swaying as if she was a marionette suspended from an unseen puppeteer. And maybe that had been the case all along. Blood trickled down the bridge of her nose, forming a red line to her chin, where it gathered momentum and dripped to the floor. Her knees buckled and she collapsed.

'You were expecting cake?'

The rear of the sweeper had been converted into a utilitarian sitting area, with several steel chairs fastened into position around a large steel table. A round drinks holder had been attached with a hinge to the end of each chair's armrest, allowing them to click into an upright position—like a clamp. Arid noticed that the front legs of the chairs also had some, but they appeared to be broken, as though cut in half on one side. Behind them, a stark wall across the entire back of the vehicle defined a storage area, taking up about a third of the interior, with one solid door in the centre.

The sweeper had a minimal crew: driver, navigator, captain, and two deckhands. They were dressed in dusty-red uniforms, something that would blend in with the world outside. Other than the captain, the rest of the crew looked dishevelled. But the objects inside were placed and spaced with obsessive detail, an array of technical odds and ends. Weapons. Cutlery. Crockery. A shelf carried a dozen tiny flat black discs, no bigger than half a thumbnail.

The crawlers flailed ineffectually against the sweeper's panoramic windscreen, the tapping of their pincers against the glass ringing in the low-ceilinged space.

Arid sat with his forehead resting on his arms, which were folded on the table in an effort to block out the noise of the creatures.

'Where are you heading?' the captain asked.

'We're trying to get back to the *Lady Moonshine*,' Frey said.

The captain nodded her head and took a sip of her coffee. 'We'll see what we can do. Do you want any more water?'

Arid shook his head. Frey smiled and held out her glass. One of the deckhands filled it from a chilled steel container with condensation running down the outside. The deckhand smiled through cracked teeth.

'You were lucky we found you,' the captain said. 'Another

half-hour and you'd probably been dead. What are your names?'

'I'm Frey. This is Arid.'

Arid raised his hand, but not his head.

'What are *your* names?' Frey asked.

'I'm Jozee,' the captain replied.

'What about the others?' Frey asked, after no further information was forthcoming.

'They're not really ones for identification. We like to keep a low profile.'

Arid glanced up, and Jozee turned her attention to him. 'What are those black discs?' he asked.

Jozee looked over her shoulder, slowly turning back and giving him a wry grin. 'Trackers. I like to see where my'—she glanced at Frey—'investments are. Or potential earners. Tell me about your girlfriend. She looks familiar.'

Arid nearly fell off his chair. 'There ain't no way she's my girlfriend. Good lord, no.'

Frey's face folded in fury. She crossed her arms and turned away.

'You could have phrased that better,' Jozee said.

'But I don't like her.'

'You don't know many girls—no, *people*—do you?'

'I know heaps, I'm really popular.'

'I can see. You must have them lining up at the school dance.'

'What *exactly* are you doing out here?' Frey asked.

'I have a brother, Andana, who's experimenting with airships. He's an up-and-coming name in urban sky logistics.'

'Flying? Wow.'

'Yes. We'll finally get to avoid individuals with unwanted questions and paperwork at the Belt.'

Arid held his breath. Only one kind of person wanted to avoid the Belt authorities.

Jozee peered at Arid as she spoke. 'Good times ahead. Lots of interesting things happening over east.'

'Y' haven't asked us where the *Moonshine* is,' he observed.

'All in good time. You know there's a reward out for you.'
'Why? What did we do?' Frey said.
'You attempted to assassinate the queen.'
'I did not,' Arid blurted.
Jozee shrugged. 'Just saying what the widecast said.'
'Are y' going t' turn us in?'
The captain hesitated, her eyes sweeping over them. 'Nah. I'm not going to drop anyone into the Feds. In the meantime, I need to keep you safe.'

Byrne had barely been on the *Hawkesbury* ten minutes before Hunter was pestering him. The man sat with his usual relaxed and insulting demeanour.

'Hunter, there's been some disturbing news,' Byrne said. 'Maria has disappeared.'

'Has she left any instructions or information about where she went?'

'It appears not. We need her skills on the bridge. I suggest we draft in Lieutenant Cosgrove as acting logistics head.'

'Cosgrove? The man is a long-time friend of yours, correct?'

'I know him. He's loyal. That's how I can highly recommend him,' Byrne replied.

Hunter rose to his feet and stood still, with his hands behind his back, an uncharacteristic pose for him. 'Something seems afoot. You've lost a few high-command personnel of late. It could be considered bordering on careless.'

'Only one or two.'

'I thought it was five. I heard it was five. Not that it has anything to do with me what you do on your ship.'

'That would be an inaccurate figure. The real number is low. We still have some, just locked away in the cells.'

Hunter shrugged and turned away to gaze through the command-deck window. 'As you wish. Is there anything you want to discuss? Your key resources?'

'No.'

'The plan continues as, er, planned?'

'Yes.'

'I only ask since those who are connected with the plan seem to be disappearing.'

Byrne paused. The moment to test Hunter's alliance had arrived. 'It's a turbulent time. I think we should head to Broome.'

'Why?'

'It's strategically important. And has very nice beaches. You already have the attire.'

'In what way is it strategically important?'

'The inlet provides only a narrow entrance. If we control that we will have complete control over resources and the shipping line. There's good profit to be made.' Byrne hesitated, letting the positives sink in. 'That's if we can get there without them knowing.'

'I'll think about it.'

The trap had been set. Byrne suppressed the urge to rub his hands together. 'You must excuse me, I have places to be.'

'Besides Broome?'

'Why didn't you say they were pirates?'

Frey glared at Arid. The prison at the rear of the vehicle had no windows, only a vent at floor level that sucked in air that was pumped from an undisclosed point.

'It ain't as if they're flying a flag. A sweeper can be aligned with anyone. I saw some in the *Moonshine* as well, y' know.'

'You're the big desert wolf who's supposed to know this kind of thing.'

'Well, a bit more time and I could have, y' know, got … stuff.'

They sat in silence as the sweeper turned and picked up speed.

'Where are they taking us?' Frey asked.

'How should I know?' Arid replied. 'Pirates do what they do. Y' don't ask, and y' steer clear of them. That's all I know.'

'Should it matter that they have cells?'

'Yes. Means they trade in people.'

'Like, for new ones?'

'Could y' ask less-dumb questions!'

'I wish I had the TEER.'

'Yeah, y' probably shouldn't have pointed it at them. Unless y' were prepared t' use it.'

'Of course I was.'

'Pointing it is one thing; pulling the trigger is another thing all together. Y' never know what kind of person y' are until yer put in that position. Me, I would've fired, no probs.' He raised a foot to rest it on the bench and leaned back against the wall.

'If only you knew how to turn it on. Anyway, it hardly had any charge left.'

'Well, now they've got the gun and are recharging it. Because *you* couldn't pull the trigger.'

'Being out here is hard enough. It would help if you weren't so difficult all the time.'

The sweeper bounced along, rocking their bodies as it sped over the uneven terrain.

'Won't the queen notice yer missing?' Arid asked.

'Only if I'm summoned, and even then she might think I'm being difficult.'

'What about Ella? Surely she'd say something.'

'Her? Only if she can be bothered. She'll be happy to be rid of me so she can have Mama-Bea to herself. And do you think she'd want to confess to helping a prisoner escape?'

'Sounds like y' got a good family dynamic.'

'It's difficult. You try being part of royalty.'

'Strangely, I'd like a family so I could be annoyed at them.'

'You know nothing about families.'

'I know mine would be here right now, sorting this out.'

Frey snorted. 'Adults can't sort anything out. They're useless.'

By unspoken agreement, they decided it would be best not to talk for a while and wait out the journey.

The jolting and rocking of the sweeper finally stopped. It had been hours. They'd both slept on and off.

After several minutes, the cell door opened and Jozee peered in. She gave the youngsters a brief smile. 'We're here.'

'Where? The *Lady Moonshine*?' Frey said.

Jozee laughed as she pointed the barrel of her gun into the cell. 'Sort of.'

They moved out into the central seating area, Arid leading the way.

Jozee patted Frey on the back as she passed by. 'Good luck.'

The sky through the windscreen was black. Nighttime. No stars. The deckhands formed into a circle around them.

'Time to get paid,' Jozee said.

'Y' said y' weren't going t' dob us in to the Feds,' Arid said.

'I'm not, not to the cops, that is.'

'You don't need to pay us,' Frey said.

'No, we're going to *be* paid. For you.'

'What?'

'Welcome to the Battery.'

'The what?' Frey asked.

'It's a place where illegal trading is done,' Arid said.

'Home,' added Jozee.

'Hey, you can't do this,' Frey said, 'I'm the daughter of Queen Bea.'

Jozee paused, her eyes scanning the young girl. Then she shrugged. 'Deal with it. Out here, a body is a body. Doesn't matter who owns it.'

'You know, I'm sure there's somewhere in the world where everyone isn't horrible all the time.'

'Go for it, princess.'

Frey tried to twist away from the deckhand, but his grip was like steel and they were forced to wait as the team suited up with an armoury of weapons.

The door hissed open. Warm air rushed in. clearing out some of the smell, but instantly raising the temperature. Arid and Frey followed Jozee out. The sweeper was parked among several other vehicles—modified sweepers, screamers and rollers—all forming a semicircle at the mouth of a large mine that was underground rather than the usual open cut. Lights buried in the ground marked out the perimeter of the entrance, and a solid wall curved behind it, rising to a tall crest at the rear. Only one way in.

The tunnel stretched downward, with lights along the base highlighting the path, sloping down until they disappeared into impenetrable darkness. Sounds of industry floated out: the screams and pounding of metal being hammered, sheared, burnt and blasted.

Rain was beginning to fall in large drops, kicking up the dust.

'Looks like change is coming,' said the sweeper's driver from the rear of the pack. He stamped his foot into a puddle and chuckled as the mud splattered over the rest of the crew.

A lowered boom gate blocked the mine entrance, its bright red-and-white stripes glistening as the rain washed away the dust. Jozee left them and spoke at length to the guards stationed to the side. They were huddled in a control booth with three walls, one table and an extended roof. The booth was large enough to hold half a dozen guards.

Arid tried to recall what he'd heard about the Battery. What had his parents said? Was it a bad place? They'd visited it, spoken about it in an unbiased way. It was a place you went when you needed particular equipment, or needed something to be made that a registered engineer wouldn't touch, for whatever reason. So it wasn't necessarily a bad place, more of a freethinking place. He felt more confident.

A guard pulled on a raincoat and approached the group. 'Names,' she said. The crew presented their arms, which had numbers tattooed along the inside. The guard pointed at Frey.

'Princess Frey,' Jozee said.

The guard looked unimpressed. 'Unless you're in No Bearing,

you're going to need a surname.'

'Frey Smith.'

The guard snorted. 'Sounds authentic to me.' She looked at Arid.

'Arid Geiger.'

The guard paused her writing and slowly looked up at him. 'Wait here.' She turned and went back to the control station. The guards formed a tight group and whispered among themselves.

The rain fell heavier, and a wind blew in around the barrier created by the entrance.

The guard returned. 'I have been instructed to tell you that you are not allowed in with your current contingency.'

'Oh, come on,' Jozee complained.

'The answer is no. And you know why. You were here when it happened.'

'It was years ago.'

'You know. We know you know. You know we know. Banned means banned. Don't believe that we'll forget. Ever.'

Jozee shook her head. 'I didn't want it to come to this, but I've got debts to pay.' She put her fingers in her mouth and whistled. The sound cut through the air, piercing and almost painful.

The crew withdrew their weapons.

Jozee aimed the TEER gun at the guards.

'You want to be banned, too?' the guard asked.

'Can't be banned if no one knows about it.' And with a smile, Jozee pulled the trigger.

The control booth exploded.

The crew ducked against the blast as splinters rained over them.

'Double time, everyone,' she shouted, signalling for them to descend into the mine.

Arid and Frey stepped delicately over the deceased guards, the brutality of the TEER shocking them. Two deckhands bumped them into the mine. The darkness quickly enveloped them as the floor lights became less frequent, and they stumbled blindly along. The occasional side tunnel branched away, with more sounds of industry and manufacture floating out.

After several hundred metres, the tunnel flattened out into a small chamber, poorly lit with only a few lanterns tacked to the walls. The area was cool, but the warm air had condensation running down the rock walls.

'Where to?' asked one of the deckhands.

'I'm not sure,' Jozee replied. 'I'm trying to remember. Probably shouldn't have shot the guards. Just keep going forward.'

The tunnel spiralled down, the wide, broad walkway opening up into long offshoots.

'Aren't we meant to be meeting Byrne?' the same deckhand asked.

'Those who will pay on time get our priority,' Jozee said.

'Who are we meeting?'

'The bid note said someone called Iris. I think we were meant to meet them in the pit. And I haven't been down there since we broke out.'

'What's the pit?' Frey whispered to Arid.

'It's where the black-trade deals are done,' he answered.

'What's black trade?'

'The illegal and cool stuff. Don't ask what illegal is,' he said.

'What if Byrne catches us?' the other deckhand asked Jozee.

'Shut up,' she replied.

The party reached a junction. Two identical tunnels led down into the dark. Jozee peered into each, muttering under her breath as she glanced between the two. She shook her head and ran off down the right-hand passage with the others close behind her. The gradient dropped and the tunnel became almost impossible to run down without losing footing. A combination of sliding and rapid footsteps soon had them at the base, where the tunnel flattened out. The lights illuminating the descent stopped.

Jozee halted and the others pulled up behind her, catching their breath. The deckhands took hold of Arid and Frey.

'Are you @scott2Morryson?' Jozee called into the darkness.

'I the designated representative,' a rasping voice replied. The first visible sign was a glowing red eye. Out of the shadows stepped a figure. It had a flesh face, but the body was metal, grim and cold. The light caught the rough edges of the worn body parts; it had seen war. 'Call me @redFive.'

Frey clapped her hands. 'It's a cyborg. They're all right. We've used them all the time. Good workers. Great at fixing things.'

'I don't like it when plans change and it's not me doing the changing,' Jozee said. 'What happened to @scott?'

'Iris disappointed in his performance,' @redFive explained. 'Replacement is sought.'

'You guys change representatives more frequently than I have hot dinners.'

Arid relaxed. He, too, had had positive experiences with cyborgs. Honest, sort-of-people that were happy to work hard in difficult situations. And they *could* fix anything. Amazing tech. But this one had something unexpected on its back.

'Yeah, cyborgs. Great,' he said.

But it concerned him that this one, who honestly looked the worse for wear, was here. Cyborgs never went in the Battery. They couldn't get to grips with the haggling process. Too honest. The way the cyborg stood also troubled him. They generally stood tall, often with a vacant expression, as though waiting to be told what to do next. This one was acting differently, almost as though he was commanding himself. An untamed cyborg with all that strength would be … concerning.

Frey said, 'They generally do as they're told, and they love money. Watch this.' She turned to address the cyborg. 'If you take us to the *Lady Moonshine*, you will be richly rewarded.'

@redFive looked down at the display wrapped around his wrist. 'No.'

'What?'

'You be harvested for parts.'

'*What!*'

'Times are changing, princess,' Jozee said.

'How you like payment?' inquired @redFive. 'Credit transfer?

PayWave?'

'I'll take cash, if it's all the same to you.'

'As requested.' The side of @redFive's leg opened to reveal a cavity. He removed a bag and extended his hand.

Then Arid worked out what the object on the cyborg's back was. It was a gun. He'd never seen one with a weapon. It was long and black, with a claw-like attachment on the barrel. The thing almost looked like a part of the cyborg, and an extension of ill intent.

Jozee checked through the contents of the bag. 'Seems in order. You can take 'em. Have a nice life, kids. Or whatever's left of it.'

The deckhands released their hold on Arid and Frey, and @redFive grabbed them, metal fingers clamping deep into their shoulders and causing both to cry out in pain. The cyborg dragged them down a short corridor that ended in a long staircase, their young feet struggling to keep up with his pace, often stumbling down the stairs. A heavy thumping resonated through the walls, with screams between each thud.

There were no more lamps. Darkness welcomed them in, with the only light radiating out from the cyborg's eye, bathing everything in a faint, deep-red glow.

They entered a space where the walls fell away. The expansiveness became overwhelming, and subconsciously they were drawn closer together. The noise of toiling machinery hummed in the background, punctuated by the repetitive scream of saws slicing into metal. Several red lights appeared ahead, oscillating back and forth as they approached.

'What's going on?' Frey whispered to Arid.

The distant red lights highlighted a face as they neared: another cyborg.

'@redFive, update status,' the second cyborg said.

'Two bodies for yield, @rockinCollette45.'

'Good.good. Iris notices your good.good dedication.'

@redFive handed them over. Before they could move away, @rockinCollette45 acquired her own tight grip on them and dragged them towards a soft glow at the far end of the cavern that slowly illuminated the vastness of their surroundings. To their left, a long orange streak appeared and intensified as they came closer.

'You are harvested,' @rockinCollette45 told them.

'That doesn't sound good,' Arid said.

'Um, what do you mean?' Frey asked the cyborg.

'Slicer dismembers your body. We redistribute for parts and contribute to cyborg war effort.'

Frey gasped, covering her mouth in horror. The orange streak outlined dozens of cyborgs walking past in their determined yet plodding fashion. They carried bits of machinery, large blades and mystery items wrapped in white sheets that leaked a dark liquid, a deep crimson in the orange light. Then they heard the screams.

'No!' cried Arid. He twisted and kicked against the cyborg, but it was pointless. The cyborg pulled them forward toward the horrific sight.

Above, a steel frame rose high above the ground and across the glowing fissure. The frame supported a row of human-sized, X-shaped structures. Each held a person with a limb secured to the points of the X. Terrified prisoners queued up on the opposite side. Cyborgs placed each one into the X structures as they progressed, slamming the people's wrists and ankles into place against the steel, then fastening the restraints. The buzz of the saw revved up, followed by a shriek as it cut into metal. Except the screams now took on a new edge—not of metal, but people.

Arid and Frey were pushed to the front of the queue and thrust against the X structures, kept in place by two cyborgs while a third adjusted the restraints to match their smaller size.

The cyborgs stepped away, focusing on the next person in the queue. The slicer lifted the pair and soared over the fissure. Their stomachs tumbled. For the first time they could see down into the horror the fissure held.

Multiple furnaces radiated light, showing the floor awash with red. Scalding waves of intense heat coursed over them. A large, clanking chain ran from a motor in the lower level, up and around a large cog that propelled the X structures along the frame. Tucked away nearly out of view was a large grey cylinder. Ahead, Arid and Frey could see a circular saw as large as a person that spun up as each victim approached. It swung out and … they couldn't look. The screams were bad enough.

And they headed straight for it. The restraints were tight, and no matter how much they struggled, there was no escape.

The man in the line before them screamed as the blade sliced into his leg, severing it. It tumbled downward into the pit. Blood sprayed out. On the third pass, the man was silenced. The saw swung away, spinning down and slamming to a halt in a clasp. Bits of bone and tissue tumbled down as the blade jarred. The glow caught the blade edges, which were pitted and scored. It paused momentarily, with the silence filled by wailing.

Hanging. Waiting. Menacing. Getting closer. Only a matter of metres now.

The clasp snapped open and the saw spun up, shrieking like a demon.

A wave of despair swept over Arid as he fought against the immovable restraints. He closed his eyes and braced against the end. Would he feel anything? Would it be over quickly? The world became the noise and fury of the blade, leaving only hopelessness. The air from the rotations blew over him, filling his nose with the stench of death.

The frame swayed and twisted, jerking him sideways. The saw hammered against the twist, bouncing back before swinging in again.

The leg restraints snapped open, leaving Arid and Frey hanging by their arms and cutting off their breathing. The conveyor stuttered to a halt, and the bandsaw, pushing through the twisted frame and slicing in, missed them by centimetres.

Through his dazed view, Arid thought he could make out a man, one with long white hair that caught the glow from the furnace. He had a long silver object in his hand, which he had brought down with such force that the drive chain had bent and buckled.

The harnesses dropped, bringing Arid and Frey within range again of the swinging saw, forcing them to raise their legs in an ungainly dance as it sliced underneath them. The intense whine of the saw diminished as it slowed, until the racket was replaced by the pounding and hiss of work in the fissure. The drive chain swung free, disengaging from the mechanism and releasing all the restraints. The prisoners dropped like falling dominos, rolling to safety before hurrying away.

Arid and Frey landed on their hands and knees at the edge of the fissure, shaking and breathing heavily. The line of prisoners had disappeared. Arid peered over his shoulder down into the abyss. The majority of the cyborgs stood still. Some continued to work on the large grey cylinder.

He glanced up, and a couple of heavy boots stepped in front of him.

[6]

A LARGE HAND DESCENDED from the heavens and lifted Arid and Frey to their feet. The man, or possibly a god, stood before them, towering above them. His long white hair was tied back in a ponytail. His movements, considering his size, were precise and lightning fast. He wore an unfamiliar brown-and-black military uniform with a circular badge on the sleeve: STEAM ACADEMY.

And there was no getting around it—he had a damn huge sword strapped to his back. Who carried a sword? Surely it would rust in the rain, or something.

Frey held out a shaking hand. 'Hi, I'm Frey. I'm a princess. Thank you so much for rescuing me, um, us. You were amazing. Did I mention I was a princess? Do you do that a lot, rescuing people in such a heroic way?'

It was painful. But the man smiled, took her hand, and held it as she calmed. Colour returned to her face, mainly red as she blushed deeply.

'Stop it,' Arid hissed. He cleared his throat, put his hands in his pockets and rocked back on his heels. 'Yeah, thanks for helping out,' he said to the man. 'I had it under control, going as I'd planned, but it's always handy getting support. Even if y' don't need it. We should team up.'

The warrior smiled at both. 'Glad to have met you. I suggest you make tracks out of here.'

'So you're not here to rescue us?' Frey said.

'Sorry, Frey, and ... what was your name?'

'Arid. Arid Geiger.'

The soldier raised an eyebrow. 'Really?'

'Why is everyone doing that?' Arid asked.

'You know much about this place?'

'A bit,' Arid replied.

'You know about down there?' the man inquired, nodding toward the fissure.

'Er, no. I've never been t' the lower depths of the Battery. I don't even know where it is in actual terms. My parents used t' come here, but I was too young t' understand.'

'Maybe for the best. You need to go. This is a dangerous place.'

'How did y' find it? This place is impossible t' get to.'

'We've been following you. Well, the pirates, until we lost them.'

'Why were you after the pirates?'

'Always a good source of information once they're given the incentive to talk.' The man gave them a disconcerting smile.

'If you weren't following,' Frey asked, 'how did you find us?'

'Was it you who fired SOS out on the edge of the battlefield?' the man asked.

'Yes.'

'Good idea, that. Smart.'

Frey giggled. Arid rolled his eyes.

'Sorry we took so long,' the man continued. 'The driver was unwilling to change course. You have ... spirited independence, with a unique deference to those from the east coast.'

'Wow, so you're an exotic foreigner,' Arid said.

'We're actually in the same country, although most of you seem to have alternative opinions on that.'

'Can y' get us out of here?'

'You're not my concern here. You're free now, so make a break for it. I've got a lot to do here.'

'We need to get back to the *Lady Moonshine*,' Frey said.

'Try Marble Bar. It's only around the corner, and I'm sure you can get a lift. I'll be there in a day or so as well, if you need extra help.' He flashed Arid a smile.

'Marble Bar? Where are we?' Arid asked.

'I think it's called Telfer.'

'Telfer. That's in the middle of nowhere. Literally,' Frey said.

'You can say that,' the man said. 'The pirates put in some decent kilometres to get here.'

'How far are we from Tom Price?' Frey asked.

'About six hundred kays.'

'Six hundred!'

'Do y' have t' repeat everything he says?' Arid said.

'This is a lot to deal with,' Frey answered. 'How on earth am I ever going to get back home?'

'Ask your friend,' the man said, indicating Arid. 'He seems confident of his abilities.'

'He's not my—forget it. I've had enough. I'm going to get out of here, overcome the tiger, navigate across six hundred kilometres of hostile terrain, find a relatively small object in about a million square kilometres, lie in my bed, then cry for a week.'

'What tiger?' the man asked.

'Isn't there always a tiger a heroine has to defeat?'

'I'm glad you've got a plan. Good luck. Maybe we'll meet at Marble Bar.'

'But how can we get there?' Arid asked.

The man shrugged, an impressive movement with his broad shoulders. 'This is a den of thieves. Steal something.'

Frey led the way out, back through the dark chamber. Without the glow of a cyborg's eye the pathway became treacherous, and they stumbled over the uneven pathway, aggravating Arid's ankle.

They were unable to determine the exit.

They reached a wall and tracked along it, running their hands along the cutaway stone until they found a tunnel that was just as dark as the chamber. It curved down in a tight spiral, disorientating them. A glow appeared, outlining the end of the tunnel, and they emerged into a lower chamber. The broken frame stuck through the hole in the roof, with the twisted X structures hanging loosely. They shivered at the thought of their recent experience.

A dozen cyborgs occupied the level; most stood still, awaiting instructions.

Frey gasped. 'They've got weapons. Cyborgs don't fight.'

A small group of cyborgs attended to a thick collection of wires running around the outside of the enormous double-wide grey cylinder that stood three metres high. A door on the edge of the curve was closed, a black hand-sized panel next to it. A cyborg was staring at it.

Arid moved toward the door, curiosity overcoming his common sense. A thick dark line ran down one side of the cylinder. Something about it called out to him; a long-forgotten memory. But it didn't look right, as though it was the wrong shape. Or not in the right configuration.

'It's the Omen,' Frey said.

The word twanged in Arid's head. 'The what?'

'Omen. Some superweapon. I recognise it from the description. My mother was always talking about it when I was younger. Your parents were meant to have built it.'

Arid stepped toward it. 'I know this.'

As he approached, the idle cyborgs turned toward him in a synchronised movement. A moment hung in time as everyone stood still.

The closest cyborg tilted his head. 'Database match. Arid Geiger. Surrender.'

The cyborgs stepped forward, picking up their pace as they neared him.

Frey grabbed Arid and they ran out another exit. She glanced back as they charged away, terror drawing her attention to their pursuers. Above the exit, a word or name had been chiselled into the rock.

She gasped and placed her hand on Arid's arm. 'Look,' she said.

Arid stopped and spun. GEIGER had been imprinted above the entrance.

'Is that meant to be your name?' Frey asked.

'I don't know. Is it a common word?'

'I thought you'd been here heaps of times.'

'I ... I don't know. It feels familiar. But I'm sure I've never seen it or been this low in the mine. My parents made me stay up top when I was here with them.'

The cyborgs' first volley shot over them and impacted the ceiling, forcing Arid and Frey to put their heads down, fear hastening their steps. The armed cyborgs continued to follow, striding behind them in two symmetrical rows.

Arid stumbled along, lost in thought, causing Frey to half guide him, half chase him around random corners. This protected them against the pulses from the cyborg weapons, but the cyborgs were impossible to shake. They finally emerged in a familiar tunnel and ran straight into a man charging in the opposite direction. A blast from the cyborgs seared past Arid's head, slamming into the wall, and the rock face exploded.

The man hit the ground, rolled up onto one knee, pulled out a pistol and fired. Frey and Arid dived for the ground as bullets flew over them. With his hands clasped around the pistol grip, the man emptied his clip.

The cyborgs jerked with flailing limbs before collapsing with bullet-riddled bodies and heads.

The man wore a dark uniform without an insignia or rank. He looked like a soldier, but the lack of identification was unusual. The mechRig teams, especially the combat forces, were intensely parochial and loud in their allegiance. He held himself with a casual authority that said he was more than one of the rank and file. He had the regulation short hair, and looked well muscled under his clothes, but he seemed to lack the presence and sheer energy of the Steam Academy soldier who'd saved them earlier.

The man stood and dusted himself down, keeping an eye on the dead cyborgs.

Frey took her hands off her head and looked up at him. 'You're bleeding.'

'Don't worry, it's not mine,' he replied. 'Consider it donated.' He stretched out his hand to her. 'Let me help you.'

'Hi, I'm Frey.' She took the man's hand and he lifted her easily to her feet.

Arid scrambled up, dust cascading off him. He noticed that Frey had not mentioned her royal-ness to the less compelling man.

The Battery had fallen silent, with the hive of activity abandoned after the violent turmoil.

'Did you see a group of people come back up? A lady with short hair surrounded by a couple of deckhands?' Frey asked.

The man pointed at her with a casual gesture. 'You're Frey.' He looked at Arid. 'Who did you say you were?'

'Arid,' he replied.

'Pleased to meet you. I'm Mathias Byrne. I may have run into some of them,' he said to Frey.

'What happened?'

'Run over and now flat.'

'All of them?'

'Not the short-haired *lady, as you called her*. She managed to slip through like a greased rat,' he said through gritted teeth. 'Were you looking for them?'

'Trying to escape them. They brought us here and sold us to the cyborgs.'

'That's disturbing news. Selling children is never a good look.'

'I guess that's one way of looking at it,' Frey said, giving the man a suspicious stare. 'I'm pretty sure it's also illegal. Mathias is a fairly unique name. I think I've only heard it once—'

'Anyway, you look like you escaped. All's well that ends well.'

The man clapped his hands together, producing a cloud of dust. 'I assume you don't want to live here. Do you need a lift somewhere?'

'Um, Marble Bar,' Arid said.

'What a coincidence, that's where I'm going, too. We can have a good old time together.'

'We ain't five years old, y' know,' Arid said.

'My apologies. I'm not used to dealing with, er, small people, or non-staff. Anyway,' he continued, glancing down the tunnel, 'I'm guessing we should get a move on before the deceased's friends turn up.'

Byrne led the way back to the surface. There appeared to be several more dead bodies than when Arid and Frey had come down. By the entrance, an oversized lux roller sat gleaming in the morning sun, the light reflecting off the polished brass surface. Byrne reached into his pocket and pulled out a small black fob. It clicked as he pressed the centre and the doors on the roller lifted open.

'Cool,' Arid said, his face lighting up.

The lux roller was a roomy four-seater, nearly twice the size of the standard roller model, and used only by celebrities and mech leaders. Inside, a row of oversized pressure gauges ran along the dashboard. The steering joystick sat between the front seats. Byrne flicked a lever at the base of the passenger seat, which moved forward and allowed access to the rear, smaller seats.

'Sir, if you would honour the lady in the front seat,' he said.

Arid looked at him, suspicious of what he meant by 'honour'. Did it have a secret meaning, like holdings hands or something?

'It's gentlemanly to sit in the back if you're not driving,' he explained, 'and let the young lady have the comfort and space for her ... thoughts.'

'I'm not sure how that's fair,' Arid said with a scowl, but he clambered into the rear and struggled to fit his legs into the limited space behind the reclined front seat.

Byrne slipped into the driver's seat from the opposite side and pressed a large button in the centre of the dash. The ignition sparker clicked away as the gas heaters caught fire and warmed the boilers. The intense roar of the burners filled the cabin, gently shaking the vehicle. Byrne squeezed the engine-engage lever on the top of the joystick and pushed it forward. The gyroscopes spun up and the roller settled into a smooth purr as it cruised out into the desert.

'So, what were you two doing at the Battery?' the man asked.

'We said. The lady with the short hair was selling us to the cyborgs for body parts,' Frey replied.

'Really? I wonder what they're up to. Makes you wonder how she knew about it.'

'She said her brother is big in hot air over east.'

'You can say that again.' Byrne let out a low chuckle. 'I mean, she took you to cyborgs, which is a low rate of return on value.'

Arid had leaned forward against the backs of the front seats and was listening to the conversation. 'What do y' mean?' he said.

Byrne looked into his rearview mirror. Arid caught the man's eyes framed against the glass. 'You know there's a reward out for your capture.'

'The pirate told us, but we didn't do anything,' Frey said. 'Certainly not me.'

'Hey, that's what I say. You're kids. What are you going to do? Don't worry, you're safe with me.'

'What kind of reward?' Arid said.

'Nothing much really. Beatrice is only a minor leader. What does she run, some small and ancient megaRig out in the sticks? Not like a mechCity.'

Frey narrowed her eyes at him.

'You're getting a bit of a reputation, though, young man,' he finished.

'Me?' Arid squeaked.

'Yeah, the queen killer.'

'But I wasn't even in the room.'

'So, it's true. There was an assassin.'

'Yes. But it wasn't me. Swear.'

'Either way, word has got around.' Byrne glanced over at Frey. 'What's your relationship to the queen?'

Frey hesitated. 'Handmaid.'

'Ideal position to gain her trust.'

'I *really* had nothing to do with it. That you can take to the bank.' Frey ran a hand over the leather armrests that were fastened in place with brass rivets. She glanced at Byrne. 'What will you be doing at Marble Bar?'

'Catching up with a few friends before heading out,' he said casually. 'There's going to be a big council meeting of the commanders, with a few district disputes to sort out, tenements and whatnot, and I've got to get ready. Lots of powerful people, going to be a great opportunity to make some money.'

'Shouldn't peace be the priority?' Frey asked.

'Of course. Number one.'

Arid reclined in his seat and laced his fingers behind his head. 'Although I ain't one t' turn down a quick roll of notes, I prefer t' do it away from the eyes of the most powerful lawmakers in the land.'

Byrne laughed. 'You don't think they're thinking the same? Anyway, each to their own. Where are you heading? For the *Moonshine*?'

'Yes, how'd y' know?' Arid asked.

'I must have heard you say it.'

'I can't remember—' Frey started.

'Do you know how t' find it?' Arid asked Byrne.

'My guess would be at the gathering. In a few days, all the megaRig and mechCity leaders will meet. And as Queen Bea owns the most tenements, she'll need to be there to negotiate deals, form alliances, that kind of thing.'

'Are you going to Tom Price?' Arid said.

'I'm sorry, I'm not a rig leader.' Byrne gave them a muggy grin. 'Just a lone traveller wanting to help out a couple of lost kids looking for home and cookies. You like cookies, don't you?'

'Um, okay.'

'I've got some in the back if you're hungry.'

'That would be great—' Arid said, reaching for the bag behind the driver's seat.

Frey put her hand on his arm. 'No, I think we're okay,' she said.

'Up to you,' Byrne said.

Arid gave Frey a narrow-eyed stare.

'We don't want to leave any crumbs,' she said.

Two years ago …

The smell of stale cigarettes drifted on the air. No light entered the preparation room. Anonymity of the other occupants led to someone less to betray.

'We live in difficult times,' the speaker said.

The voice swirled around Alex's head. So tired. The training had taken its toll, but they had been clear about it from the start. Heat and claustrophobia crept in. At times it felt as though the whole world was metal, decaying under the strains of an unrelenting environment.

'Do you understand how important your task is?' the speaker asked.

'Yes,' Alex replied.

'The imperial cow threatens our security and happiness. The forces at the Belt amass and she refuses to bring the factions together. We will fall under their might.'

'I am aware of the complications.'

'This will be the most dangerous mission you'll ever have been on, but there will be an opportunity to set us free. The rewards will be great. You need to live the life. It needs to be totally believable.'

The speaker took a puff on his cigarette. The end glowed and the burning ash fluttered to the ground.

'They may never come,' he finished. 'Will you take the assignment?'

The cost to this point could hardly have been called minor. Loss of family and friends. Continual danger. Ultimately betraying so many people. They'd said the last mission was going to be the last one. One day you'd be recognised, and it was going to be game over. Until then you played the game.

So tired. Alex nodded. 'Yes.'

[7]

THE ROAD SIMMERED into a straight red line disappearing into oblivion, capped by a fierce stormy sky threatening a biblical tempest. The dirt track gave no sense of distance; the scenery was measured only by the irregular occurrence of trees that undulated through otherwise unchanging landscapes. The world was made up of two colours: red and grey.

'Has the apocalypse happened here and we missed it?' Frey asked.

'It always looks like this,' Byrne replied. 'The place is what it is. Maybe the end of the world did happen, and we're living in the aftermath. Maybe it's not even an external thing; we face it individually and our actions shape the world. We plundered the land and polluted the skies, *poisoned the water*, diminishing nature for greed. And as punishment for the ills of previous generations, we're forced to live a life in this. The apocalypse is what we make it, and hell is a place called home.'

The roller bounced along in silence for a few moments.

'Y'd need t' be a top diviner t' find any water out here. Could easily end up with bad data,' Arid said, watching the scenery roll past.

Frey noticed Byrne's knuckles whiten on the steering at the words 'bad data'. 'Have you got any family?' she asked him.

He peered at her, his eyes dark. 'No.' He returned his attention to the road. Under his breath he added, 'Not anymore.'

The roller crested the hill and Marble Bar revealed itself like an intrepid cockroach: a collection of a few dozen low structures, a combination of old stone buildings and wooden houses with expansive verandas, huddled in a wide hollow. A towering transmission post soared into the sky on the far side of the town, its white paint in contrast to the deep red of the distant rocks of the surrounding hills.

Byrne killed the engine and the vehicle wheeled down into the main street, slicing through the centre of the town. The doors lifted and the baking air flooded into the cabin.

Frey stepped out, and Arid scrambled out after her. In the middle of the road, surrounded by the silence of a terrain suppressed by the incandescent heat, they took in the bastion of human defiance.

Byrne reached into a dashboard compartment and pulled out his pistol, slipping it into a loose holster strapped to his belt.

'Whoa, this place is hot,' Arid said.

'And the origins of life on Earth,' Byrne said as he pointed to a colourful rock formation jutting up from a nearby hill.

'Not much evidence of that now. Do people actually live here?' Frey asked.

'People will always live where you can get a cold beer. Speaking of which, I might grab a swift one at the Iron Clad.'

'The what?'

'The pub.'

'Can we have one?' Arid asked.

'Yeah, why not. Buy yourself a milkshake or something from Mad Clapping Harry's Café.'

'What about a beer?' Arid persisted.

Byrne laughed and shook his head. 'You got any cash?'

'Um, no.'

Byrne fished in his pocket, pulling out the payWave card and a handful of colourful notes. He handed over an orange bill and pointed back up the road to two stone buildings. 'I'll see you later.'

As Byrne turned, a figure blurred by the haze strode toward him. Byrne was jolted backward, a palm against his chest that kept him off balance. He staggered back and then regained his footing, spinning and grabbing the arm pushing him. The two locked in a brief altercation where neither could best the other. In the end they separated, and Byrne realised who his attacker was.

'You owe me,' Jozee said. 'I want my money.'

'I owe you nothing. I don't even know you.'

'What are you talking about, Byrne? You've left me with no crew and banned at the Battery.'

'Well, that was mostly your own doing. You shouldn't kill guards. And your crew shouldn't open fire at innocent businessmen visiting the Battery.'

'You forget I know things.'

'Do you? Obviously not enough to survive. Not enough to bring a weapon.' He tapped the side of his belt, indicating his pistol.

Jozee raised her hands and backed away. 'This is not the last you've heard of me,' she warned.

'It is.'

The two stared at each other as Byrne's hand hovered near his pistol. Jozee's eyes flicked down to his weapon before scowling at him. She stepped back and turned away, then her shoulders hunched forward as she stalked off.

Byrne returned his attention to the youngsters. 'I'm sorry you saw that. That's the problem with these isolated places—you get all kinds of delusional crazies. Get something to drink,' he said, pushing them in the opposite direction. 'You can tell me about your adventures after.'

Jozee came charging back, jumping on Byrne's back and knocking him to the ground. Her arm wrapped around his neck, turning his face a deep red as he struggled against her. She certainly was a match for him. They grunted and shouted as they rolled on the ground.

Frey grabbed Arid's arm and dragged him away from the confrontation, back along the street.

'What're y' doing?' he asked.

'I don't trust him. There's something suspicious about how much he knows. How come they know each other? Jozee tried to sell us, and no one mentions it. That doesn't wash with me.'

'Stop worrying. He's all right. He's an adult. They know stuff.'

'We need to ditch him and make our own way,' Frey said.

'And how exactly do we do that? Got a vehicle? Money?'

'Can't you sell something?'

'How about you?' Arid said, jabbing his finger into her arm.

They charged up the slight incline toward the tallest buildings in the town, rising to a mammoth two floors hidden behind a short row of white gum trees. Inexplicably, the building had a steep sloping roof, which was out of place in an area where it obviously never rained. Both floors were stone and looked a thousand years old. The exterior walls had been worn smooth, with the colour baked out. They opened the wooden door, which caused a light bell to tinkle, and entered into the shade. The effort of the run had zapped their energy and they sagged against the wall.

An ancient man sat behind the counter, staring at them.

'Are y' Mad Clapping Harry?' Arid asked.

'No,' the man replied. 'Otherwise I'd be twelve hundred years old.'

'Y' look it.'

Frey elbowed Arid.

'Y' got any beers?'

The elderly man scowled at them. 'You can have shakes.'

'Beer shakes?'

'Beside that sounding like the most disgusting thing on the planet, I don't think it's technically possible. The hops would have everything frothing over the lip of the glass. It reminds me of a time when a group of out-of-towners came in, sat down over there,' he said, pointing to a small round table in the corner, 'and ordered water. Then things got really weird.'

'Y' know, as stories go, that's probably the lamest one I've ever heard.'

'That's the problem with you kids today, wanting things all fancy. Like beer shakes. Sit down and wait your turn. And don't do anything weird.'

'Do you want to know our flavour choices?' Frey said.

'If I gotta.'

'I'll have mint.' Frey turned to Arid. 'You want mint, too?'

'What? No, it's disgusting. I'll have chocolate.'

The man held out his hand and they handed over the note they'd gotten from Byrne. There was little change. They made their way over to a table and sat.

'How on earth are we meant to get t' Tom Price now?' Arid said, as he counted through the coins.

'Didn't the big guy back at the Battery say you were resourceful?'

'Well, yes, of course. But, y' know, I've got t' think about it, plan something, which takes time.'

'Yeah, we've got a day or two to get there. You'd better start thinking quick.'

The elderly man appeared with two tall glasses, one white and one brown. He placed them down on the table with a serving finesse that had him wobbling erratically while holding the glasses perfectly still.

After he had gone, they sucked through the straws and then both looked up in surprise.

Arid screwed up his face. 'What flavour is yers?'

'None, it's just milk,' Frey replied. 'Yours?'

'I think,' he said cautiously, 'it's all of them.'

Frey pushed her glass away as Arid attempted another mouthful of his drink. She watched his face sour before rolling her eyes and looking at the old man. He stared blankly at a carousel of battered cards depicting flattering renditions of the local area.

'Maybe he knows how to get to Tom Price,' Frey suggested. 'I'll ask him. These country folk love royalty.'

She stood, smoothed down her dress, brushed back her hair, and approached the counter. 'Hey, old man—'

'I ain't an old man,' he grumbled, as he turned to face her. His withered face wrinkled up as he chewed the side of his top lip.

'Whatever. Old individual, we have no money, but we need to get to Tom Price.'

'I ain't takin' ya.'

'No, that's not what I request, nor would it be appropriate. We simply need advice on how a couple of unfortunate travellers can get to their next destination.'

'We get all the weirdos in here. A while back we had a group in here asking for beer shakes. Then it got really weird—'

'Yes, that was us. And we're not weird. Anyway, how do people get to Tom Price from here?'

'They don't. Why would ya want to leave this piece of paradise?'

'But if, for some crazy reason, someone needed to get to Tom Price, how would they do it?'

'Only way is by dirt track. Ain't nothin' else out here since the rail tracks crumbled.'

'Thanks, you've been so helpful,' Frey replied, doing her best not to gouge out the man's eyes. She returned to the table.

'Didn't the Steam Academy guy say he'd be here?' Arid said. 'It's not a big place, we should be able t' find him. He's got a sword. That should stand out.'

'And if we don't? We don't have the time to wait around,' Frey said.

'I don't suppose we can walk …'

'Three hundred k's?'

'Just a thought. So, what've we got?'

'No food. No money. No weapons. No transport.'

Arid nudged her. 'What if we steal Byrne's roller?'

Frey gave him a flat stare. For a long time. Eventually, she said, 'It's stupid, but it's all we've got. Let's go.'

The street was devoid of human activity. You'd easily think the place was a ghost town. Even their footprints quickly disappeared in the sand. They crept over the street to the Iron Clad. The small windows were set high, allowing them the opportunity to peer in without being seen from inside.

Byrne sat at the long counter with two other men, one young with a shaved head, and the other old with neat grey hair. They all sipped on their beers as they spoke.

'Who are they?' Arid whispered.

'Theo is the chair of the council,' Frey explained, pointing at the grey-haired man. 'And Randy is trouble. He's commander of the Larrakia, which used to be friendly before he turned up. A dead nasty piece. Hide! Byrne's coming.'

Byrne stood and shook hands with the men before heading out.

Arid and Frey raced down the side of the building and watched Byrne as he strolled across the road back toward his roller, then followed, keeping low. On the far side, he turned to check over his shoulder, forcing them to duck behind a stack of empty pots piled out the front of a closed store. They edged around the rear of the building to the opposite side and took up stations behind a pile of rubbish bins. Peering around the side of the building, they spied Byrne sitting in the roller with the driver's door raised. He had his legs crossed, with his feet hanging out. Something held his attention through the windscreen, and he whistled tunelessly.

'I have a plan,' Arid whispered into Frey's ear. 'I'll sneak around t' the other side while y' go up by the door. I'll keep an eye out while y' place a bucket on the inside. Y'll need t' break in somehow. Then get ball bearings, so when the bucket falls on his head he'll slip over. I'll hotwire the roller.'

'That seems awfully complex,' Frey replied. 'Are you sure it'll work?'

'Yeah, totally. Ready?'

Arid stepped out from behind the bins, misjudged the step and stumbled sideways, causing the bins to crash to the ground and scatter. The racket continued as a lid rolled toward the car before it spun on the spot, with a ringing rattle as it eventually settled.

Byrne searched for the cause of the noise. Shock registered on his face when he saw Arid standing among the debris.

'What are you doing back there, idiot?' He stepped out of the roller and ran toward Arid, raising his gun. Something caught his eye, stopping him mid-stride.

Arid followed his gaze. Byrne was staring at a man crossing the street, dressed in shorts and a wildly colourful shirt. Arid heard Byrne whisper, 'Hunter.' Arid didn't know how he could tell the other man's profession from his clothes.

Byrne switched his attention between Arid and the man he called Hunter. Then he charged after Arid, who turned and fled, quickly outpacing Byrne, who gave up and ran off after Hunter.

'Let's go,' Arid shouted, and they leapt into the roller and pulled down the doors. Arid stuck his tongue out the side of his mouth as he ran his eyes over the dash, nervously tapping his fingertips together.

'One thing I forgot to ask about the plan: you do know how to drive a roller, don't you?' Frey asked.

'Yeah ... of course. I was watching him all the way. Shouldn't be too different to my dowser.'

Hunter made his way down the main street. He walked with confidence, with the air of someone looking like they wanted to avoid attention. *Nothing to see here.* There wasn't much to the town, but he still travelled a crooked mile to get to his location. And Byrne tracked him, corner by corner, matching the pacing of his footsteps. Silent footfalls. Nothing more than a shadow.

Of course, Byrne was going to have to test Hunter at some point. Everyone needed to be loyal, even if they didn't realise it, or even if they didn't think loyalty applied to them.

Shade flashed across Hunter's face as he stepped into a derelict building made of nothing but crumbling walls and broken floors.

Byrne moved in closer, concealing himself against the wall and listening through a boarded window. The man hadn't even looked back. How over-confident was he?

Byrne checked his watch. The oversized bronze dial clicked the minute hand around with precision, approaching the hour. He had a minute before his meeting.

'You got the new location?' said an unfamiliar voice.

And which location will it be, thought Byrne.

'He suggested pushing toward Broome,' Hunter replied.

Click. The first piece fell into place.

'Broome? Why?'

'It could be to do with an alliance or an ulterior motive. There've been reports of the cyborgs working on some old tech. I think it might be a distraction, covering for the real destination.'

'Do you think it's a legitimate attempt toward an alliance with the east?'

There was no response from Hunter.

'Do we need to get there now?'

This was the point, Byrne thought. The answer would reveal whether Hunter was the leak. A roller drove past, sounding its horn and concealing Hunter's response. *Damn.*

'In that case, do we have a name?'

Byrne held his breath as he searched for a crack in the boarding, finding a sliver at the edge. He peered in, and the limited view allowed him to see Hunter. If Byrne swivelled, he could see part of the other man, but not both together.

'Major Maria had said she had suspicions about someone. She'd been afraid to say the name or give much detail until she'd investigated further,' Hunter said.

'And?'

And? Byrne's interest bordered on obsession. Had Major Maria given him away? Everything rode on Hunter's response.

'She disappeared.'

'So she was probably right, and she never told you.'

This time there was no response from Hunter.

It could be coincidence. Had they been able to tie Byrne to the plan? Was there enough evidence to tie Hunter to the leak? His inability to see Hunter's non-verbal responses was infuriating. Byrne had told a few people about Broome. To accuse Hunter, he needed to be certain. Evidence needed to be beyond doubt, and at this point it wasn't. But that could be done by tomorrow if he was quick enough.

'So, what next?' asked the other man.

'I believe—'

Byrne's watch hit the hour, clicking loudly enough to be heard inside the room. He turned and ran. Time was up. In the last moments he'd seen the other man's *Moonshine* uniform. Whether Hunter was the leaker or not, talking to the enemy was a foolish mistake.

Arid pressed a big button on the dashboard and the igniters flared. The engines rumbled into life, making the roller vibrate. A mix of nerves and excitement filled him as he wrapped his hand around the joystick. He pushed, and with a horrific grinding of metal the roller jerked forward, its engine hammering as the furnace blasted out extra heat.

Frey turned her head away and closed her eyes each time Arid rammed the lever forward. 'You know, Byrne squeezed the top grip each time he changed gears.'

Arid compressed the grip, the engine revved up, and he pushed the joystick. The gearbox clicked and he released the grip. The roller hurtled forward smoothly, the acceleration making them giggle with excitement.

'Told y' I knew what I was doing,' Arid said. 'We should be there in a couple of hours. Probably sooner now that I've mastered it.'

The roller zoomed along the dirt track, drifting from side to side as Arid twitched the joystick. The vegetation thinned out and gave way to endless red sand and the occasional bush hugging the ground. As they made their way west, the clouds darkened, black rolling in like a poorly painted ceiling. A lightning sheet illuminated the sky, turning the clouds a patchwork of pink. A thunderclap followed, cracking the air and shaking the ground. It dragged on in waves of elemental anger, frowning at the world. There was a moment of stillness across the plain. Arid pushed the roller on against the changing weather.

They managed to make considerable headway into the long journey. As they approached the third hour, the ceasefire in the weather cracked and raindrops splattered across the windscreen.

'Have you driven in the wet before?' Frey asked.

'Yeah, yeah. Of course.' Arid rubbed the back of his hand against his nose and hesitantly looked over at Frey.

The rain fell heavier, cascading down the windscreen and obscuring the view.

'Make sure you miss the tree,' she said.

'What tree?'

'There's only one on the whole plain.' She pointed to a green blur to the right of the track.

The rain lanced down, providing a deafening soundtrack inside the cabin and blurring the view out through the front. The roller lurched to the right, losing traction and spinning out onto the sand. Arid fought with the controls, randomly jamming the joystick back and forth. In the turmoil of the blurring exterior, colours flashed by as the roller rocked onto the right-hand tracks, with the opposite side rattling noisily as they fought for purchase. The roller straightened, the tracks bit into the dirt and it shot ahead—directly into the only tree on the plain.

Steam poured out of the ruptured boilers, and the remains of the engine pinked as it cooled in the rain.

Frey's door clicked and hissed as she attempted to open it. Smoke coiled out of the small gap. Her leg thrust out, forcing the door completely ajar and off its hinges. The door spun across the ground and landed in a puddle. She staggered out.

'What have you done?'

'I think it's pretty self-evident,' Arid replied, climbing out his own side. 'Y' put me off with all the shouting and giggling and stuff.'

'Don't you dare blame me for this. You were driving, like everything you do, charging ahead without thinking or checking things out.'

'That's the thing with some people,' he said, looking pointedly at her. 'They hang onto the excitement created by others because they're afraid t' take their own risks. They get t' enjoy the thrill then blame the other person if it goes wrong.'

'It's called trust. I trust that you know what you're doing and can be responsible.'

'Responsible? We wouldn't be in this position if y' hadn't blown a hole in the *Moonshine* t' start with.'

'And you would be facing the death penalty for attempting to assassinate my mother.'

'*I didn't do it.*'

'Well, who did? You were the only new person on the rig.'

'How should I know? Y' need to believe me. Ella did.'

Frey sighed, and wiped the water off her face. 'My sister believes everyone. What do we do now?'

The alley between the local store and the bank was dark and provided little protection against the elements. After the meeting had been rescheduled due to an 'update', Byrne finally met the cyborg. Rain cascaded down the cyborg's body, the red eye shining dimly in the darkness.

'What was the update about?'

'Security patch.'

'Down at the Omen?'

'No. Cyborg operating systems.'

'*You've* been updated? What's new? Waterproofing, I hope.'

Byrne wore an Akubra hat and stood against the wall, getting some shelter from the angle of the rain.

'A new settings icon,' the cyborg replied.

'How about an update on the Omen? How far you have got? Did the incident have an impact?'

'Iris is sad.sad about delay. Iris warned about uncontrolled distribution of sensitive information and the ramifications, resulting in the disruption of the harvesting.'

'It was hardly my fault that the pirate took matters into her own hands against my orders.'

'Everyone owns and is responsible for destiny.'

'So you say, yet here you are talking to me after an update. So, what are you going to do?'

The cyborg went quiet, his eye dimming. On his arm, the miniIris went blank and a series of lines appeared, spinning in a circle. 'Iris continues to co-operate with agreement.'

'Good to hear, after me paying and everything.'

'We note funds not received yet.'

'Only an administrative oversight. What have you learned?'

'The Omen is not a single thing. It has complex components.'

'I didn't assume it was a great thumping piece of concrete. That wouldn't be much of a high-tech superweapon. Unless you could drop it on someone. Then you wouldn't build it underground.'

'The components must be separated for it to work. And it requires a power source.'

'Such as?'

'Hydrocarbon gas will be sufficient.'

'How much?'

'Fifty thousand litres.'

'Struth.' Byrne went quiet. 'That's quite a lot. I'm going to need a bigger rig. And possibly some help.' He turned to run back down the road to the Iron Clad. 'Keep in touch.'

DRIVING TWENTY KILOMETRES felt like a fantasy as Frey and Arid trudged through the mud. At least the rain cooled the stifling air. Actually, it didn't. The humidity descended like a blanket, making each step a misery. They chose not to talk. Arid pulled the hood of his top over his head, but the rain soaked through and he felt as though he had a wet towel draped over him. It was better without.

Eventually there was a break in the clouds and the rain eased. The heat intensified even as the sun set, and steam bubbled up out of the mud. It was the kind of weather insects loved. Mosquitoes buzzed in clouds around them, and they trudged on in silence, slapping away at their exposed skin.

Relief came as the moon disappeared behind an endless bank of clouds running from horizon to horizon. Rain returned in full strength, tumbling in all directions, caught up in the swirling winds, forcing its way in under their clothes.

Frey pushed forward, her steps slowed by the weather's onslaught.

'I've never seen so much rain,' Arid shouted. He wiped his hand across his forehead, wiping away the water.

'Must be a cyclone.' Frey lifted her hand to shield her eyes. Ahead lay a small collection of buildings. 'The kind of weather where it would be good to be in something like a roller.'

'Give it a rest. It was an accident.'

'One that could've been avoided.' She pointed ahead to a dim collection of lights. 'At least we made it.'

They tried to run, but the mud dragged at their feet, forcing them to give up after a short distance. Then a solitary streetlight, standing tall against the weather. A building. It provided a veranda, where they collapsed and took a moment to rest. A large bin sat at the end of the veranda.

Arid flipped it open and looked inside. He pulled out a couple of plastic bags that were struggling to decompose. 'Here,' he said, handing one to Frey. 'Put this on yer head.'

'I'm not wearing garbage.'

'It'll keep y' dry.'

She sniffed it before tying it over her head.

'They banned these at some point. Now they're worth a bomb on the black market,' Arid said.

'So why is someone throwing them out?'

'The house looks vacant. Maybe the bags were part of an inheritance that no one wanted. Like some hidden treasure.'

The buildings blossomed into a street, then into a suburb. Lights were out and the windows shuttered against the storm. Only the occasional person braved the weather. A homeless man staggered across the street in front of them, eating a carrot.

A hall lay at the centre of the town, with a carpark packed with dozens of vehicles.

'If the meet is here, where are the rigs?' Arid asked.

'They won't turn up in a rig. Where would they park it? Even if they left it nearby out on the plain, the leaders will just come in a diplo-sweeper,'[1] Frey replied.

The main street continued on between the darkened buildings.

'We need to find somewhere to stay and dry off,' Arid said. 'Just for the night. Inside.'

'The place looks deserted. Let's keep going.'

Dashing from building to building, resting under the eaves before running to the next one, the isolation of a day alone on the plains only to end up in a ghost town played on their nerves.

Finally, buildings in the town centre offered light and noise. After the hours of marching through vacant wasteland, the small town felt like a buzzing metropolis, lifting their spirits. They passed a general noticeboard fastened to the front of a farming supply store. A single bulb swinging in the wind cast light over the front of the shop.

Frey pointed to a poster stuck to the wall. 'Is that you?'

Arid ran his hand over the picture before ripping it off the wall.

'I'm sure it's the only one,' Frey said, folding her arms and staring out into the street.

Arid examined the picture. Clutching it tightly between both hands, he stared at it, feeling conflicting emotions. Infamy was pretty cool and would boost his reputation on the plains, but he could also get caught and be thrown in jail forever for something that, ultimately, he didn't do.

'What the … How come I'm in the wanted section? Why ain't you?'

'I'm the queen's daughter,' she replied haughtily. 'Why would I want to kill her? You'd better keep your hood up. At least the rain gives you an excuse.'

'Wanted.'

'Ooh, a dangerous man. Do you feel dangerous and, um, manly?'

'Leave me—' He interrupted his own sentence and grabbed Frey, pulling her around into the rain by the side of the store, out of the reach of the light.

'What are you do—'

'Shh.' He pointed across the street to a roller arriving. An interior light switched on as the passenger door opened, clearly identifying the occupants. Theo, the chair of the council, and

Byrne.

'Is he tracking us?' Arid asked.

'He said he was coming here,' Frey reminded him. 'The big council meeting is tomorrow.'

Byrne stepped out of the roller. He turned and placed his hand on the roof, leaned back in and grabbed his Akubra. 'Thanks for the lift. Meet me in about an hour. '

The hatch closed and Byrne, fitting his hat, made his way down the street.

Arid was about to step back into the light when Frey grabbed him. She pointed across the road.

Another man appeared out of the shadows of the opposite building. A man in shorts and a colourful shirt. He watched the roller draw away slowly, its steam fighting against the downpour. He glanced at his watch and made a note in a small book.

Hunter. Again, in the same place as Byrne. There was definitely something suspicious going on between them.

Most of the nightlife rotated around a large hotel called the Colonial, an ancient and sweeping building built out of nostalgia for an age of empires. Byrne hesitated at the front before heading off in a different direction. Hunter disappeared into the main entrance.

Arid and Frey kept track of Byrne through the empty backstreets, staying a couple of buildings behind, until he reached a dark house with a solitary light glowing red on the outside. Byrne tapped a pattern on the door. A small hatch opened at eye height. Peering out was one normal eye and one glowing red.

Byrne shook the water from his hat, leaving a pool on the wooden flooring. His eyes scanned the rundown room. For every upmarket Colonial pub, there was a dive the disreputable believed was theirs. A source of pride and a badge of honour.

Randy sat quietly at a table, relaxing in his chair and sipping on his beer. Byrne sat opposite, the two men staring into each other's eyes, searching for a weakness.

'Beer?' Randy asked.

'I'm good.'

'Suit yerself. Your loss.'

Byrne leaned on the table and the slat lifted up. Randy picked up his beer to avoid it being spilt.

'Table's a bit wonky,' Byrne said.

'Musta been built by your lot. What did you want to say that old man Theo couldn't hear?'

'Randy, I need gas.'

'Change yer diet.'

'Thanks for the insight to your intellect. Fifty thousand litres.'

'Only the mechRigs carry that kind. And only drillers.'

'Like the *Moonshine*.'

'That's the one.'

'Typical.'

'And with the meet, ya know it's going to be the closest gas rig. Unless ya can find a contract driller. And we all know how elusive and booked up they are.'

It wasn't that Randy was incompetent; he had excellent skills and a mean streak that had placed him on top of the heap in the north. He was wilfully unhelpful unless there was something directly beneficial to him.

'Right. You're going to have to do a few things for me.'

Randy laughed and shook his head. 'Nah.'

'You want to rethink that? I don't find your response very loyal. It's not the thing I'm going to forget or forgive.'

'Ya can *try* your tough words on me, but I'm not buying. The other commanders might fall for the big talk and threats, but we're bred different up north.'

'Yeah—*in*bred. Look, you might think you're getting a bit ahead of the game, but don't forget where this is all heading. You want to be on the wrong side? Because, believe me, I will make it priority one on day one to …' Byrne thrust down on the table, and a slat sprang up on the opposite side into Randy's face, forcing him to drop the beer. Byrne grabbed Randy's head and smashed it onto the table and pressed down. '… hunt you down like a diseased three-legged dog.'

Randy squirmed under Byrne's grip. 'Yeah, all right, all right. My beer!'

Byrne released Randy's head and let him sit up with a degree of decorum. Then he straightened his collar and smoothed out his hair. 'This is what I want you to do.'

The cyborg standing beside the door turned his head sharply, staring at the door. He grasped the door handle and quickly forced it open.

Arid and Frey glanced at each other, their ears pressed against the wooden wall, as the cyborg stepped out, his menacing eye glaring at them.

'What you doing here?' the cyborg demanded.

Frey went quiet as the creature took on an aggressive posture.

Arid stuttered out a few syllables.

The cyborg stepped forward, looming over the teens and repeated the question.

'Beer,' squeaked Frey.

Arid gasped. A brilliant idea that could either get them out of trouble, or a free beer. 'Yeah. We'd like two beers. Not beer shakes, mind.'

'What is your age?' the cyborg asked.

'I'm going t' be eighteen,' Arid replied, finding his voice.

'When?'

'Soon.' He let the vowels ring out, and waved his fingers as though casting a spell.

'I calculate this to be in five or six years.'

'Hey, it's only four—*damn*.'

'Return to location of domesticity.'

'I'd love to,' Frey muttered, pulling Arid away from the confrontation.

Arid thought about Byrne as they followed the man at a reasonable distance. 'Y' going t' let some meathead cyborg push us around?'

'He had a pistol on his belt. They're changing. We shouldn't risk it.'

Arid and Frey made their way back to the main street, with Arid jumping in the puddles as they went. They emerged opposite the Colonial. The lights shone from each window of the two-storey building and rowdy voices echoed out into the silent street. They ran across the road and took shelter under the veranda of the public house. The smell of beer rolled out.

'We should go in,' Arid suggested. 'They won't have a cyborg bouncer.'

Frey made a face. 'We should *not* go in. What kind of people are going to be in there? Troublemakers.'

Arid sighed. 'Y' don't have to talk to them. Or interact. Just don't cause a scene. Or stay out here. I don't care.' He pushed in through the door.

Frey hesitated, peering in at the smelly, crowded but, more importantly, dry room. Her dress was soaked, and even in the heat she was beginning to chill. She closed her eyes and followed.

Inside, the room was full. Men of expansive seat pants stood by the bar as young women expertly poured drinks and slid them across the long wooden benchtop. Large fans in each corner blasted air into the room, but their hum was drowned out by the rain on the tin roof. Women collected in the corner sat on high chairs around tall round tables, their legs crossed as they drank from large wine glasses.

An old lady with a friendly face stood behind the end of the bar, keeping note of the change handed back by the bartenders.

Arid approached the bar and waved at her. 'Can we have two beers, please?'

'No. You're kids,' the woman replied.

'Please.'

'You know it's illegal. And do you know who these people are?

People who set the laws and enforce 'em.'

'How about a drink of water.'

'Are you cyborgs?'

'What? No!'

'Then go outside and open your mouths.'

'Y' ain't a very nice lady.'

'Just following the rules. And if you don't got a guardian, then you can get out right now.'

The youngsters glared at her as they made their way back to the door. As Arid reached to push against the wood, large hands fell on their shoulders.

'Fancy seeing you here,' a deep voice said.

They turned and were greeted by the smiling face of the large Steam Academy man from the Battery.

'Y' said y'd meet us at Marble Bar,' Arid exclaimed, at a volume that surprised him.

'Yeah, sorry, I was distracted. I can get you some food if you want.'

'Oh, yes please,' Frey panted. 'We haven't eaten in days, weeks possibly.'

'Come, join my booth.' The man waved for them to follow.

The owner scowled at the trio as they made their way through the crowd. Arid flashed a cheeky thumbs-up. The man signalled the barmaid and ordered drinks.

'Yer lucky they let y' in with the sword,' Arid said. 'Most places have rules about exposed weapons.'

'I keep to myself. They know me. You both look exhausted. And wet.'

'You wouldn't believe what we went through to get here,' Frey said.

'They've got a sign up about you,' the man said, looking at Arid.

'Yeah, I'm a wanted man. Ain't no cell can hold me.' He leaned back, attempting to give the air of a casual rebel.

The man grinned. 'Might be best to keep a low profile while

they sort out your situation. A good idea to keep the hood up.'

'That was my idea,' Frey said.

A barmaid delivered two beers and two waters, placing them in the centre of the table. Arid slowly reached for the beer, but the man took it away before he could wrap his hand around it. The man slid the water towards them. Condensation rolled down the outside of each glass.

'My mother lets me drink all the time,' Frey said.

'I'm not Queen Bea,' the man said.

'How do you know my mother is a queen?'

The man hesitated. 'You said you were a princess. And there aren't too many queens on the plain.' He sat back in his seat and took a sip of his drink. 'So, how did you get here?'

'We stole something, like y' said.'

He raised his eyebrow. 'Really? I think I was joking. Lucky you could drive.'

'Yeah,' said Frey, giving Arid a sideways glance. 'What are you doing here out west?'

'Scoping the area for my boss.'

'Who's that?'

'I have a commander who reports to Number Two.'

Arid and Frey laughed.

'What's your name?' Frey said. 'Mr Ploppy?'

The man paused for dramatic effect. 'I am Captain Nikola Tasman.'

Arid and Frey went quiet as they stared at each other.

'Never heard of you,' Arid said.

Frey nodded in agreement.

Another large man approached and sat down next to Nikola. He was dressed in the same uniform, but in comparison to the captain's good looks, the newcomer had a battered and scarred face. Although not as bulky as the captain, his body radiated a sinuous aggression.

'And this is my most trusted man, Lieutenant Parker,' Nikola said, indicating the other man.

'I've got a message from'—Parker looked at the teens—'the contact.'

Nikola also glanced quickly at Arid and Frey. 'Is it urgent?'

Parker hesitated. 'I think it can wait, but they'll be here as expected. But the next phase needs work.' He returned his attention to the two across the table, who were eyeing up his beer. He pulled it closer, out of their reach.

The lieutenant sat quietly for a moment, staring at the teens and tapping his fingers on the table. He leaned over to Nikola and whispered in his ear.

The captain shrugged. 'If that's the order, then it's what we do. We stick with the plan.' He turned back to Arid and Frey, and smiled.

Parker drained his beer and nodded across the table. 'Nice meeting you. Let's talk again.'

'But we didn't say …' Arid began.

They all watched Parker disappear into the crowd and out the door.

'Why are you out here spying on the cyborgs?' Arid asked Nikola.

'Your relationship with the cyborgs is different to ours. We've been at war with them for centuries, but it's been getting worse over the last decades. They're up to something and they're using you lot to help, whether you know it or not,' Nikola replied.

'Like what?'

'A new weapon. We operate on steel and steam, and a few secret ideas, and we're able to keep them at bay. But if they get something new it will tip the scales in their favour. We defend a lot of people on the east coast. If we fall, the entire seaboard could be threatened.'

'You're talking about cyborgs?' Arid said.

'Yes.'

'You've been at war with the cyborgs for centuries?'

'Not me, personally.'

'Cyborgs. But there are, like, a couple of hundred of them

here.'

'We have hundreds of thousands. Let's hope they don't construct their own mechCity. Look, we need to focus. With ecosystems dying and water increasingly scarce, people are frightened and prone to making bad decisions. We hear horrific stories from across the sea—the collapse of empires, utter devastation.'

'Why?'

'The sky is being ripped apart.'

'Is that the booms we hear at night?' Frey asked.

'No. You have a diminished ozone layer. You can hear celestial sounds. I believe the booms are from the sun. Turns out you can hear a sun scream.'

'Ozone?' Arid said. 'Doesn't that protect us from radiation?'

'Yes. The planet is dying, and us with it.'

Arid and Frey went silent, staring at Nikola's impassive face.

'Don't worry, it shouldn't happen in your lifetime,' he continued.

'How do y' know?' Arid said.

'On the east coast we have something called the Omega. It's the remnants of an experiment that went horrifically wrong on the other side of the planet. It gives us unique insights into how the world is going. It's been explained to me, but the physics are too complex for my brain.'

Arid and Frey sagged. The weight of the day lay heavily on them.

'You should get some rest,' Nikola said.

'Before everything dies?' Arid replied morbidly.

'As I said, you don't need to worry about it yet.'

'The 'yet' part is the bit that's worrying me.'

'Can you pay for a room or something?' Frey asked.

'I have to walk lightly, so, sorry.'

'Great,' Arid grumbled.

'It's a warm night. See if they've got some spaces in the visitor shed.'

'Great,' he repeated. 'All in all, y' haven't been an evening of light entertainment.'

'Here, have some chips.' Nikola threw a bag of salt-and-vinegar chips across the table.

Frey got up and stalked away. Arid followed, then ducked back and grabbed the chips. When he came out the door, Frey was nowhere to be seen. It would be typical for her to get lost in ten paces.

There were three heavy footsteps behind him, and a hood was pulled over his head. The bag fell to the floor and chips scattered across the wooden boards, crushed under a pair of dusty boots.

'You!'

'Hello, Arid,' Suzie said.

The door slammed closed behind him. The rumble of the patrons from the floor below could be heard. She sat alone in the hotel room, on the edge of the bed. A breeze through the curtains. Heavy footsteps in the hall. The bed sat high off the floor, its mock-colonial frame containing a thick but hard mattress. One pillow. The whole thing covered in pale green. The rest of the room was oddly empty. *Like her heart*, Arid thought.

'Do y' know the difficulty y' caused me?'

'I'm sure you're just exaggerating,' she replied, examining her fingernails.

'You blamed me for trying t' assassinate the queen,' Arid exclaimed.

'I believe the evidence was striking, and part of me still thinks so. No one had even given Queen Beatrice a harsh word. You turn up and there's an attempt on her life.'

'But cause doesn't equal effect.'

'But it cannot be ignored.'

'But—'

Suzie raised her hand. 'Or someone who was on the *Lady Moonshine* wanted to use you as an excuse. Someone who had been waiting for a long time. The queen will be here tomorrow, and so will you. One would think that would be another perfect opportunity for another attempt. And, of course, pin it on you.'

'That's it, I'm out of here.'

'We need you.' Her voice took on a pleading tone.

'What?' Arid froze with his hand on the door handle.

'We need the assassination attempt, otherwise we'll never know who the killer is. And her life will always be in jeopardy.'

'No way.'

'I would do anything to protect the queen. I would sacrifice myself if I could save her. I would do *anything* for her. Anything at all.'

Arid found the statement a little confronting and obsessive. 'I'm sure she's grateful.'

Suzie's face didn't move, but he thought he detected something between a sneer and sadness. It reminded him of Revvy, when he said he wouldn't go to the No Bearing show. He turned the door handle.

Suzie grabbed his arm and pulled him back. 'Please, I can't let her die. She means …'

The aggression startled Arid. He looked into her face. It was pale and tears welled in her eyes.

'Everything. She means strength and stability. To us all. There are huge plans in the works that she's pivotal to.'

'Yeah, *you* might be happy with jumping in harm's way, but I'm—'

She stood back and rose to her full, slender height. Her face morphed, the desperation melting away to be replaced by an incoherent fury, a love letter to unearned nobility. 'You're a wanted criminal. If you don't help her, I'll make sure you're hunted down, starting with the men standing outside this door. You will never be free.'

One and a half years ago …

The barracks on the Hawkesbury are hot and overcrowded, with insufficient facilities, clean water or air. The smell is unbearable, deteriorating over the months as more recruits are crowded in. The mechCity has its security concerns and soldiers are always required, but the conditions in the cells the recruits are forced into are inhuman. And now the older recruits are causing a stir. Chanting, banging on furniture. And the guards come charging in wearing full riot gear: black suits and helmets, weapons. They've been here before, with dozens of recruits ending up in the medibay or jail. Their crumpled and lifeless bodies are even thrown out with the trash onto the endless plains, to be picked apart by the army of unspeakable and diseased creatures that followed the rig.

Several older teens next to Alex shout and throw whatever is at hand. It's pointless. Without any kind of organisation, it's just a frantic tantrum.

A guard shouts and pushes through a group of smaller children, forcing them to the ground, and chases down the teens. Cameron, who is the eldest, tries to defend them, but he's too young to be any help.

Alex reaches breaking point as the dark memories of childhood flood back. They weren't causing a scene or presenting a security threat, they only want a safe place to sleep. It shouldn't be this way, and enough is enough.

Alex picks up a large bin overflowing with trash and swings it into the head of the nearest guard. It hits with enough force to dent the cylinder. The guard crumples to the floor, scattering his weapons. Alex scoops up the baton and shield and charges into the other guards.

It's ridiculous, Alex thinks. The recruits easily outnumber the riot squad. Sheer weight of numbers should be enough to send a message to the command. Alex shouts to the other recruits to pick up their beds and use them to push back against the guards' attack.

But in the end, Alex is surrounded, taken down and dragged out by a guard on each limb. Is it a planned humiliation, a visible takedown in front of everyone?

And now here...

Is the room a prison? Alex can no longer tell the difference. Without warning, the door opens. Someone comes. Alex understands it's all for show, but it still leaves bruises. It still cuts into you, making you feel weak and unimportant. Life is a chain of confrontations and the resulting injuries. It defines you in the end.

Byrne spins the opposite chair so the rear faces Alex and sits with his arms on the back. It's a casual move by a man who feels he needs to show he's in control.

'I trust all is proceeding as planned,' Byrne says.

Alex nods.

'Have you made any friends, anyone that could cause complications down the track?'

'No friends, just followers.' Alex's response is flat. You cannot trust anyone, especially those who say you cannot trust anyone.

'It may be time to invoke some of those followers. We've had word that there could be a potential opportunity to intersect with the target. Our source can never be certain, but we roll the dice and see. We need to ensure that believable evidence is in place to match expectation.'

Alex sits quietly. There doesn't seem to be much to say.

'Are you ready to go?'

'We can only find out when the time comes,' Alex replies. 'It's a big deceit.'

'Not exactly the answer I was after. But better to be honest than lying and failing.' Byrne takes a long drag on his cigarette and lets out the smoke in an equally long breath. 'You've been in the system for several months. What have you learned?'

'I've learned you need to be patient.'

Byrne lets out a low chuckle. 'What do you say if you're asked about command?'

'They're a spoiled group of over-privileged bullies whose incompetence is only outweighed by their greed and laziness.'

'Very good.' Byrne smiles and nods. The end of his cigarette glows brightly as he takes a deep puff.

It doesn't hurt to pretend it's a lie.

'If and when they take you, don't go quietly,' Byrne instructs. 'After all, the queen is the enemy.'

'I'll proceed as I see fit, based on the situation and the training you have instilled. I know the process. We follow the plan.'

Byrne finishes his cigarette and stubs it out on the floor under the toe of his boot. 'Don't get complacent. If you ever find yourself wandering or being lulled into complacency, you know what you need to remember.'

'The queen killed my parents. It's not something I'm going to forget.'

[9]

ARID RAN ALONG the veranda in a panic, constantly checking over his shoulder. When he was far enough away, he slowed and thought about his run-in with the stretched-out woman, Suzie.

The situation was getting desperate. In the past, adults got him to do stuff, but it was never important. Maybe this was his chance to prove how awesome he was. Keep his head down, keep out of the way of everyone, keep a low profile. Just follow the plan and don't talk to anyone who wasn't a close friend of the queen, or anyone that wasn't sanctioned by stretched-out Suzie. That was it: keep quiet and invisible. Don't talk to anyone.

Hunter stepped out from the doorway of a barbershop. 'Kid.'

Arid jumped out of his skin. 'What?'

'I've seen you around. Have you run into the captain from over east? He's got a big sword on his back.'

He thought of what Suzie had said. *Don't tell anybody anything.* 'Uh, yeah.'

'Just wondering if you, in your inimitable style, could do me a favour. Could you bring him here?'

'He was in the pub. Can't y' go there?'

'Best if I wasn't seen there more than once.' Hunter tapped

the side of his nose. Arid had no idea what that meant. 'I'll drop a couple of goldies for you.' He pulled out a short cardboard tube that fit easily in his palm. MACQUARIE BANK was stamped on the side. In the open end was the flash of a gold coin. 'You must be on the precipice of exhaustion from your extensive gallivanting all over the place, hither and yon. It'll get you a good feed.'

Arid was tired, wet, exhausted, didn't understand half the words, but, more importantly, hungry. 'I only have to bring him here?'

'That's all.'

Arid let out a long groan. 'All right.'

He made his way back to the hotel. Nikola was still inside, deep in conversation with Parker. They stopped talking abruptly as he approached the booth.

'Young Arid. It's a surprise to see you.' Nikola glanced over at Parker, who shrugged.

'Er, yeah. Someone wants t' meet y',' he said to Nikola.

Nikola nodded. 'That is often the case. Would they like me to sign a photograph?'

Parker snorted.

'Er, no. Look, could y' come with me? He says it's important,' Arid insisted.

'Who?'

'Hunter.'

'Hunter wants Nikola's autograph?' Parker asked.

'No, no. He wants to meet him.'

'Romantic dinner for two?' Parker said, nudging Nikola.

Arid sighed. 'Look, it's been a really long day, I'm really tired and I'm getting paid for this. Or will be, I think. It's hard to tell what he means when he speaks. Then I can eat. Can we just go?'

'Kid looks dead on his feet,' Parker said.

Nikola stood and dismissed Parker for the evening, then followed Arid to the barbershop. The lights were off, but the door sat open. A large fan in the centre of the ceiling circulated the hot hair around the room. Hunter sat in one of the gas-cushioned chairs. He indicated for Nikola to sit in the one next to him.

'Hunter.'

'Tasman.'

They nodded to each other in a stiff and formal fashion.

'How have your travels been?' Hunter asked.

'Interesting. And informative, of course,' Nikola replied.

'Yes. Pray tell, what information do you have of an uprise? Is it local, or the breadth of a wide cast?'

'Right.' Nikola glanced over at Arid. 'It's narrow and specific. The lead … er is unaware, as far as I can ascertain, judging by his actions.'

'A diffusion is providing a suitable shield regarding the incumbents?'

'Yes. I think so.'

And they continued with the odd dialogue. Was this how they spoke over east, Arid wondered. It seemed an awfully complex way of not actually saying anything.

'The steps of the plan are falling within expectation, with the target's behaviour aligning to calculated conjecture.' Hunter's gaze drifted over to Arid. 'And the objective of the …' He sighed and gave up.

Nikola turned to Arid. 'Actually, you can go now. Thanks for the message.'

'Hunter said he'd pay me,' Arid said.

Nikola reached into his pocket and pulled out several gold coins. 'Treat yourself.'

'Do y' know where Frey got to?'

'She's passed out in a safe place. You can meet up with her tomorrow.'

'Can I have a safe place, too?'

'You're resourceful.'

'What's the difference?'

'She needs to be watched.'

'Why?'

'Everyone is a suspect.'

'How come it's my face up on the board, then?'

'I didn't say what she's suspected of,' Nikola said. 'Go get some rest. It's a big day tomorrow.'

Frey tried the door handle. Locked. The room was pleasant enough in its own country-town way. They loved their wood out here. It was like the people: worn down to nothing then replaced in a never-ending cycle of repair, everyone slowly falling to pieces and dying. No one flourished in the outback; it was a matter of enduring until the climate beat you. At least in the mechs you had a chance of survival. You could go looking for food or water, then shift south in the summer to avoid the heat, as long as the alliances allowed you passage.

The mech leaders were as strong and inflexible as the steel making up the rigs. Just like Mama-Bea. Everything had changed over the last decade; the rigs had gotten bigger and tougher. And it was true that the queen had also changed.

In a way, it used to be easier. You knew where you were with her. Usually hated, berated and ignored. Then, after Stephanna's death, she'd awoken. Her heart broke. She learned that some things were more important than being victorious every moment of your life. And she saw the world in a whole new light, and you were left with the bitterness of the past, of the things she'd done because you were the one who hadn't had a revelation. You didn't have permission to abandon your history, redeem your sins, because the world was ninety-nine-per cent the same. Only, one person who didn't like you suddenly pretended to like you. It was all an act, told by Mama-Bea to herself. Tell yourself a lie enough times and you'll believe it. Tell everyone else a lie enough times and they'll believe it—if it doesn't involve them. But that was probably something all leaders knew. The power of deception.

The only honest people, emotionally honest, were kids like her. They were the only ones you could really trust.

Frey found it annoying that Arid couldn't see that the adults were playing him. Like they'd tried to play her with Ella. It felt deliberate. Find a pretty young thing to be the daughter she was never going to be. The girl had been horrible, but Mama-Bea had decided she was going to be some kind of project, someone to save. The arguing had gone on for months and months. Then one day Ella was all sweetness and light. And they were all a big happy family. Except there was a favourite now, and it wasn't Frey.

But she'd been given a huge responsibility. A mission. And hadn't that gone well.

She was meant to keep something safe. Here she was, miles from home, unprotected, among untrustworthy strangers. Almost, if not exactly, the opposite of what she was meant to achieve.

She could hear Mama-Bea's voice, the intonation, the way she tilted her head and placed her hands on her hips. The task had been straightforward, not easy. A defined goal with a straight-line path to success.

Was it worth going through all this effort and heartache if Frey was just going to be a disappointment?

Could she run away? Her real mother was dead, so there were no loyalties or guilt to keep her in place. The country was a big place. The people from over east seemed nice. What was the point in being in a place where you were thought of as a second-class citizen?

This was a time when, if she had had a photograph of her real mother, she would have pulled it out and stared at it to find inspiration and strength, but Mama-Bea had thrown out all the pictures when Stephanna had been poisoned.

The chest of drawers against the far wall was completely empty. It had the musky smell of age, and the feel of thick dust recently cleaned away. A plastic film decorated with flowers lined the base of each drawer. The chest had also been secured to the floor. The window was locked. Outside, the street was dark. No lights. No signs of life. A glass of water sat on a table next to the bed. The table was nothing more than a piece of wood stuck on top of a metal frame. The bed didn't look much different. She sat on the edge and found her suspicions to be correct.

The past was a hard thing to forget. It made you, supplying your fears and insecurities. But the future was a different beast.

If they were right and Mama-Bea was going to be here tomorrow, then it was Frey who was going to be the responsible one. When something needed to be done, you had to take destiny in your own hands. No one else seemed able to do it, so she'd be the one to take care of the queen.

This time she wouldn't fail.

Arid stirred. He'd found shelter in a doorway and gotten some sleep. Nothing had attacked him, so the day was already off to a better start than the previous one. He stretched and walked out into the road. Dawn presented a clear sky, with a fierce sun already heating the day. Steam rose from the ground as the heat and humidity dried out the remnants of the deluge. Flowers bloomed in erratic clumps, tempting the gentler insect life.

People were up and working. As the cool part of the day, it was the only time anything physical could be attempted, when shop owners unloaded vehicles. He heard the whistle of a train. It would be one of the steam expresses that brought timber up from the Southern Alliance.

Alliances.

Politics.

He groaned. Today was going to be a challenge. Stay out of sight. Stay on the lookout for an assassin. Stay focused. Get ready to run at the drop of a hat. And get ready to save the day. It was a complex recipe for the most experienced hero, and here he was with the weight of an expectation that could sink a rusty rig in quicksand, with no help, or even a clue about what to do.

It was probably easy for heroes like Nikola, who probably got up in the morning and thought, I'd better go save some people, and no two shakes about it. Not beer shakes, though.

Arid sighed. Anyway, it was better to go out in a blaze of glory than hiding away.

Actually, it wasn't. But being on the run for the rest of your life could get wearing. Being alone in a dowser was emotionally demanding, and it had only been a handful of years. Always looking over your shoulder. Always under threat from crawlers, dinocrocs.

He pulled the hood over his head, and with hands in pockets he made his way toward the civic hall at the far end of town. Tom Price hummed with activity as the supporting businesses prepared for the bonanza of a political get-together. And no one gave Arid a second look as they haggled and joked with one another.

He managed to steal bits of food, wolfing them down behind the post office. A yellow roller with red stripes, covered in dust and dents, rolled into the service bay. It was a courier's rig. The far hatch opened, and the driver ran into the building.

A courier? That could be an option. Always on the move. No one ever looked at the face of a delivery boy.

Arid approached the roller. The hatch hadn't closed. It was still running, the pumping air conditioning cooling the cab. He could feel the breeze and it was intoxicating. The courier was talking with someone inside, and he heard angry voices. Arid stood still, staring at the vehicle. An argument gave him time. He could get in and drive away. Not only was it possible, but right now it was even easy.

He rubbed his fingertips on his palms as he thought about it, dreaming about life on the road, running.

But if he left, he'd never get the dowser back. And the queen had promised. And saving her, proving he wasn't the assassin, would definitely make sure she got it done. And he could get his pendant back, the last memento of his parents. She wouldn't keep that from him. He could trust her.

The courier's voice floated out from the office, calmer. He definitely heard 'goodbye'.

Time to choose. Stay or go.

He stood riveted to the spot with indecision. The pressure

built; his head throbbed.

Go.

No. Stay.

The door opened behind him and Arid ran off around the corner of the building.

'I'll keep my eyes open,' said the courier. It was a female voice, vaguely familiar. 'You should get out of town before they attack.'

The hatch slammed shut and the roller roared past at a hectic pace.

The civic hall was packed. The elevated ceiling allowed for the tall, thin windows along each side to let in plenty of light. The ancient wooden floor gleamed from centuries of wear and varnishing, shining like glass. The stone walls kept the heat out and the room cool. It was an oasis in the desolation of the desert.

A broad range of leaders graced the interior, feasting on the trays circulating on the heads of serving bots. Arid moved through the throng of people, stepping between the tight clusters and occasionally stealing a cracker smeared with Vegemite. It was the good stuff, food for kings—or leaders, at least.

He grabbed a handful of appetisers as a bot chuffed past, its steam motor leaving a trail of mist that coated the floor with condensation and oil.

Frey stood on the far side of the hall near the service door, which opened occasionally as a catering bot rolled out into the crowd. He backed against the wall, keeping out of sight of the main group.

Suzie approached, carrying a small white bag. She placed it by her feet and rummaged through it before handing him a circular piece of metal. 'It's an earpiece. We'll be able to communicate.'

'I've never seen anything like it,' he said.

'Cyborg tech. New. The future is coming.' She tapped the bag with her foot. 'Hopefully it'll work, even though we're not cyborgs.'

'It won't do anything to us, will it?'

Suzie placed one on her own ear. 'Can you hear me?'

'Yes.'

'Okay. Beatrice will be led into the hall and take the guest-of-honour chair. I'll situate myself behind her when she sits. You roam the area and search for the potential assassin. Don't trust anyone. The killer could be someone you know, or someone totally unexpected.'

A commotion grew by the entrance as the attendees rushed the main doors. Gasps and claps were heard from outside.

'She's here,' Suzie said, clutching her hands to her chest. 'Take up position.'

Arid moved slowly to the corner and munched on the appetisers. It seemed pointless waiting as more people left the hall. Surely it would be better if he followed the queen from her arrival. He moved slowly toward the exit and peered out over the crowd.

The *Lady Moonshine* had rolled into the carpark, casting a shadow over all the other vehicles and the building. The audacity of the arrival had the leaders cheering. The *Moonshine* lowered into its docking position, hisses and creaks emanating from the suspension mechanisms. A whistle from above drew the audience's attention, and the rescue harness descended from the upper levels. Bea landed gently on her feet, to the cheers of the crowd. Unclipping the harness, she stepped out. Another figure joined her and stood by her side.

Arid struggled to see through the closely packed crowd, and only caught her, dressed in her officer's uniform, as she climbed the steps to the hall. His earpiece buzzed.

'Where … you?' Suzie said. Her voice crackled over the line.

'Sorry, you dropped out.'

'Where … ell are you?'

'I'm outside. Everything looks okay,' he replied.

'Get … here …*ow!*'

Bea was greeted by the senior council members, delaying her procession, and Arid, keeping his head down, squeezed past into the hall. Although the crowd was thin, once the people from outside were in it was going to be packed. He picked the best position to see the entire chamber.

'In place,' he whispered.

The queen appeared. His heart lifted when he saw Ella next to her. She wore a long black robe, like she had the day they met. She looked stunning with her hair tied back but flowing over her shoulders. She'd made up her face and she looked like a china doll. Dark red lips contrasted with her pale skin. Eyeliner rimmed her steel-blue eyes.

There were possibly other people in the room, but for him they disappeared in the golden halo wrapping around Ella. His eyes tracked her graceful movements as she floated over the floor to the rear of the building.

The queen mounted the stage, with Suzie taking up position behind her. Ella stood at the foot of the stairs, her hands clasped in front of her and her head lowered. A familiar figure knelt next to her, engaging in a casual conversation. It was Theo. How did that work with the connection to Byrne? Here Theo was, being friendly to Bea, when he may have been involved in the assassination attempt.

People buzzed around Arid, excitement building as the event opening neared. The volume in the room steadily increased, as did the temperature. He watched those close by milling around him, absorbed with their own cliques. Then his eyes opened wide as a figure came striding directly toward him.

'You!'

'What are y' doing here?' he squeaked. Arid peered up into the stern eyes of Jozee.

'Hunting for Byrne,' she replied. 'But I'll take out anyone who gets in my way.' She withdrew a knife and held the point against Arid's throat. He gulped, feeling the point prick against his skin. The crowd around them swelled, causing Jozee to lower the blade. 'You have no idea how much you and he have cost me,' she said.

'Me? *You* picked *us* up.'

'Yeah, what a coincidence. But I have to admit you've got guts showing your face here, with the price on your head.'

The people moved on and she raised the knife back to his throat.

A woman next to them said, 'Ooh, could I borrow that? The cheese knife has disappeared.'

Jozee glared at her wordlessly.

'I'll wait,' the woman said.

Jozee returned her attention to Arid, lowering her knife. 'You see Byrne, you tell him there'll be more than one death today.'

'What do y' mean?'

'Don't think you're the only one who knows about the assassination attempt. We're all expecting a show.'

'Are y' the assassin?'

Jozee laughed. 'High risk and low pay. I don't think so. The assassin is very close to the queen. Her daughter.'

'That's stupid. How would y' know?'

'I know someone who knows someone. And, my friend, you have a leaking rig.'

'I don't believe y'.'

Jozee shrugged and smirked at him. 'Believe it or not, the assassin has actually been on my sweeper. Recently.'

He spun around. Frey had yet to reappear. After everything she had said, she couldn't be the one.

'And you know what else? I know Frey is wearing the same clothes. Since I don't trust Byrne or any of you lot, I put a tracker on her dress. CF-TX3. You need to *adopt* an open mind. Let the fun begin.' Jozee smiled and backed away into the crowd.

Arid placed his hand on the earpiece. 'Suzie, did you hear that?'

'No.'

'I just got information from someone who said the *Moonshine* has a leak and that the assassin is the daughter of the queen.'

'Which one?'

'I think she meant Frey. And I can't see her.'

'What makes you think that?'

'All the clues she gave. And she said a tracker is on Frey's dress.'

'What kind?'

'Is there one called a CF-TX3?'

'I don ... ow.'

'Do you have a scanner or something?'

'I'll ... check ... bag.'

He watched Suzie kneel next to her white bag and search through it. She pulled out a flat black box. 'I ... ot something. What ... the model number?'

Arid repeated it.

'Got it. Search ... nothing yet.'

Suzie reached out and grabbed Ella. She said something that it looked to Arid like 'Frey', followed by a long sentence. Ella tilted her head, her face becoming a mask of inquisition, maybe concern.

'Okay, I've ... signal,' Suzie said over the earpiece.

'What were you talking to Ella about?' Arid said.

Suzie responded, 'Filling her in ... details and ... keep safe. How reliable ... source of yours?'

'She was a pirate who picked us up and sold us to the cyborgs,' Arid replied. 'She said she had some trackers to follow her investments, whatever that means.'

'The scanner ... narrowing ... says ... assassin ... room. Repeat: *Assassin is in the room.*'

Arid's stomach fell. He was here. The assassin was here. If things went bad, it was going to be difficult to explain the coincidence. He moved through the crowd. How did you spot an assassin? They wouldn't necessarily look suspicious. If Frey was the assassin, shouldn't she be here now? And with hundreds of people watching, how was that possible? Surely they'd overlooked something.

His eyes caught the movement of orange: Frey's dress. He pushed through the crowd after it.

Suzie's voice crackled in his ear. 'The scanner ... assassin ... your side of the room.'

'I see Frey.'

'Can you see ... anywhere?'

'Who?'

'Ella. I can't ... see her. Did the pirate give you anything specific ... who?'

'Er, she said, um, made a big thing out of the word 'adopted'. Frey said she was adopted.'

'The assassin is right in front of you.'

His eyes darted over the crowd. 'There's no one here. No one looks familiar.'

'Arid, can you hear me? Arid!' Suzie yelled into his earpiece. 'Arid, the adopted daughter of the queen is—' Then his earpiece was ripped away. A familiar figure appeared in front of him as he turned.

'Surprise, Arid.' Alex's hand moved like lightning. Two metal prongs dug into the side of Arid's stomach and his body shook as an electrical charge coursed through him. His hood was pulled back, revealing his identity.

'Arid Geiger is here,' Alex shouted, pointing to Arid as he collapsed to the floor. The guards closed in around him, and Alex slipped away.

One year ago ...

The line had been said so many times it made up Alex's breath. A reality so deeply ingrained that at times it became a mantra. What if they never met? How many people waste a life attempting something they were never going to achieve? But a message had been sent. It had cost. People had died.

But Byrne was certain they would come. 'Inside information,' he'd boasted, then reminded: 'The queen killed your parents. Say it.'

'The queen killed my parents,' Alex had responded.

Queen Bea stands at the front of the sweeper, holding onto a handrail on the ceiling as it bumps over the terrain. It's a dark night, with heavy cloud coverage. The sweeper holds about two dozen soldiers, all she can afford to dispatch without leaving the Moonshine vulnerable. The Moonshine's armed forces approach the prison cell. Tethering to the rear of the Hawkesbury is going to be a risk, but they need the people. The driver switches the sweeper into hush mode and the electric motors take over, the mute whir replacing the regular compressions of the steam engines. The queen watches the prison cell bump erratically as it is hauled over the ground behind the megaRig. Docking is going to be difficult.

They hold their breath as the sweeper approaches. Nervous hands hold on tightly to weapons. The breach team prepares their equipment. The sweeper rocks as it crunches over the creatures that follow a mechCity.

Three.

The prison cell is a matter of metres away, a dark sheet of steel hiding the contents.

Two.

The breach team ignite their plasma cutters. They will throw a serious amount of fire and sparks behind the wall. If anyone is nearby, they will be injured. Possibly killed.

One.

On either side of the sweeper, team members secure suction cups to the prison, and seal and winch the two vehicles together. Everything goes dark. They have a few minutes before the Hawkesbury's security crew become aware of the breach and deploy a defence team.

Burn.

The welders crank up the metal cutters and the sweeper is filled with bright blue light and a sea of sparks. Within half a minute they cut an entrance into the cell.

Inside, Alex turns as the fire lances through the metal. Two vertical lines burn upwards. The guards turn to determine the noise. Alex doesn't have long if the next phase is to be a success.

'Riot!' Alex shouts.

Nearby fellow recruits rise up and charge the guards, pushing them back. Angry shouts fill the room as the guards regroup and counterattack.

'And do you remember what you will call yourself?' Byrne had asked.
'Yes,' Alex had replied.

Smoke billows out from the plasma sprays and the two glowing points *meet at the top. The cut metal swings in and smashes onto the floor. Soldiers charge in, firing machine guns above the fighting. Children scream in terror, caught between the Moonshine's forces and the guards. Then the attack forces part, and Queen Beatrice appears wearing a sleeveless T-shirt and camouflaged pants. A flamethrower is strapped to her back. She releases a thick jet of fire above the heads of the recruits, forcing them to the ground.*

'Rescue the prisoners,' the queen shouts.

The soldiers shepherd the children onto the sweeper.

Alex remains standing, and the queen approaches as her soldiers hold back the guards. The woman towers over him, her lean arms glistening with charred sweat. There is no doubting her strength and charisma. The guards herd the children. They grab Alex's arms aggressively. Pinned to the spot. Defiance is impossible.

'Cameron, keep them safe,' Alex shouts.

'What's your name?' asks the queen.

'You can never waver or hesitate when you say it,' Byrne had instructed.
'I understand,' had been Alex's answer.
'And what is it?' he'd asked.

Alex looks up into the dark, unflinching eyes of the queen. 'Ella.'

[PART 2]

[10]

FREY RAN HER hand over the enormous hub of the *Lady Moonshine*'s front wheel. It was good to be home. Bringing the monster rig to the meet was the ultimate power move. She smiled. The feel of the heavy, worn metal filled her with a sense of security. Those who lived on the rig were guaranteed safety. It was something you couldn't fight. Partly because of its size, but importantly because of Queen Bea and her unmatched strategy skills. Long live the queen.

There would be an assassination attempt today. Here, in front of everyone. How did she feel about it? Mama-Bea wasn't *really* her mother. Stephanna had barely been any kind of parent, seemingly unable to grasp the complexities of care, responsibilities or interest.

All the so-called adults in Frey's life had let her down one way or another. Anger had long packed its bags, replaced by the resigned understanding that people generally looked out for themselves. Or, more accurately, that no one looked out for her. Not anymore. Not since Ella had arrived.

Being outside the *Lady Moonshine* had let Frey's thoughts unravel. *Wrong word. Breathe.* The world was suddenly a lot bigger. But someone was coming to kill Mama-Bea. A deep dread sat in the pit of Frey's stomach. She recounted her thoughts from the previous night, where the wide-open plains had given a fresh perspective on her life. This was the time to do something, to stand up and show she could make a difference. Right or wrong, they'd know her name.

She dragged the toe of her shoe in the dirt, tracing out a semicircle. The wind covered it with dust.

Everything was so temporary.

Shouts bounced out through the entrance to the civic hall, followed by the commotion of confused people. She pushed through the crowd, grinding against the door to pass as those closest streamed out. Guards were clipping handcuffs onto Arid's wrists. Mama-Bea was talking to dignitaries, lost in a heated debate.

Ella approached their mother, oblivious to the excitement behind her. Light flashed in her hand. A blade.

Arid in cuffs.

Ella with a blade.

Mama-Bea distracted.

Ella's face set in a determined stare.

Ella with a blade, twirling and slipping it behind her back underneath the cloak.

Frey ran forward, dancing through the crowd, struggling against the evacuation.

Ella's eyes narrowed; her face hardened. She was only a few steps away from their mother.

Frey shouted, but her voice was drowned in the noise of the departing leaders.

Ella brought the knife forward and lunged. Frey grabbed her sister's arm and the two spun, wrestling for the blade.

The movements became jerky, attracting the attention of their mother. She opened her mouth to say something. The knife was gone.

'No!'

Who had shouted?

It had been Ella. She now stood behind Frey.

Blood trickled down from the queen's chest. Something heavy weighed down Frey's hand. She looked down. It was the knife.

Frey watched the blood drip from the point and fall to the ground, spinning as it tumbled and splattered into the dust. She raised the knife loosely in her palm, releasing her fingers from the grip. Her mother's face dissolved into shock. The knife tumbled out of Frey's hand and landed point down in the wood, vibrating.

Two guards grabbed her by the arms.

The queen slipped off her chair and collapsed onto the floor, her body sideways, arms at right angles, hands by her head.

Frey screamed.

And screamed.

The guards dragged her away as the dignitaries closed in around the queen. One ran his hands over her eyes, closing them.

And Alex ran.

The message went out: *The queen is dead.*

Hawkesbury guards dragged Arid into a diplo-sweeper and raced him to the megaCity. The cell was brutal: scarred grey walls with a tiny window near the ceiling. People died in here, slashing their wrists open on sharp edges. The howls and screams seeped out of the walls. No one cleared up the blood; it had crusted with age. Maybe it was a message, a warning, threat.

Everything was so temporary.

But what filled every moment was Ella. Why had she turned him in? She knew he wasn't involved. She'd been kind. She had helped him escape. He couldn't connect the glowing, smiling face with the betrayal.

Stern guards came and cuffed him, dragging him from the cell to another dark, miserable room. Pushed him into a steel chair. Handcuffed him to a table. The questions were relentless. A small room smelling of stale cigarettes. Figures without faces. Walls without lights.

'Why were you helping the assassin?'

'I wasn't,' Arid replied.

'Why did you want the queen dead?'

'I didn't.'

'How long have you been planning this?'

'I wasn't.'

'Who are you working with?'

'I'm not.'

'Did you hate her?'

'No. No. No! NO!'

A pause rushed in like a tide of respite. The chains rattled as his hands shook. A fetid breath hissed over his shoulder. 'Confess and we shall ease your suffering.'

'Why are y' doing this t' me?' Arid screamed. He pounded on the small metal table, ratting the chains, and shouted, driving out the anguish until he collapsed.

Blackness.

Why was there no light?

Fear is when you can't see a way out.

The soldiers came back. The questions continued.

'Did you want her dead because of your parents?'

'I didn't.'

'How long were you planning with Frey?'

'I wasn't.' Arid lifted his head and stared into the dark. 'Frey?' He rubbed his eyes, but it didn't help. There were voices without presence. Accusations without reason.

'The assassin.'

He shook his head. 'Frey wasn't the assassin. It was Ella.'

'Were you there? Did you see her do it? Do you have any special knowledge?'

'Ella exposed me.'

'She was doing her civil duty in identifying wanted criminals. Ella tried to save the queen. Frey was there with the knife, the queen's blood on her hands.'

'No, it was Ella. I was meant to be protecting the queen.'

'Didn't do a very good job.'

Arid folded his arms and stared down at his feet.

Fear is when you can't see a way out.

Movement. Hands on shoulders. Feet stumbling. Arid was too tired to notice he was being pushed down a different passage until he was in the new cell.

Slow rocking and a vague feeling of momentum. The *Hawkesbury* was moving again. A dim glow crept in through cracks in the wall, revealing the small space he was in. The floor felt rubbery. He tried to peer through the cracks, but they were too fine. He sat in the corner, bringing his knees to his chest.

The queen is dead.

He'd heard them repeat that news. How was it possible? Why had they called Frey the assassin?

Nothing made sense.

Arid had always done as he'd been asked. Been polite. Listened to advice. Since his parents had gone, other adults—fellow diviners—had been the only people who had helped. They'd helped him learn, helped him survive. Or so he had thought. Maybe that had been a gang thing, diviners sticking together, and it had been unique. Maybe the rest of the world wasn't like that.

It hurt. He didn't understand why.

Nothing made sense.

The motion ceased and stillness descended over the cell. The mechCity had come to a stop. The engines wound down and screamed as the steam vented, shaking the walls of the cell. It sounded as though he was directly next to the gas stacks. He clapped his hands over his ears to stop the ringing. The piercing sound subsided, and silence rushed in like soft gloves. Silence. Complete and suffocating. The room spun as he clutched his head.

Sobbing leaked in, like a child arriving late for school. Small, and trying to avoid attention. Arid followed the sound, tracing it to the corner, through a thin crack that allowed the faintest of breezes.

'Hello?' he whispered.

The sobbing paused, replaced by long, deep breaths.
'Who's there?'
'Arid? Is that you?' Frey replied.
'How did we end up here?'
'Mama-Bea ... she's dead.'
Arid said, 'I heard. They're saying I had something to do with it, too. I've tried to tell them I wasn't even there, but they just won't listen. They said you killed the queen.'
He could hear the sobs.
'They accused me of killing my mother. How can they do that? She was everything to me.'
'But they said they caught you with the knife.'
'It was Ella. She did something and made it look like I'd done it. I was going to save the day, catch the assassin. Finally, everyone would have been proud, but it went completely wrong.'
'I was helping them, too. They got *everything* wrong. What do we do?'
'Once we overcome the tiger, we run.'

Nikola sighed. 'Cameron, it really isn't that complex.'
Cameron put one hand on his hip, puffed out his chest and pointed at the soldier, which seemed incredibly brave or reckless or both, considering the man's size. His shadow flicked around the concrete walls as the solitary globe swung in diminishing circles. 'You come in here, telling us what to do, expecting us to kowtow to you just because you're an adult.'
Nikola looked at the boy in front of him. The sun-baked individual had been toughened by years of surviving the most hostile environment in the world. In all respects he was a hair's breadth away from adulthood and was more resilient than most people he'd met. But identity was more than physical. Cameron was a boy in search of recognition.
'Maybe you misunderstood when I said I need your help. Look, you want a bit of respect, to be recognised. You know the internals

of the *Hawkesbury*. I'm guessing you still know people on it. You hate the queen. The pair was a part of the assassination. See?'

Cameron scratched his head. 'I don't get it. What's in it for us?'

'Is there someone else I can talk to? Anyone at all?'

'I'm leader. You deal with me.'

'Fine.' Nikola scratched behind his ear and gazed around the room, which was hot and full of teenagers with a relaxed or incomprehensible attitude toward personal hygiene. The anger and boredom were palpable and thick enough to spread on toast. Their smash-the-system ideology, based on a complete lack of understanding of what authority was about, was scrawled over the walls. 'Are you sure there are no windows in here?'

'It's a secret sanctum. Can't be that secret if people can see in.'

'Okay. Byrne—you remember him—he wants the Omen. Arid knows how it works, which means he can destroy it. You get him, lead a charge to smash it—something you also enjoy, going by your slogans on the wall—and become heroes. Parties. Soap. Drinks all round.'

'How do you know Arid knows how to destroy it?' Cameron asked.

'I've been researching. He might not even know he can do it, but when he confronts it, not only will he want to but he'll be the only person who can.'

'It sounds dangerous.'

'Being a hero often is. But the rewards are great.' Nikola thought back to what he wanted when he was sixteen. 'Food. And girls.'

Cameron narrowed his eyes. 'Not all of us want "girls". Except for Revvy.' He then put his hand over his mouth and whispered, 'She went weird after she asked some loser to see No Bearing. Probably just a phase.'

Nikola sighed again. 'Can we stay focused? Will you assist?'

The teenager turned to the row of younger teens sitting on the floor behind him. They muttered. Hands were raised. Heads nodded.

Cameron turned back. 'It's not looking good. I think we'll pass.'

One teen, a girl dressed all in black, stood up and coughed. Her face had been covered in white powder, but in the heat it was smeared down her face.

'Yes, Del?'

'I don't know if you remember, Cam, but I spent some time with Byrne. He spoke with such a patronising tone, belittling my efforts and mocking my achievements. The years of sacrifice, focus and hard work derided by an idiot who wields unearned power. I didn't ask for advantage or privilege, just impartiality and the appropriate respect and reward. And the other things he used to do. Inappropriate. He stripped my dignity for his own self-esteem, with little recourse for redemption. So I punched him in the nuts.'

'Right on,' called out another girl.

'Calm down, Revvy,' Cameron said.

'You're the only one who thinks so,' Del continued. 'I explained the story to Hunter—I thought he was a nicer man because of his flowery language—saying that I consider it a blow for equality and justice. And he goes, "That's not equality, and the way you've explained it undercuts the whole *equality* ideology," doing the stupid rabbit-ears thing with his fingers.'

Revvy shook her head. 'It's hard to find kindred spirits in such a diseased world.'

'We have our cross to bear. The fight is long and hard, with many sacrifices, but worth it.'

'What did you do?' Cameron asked Del.

'I punched him in the nuts.'

'I like that girl,' Nikola said. 'Come to the Steam Academy and be a warrior.'

Cameron turned back to the collection of teens. Hushed voices continued murmuring. Eventually he turned back to Nikola. 'Okay, we agree,' he said. There was a cough behind him. 'Except for Revvy.'

'You know how to get in?'

Cameron nodded and smiled. 'I know a weakness in the shell.'

Byrne paced across the command level on the *Hawkesbury*, his face radiating anger as his boots clomped on the metal. It had been days, and cracks were appearing in the command hierarchy. It wasn't meant to be this troublesome.

Theo watched him stride back and forth, his hands clasped behind his back. Byrne glared over at him; the other man was impossible to read. Was this part of some plan? Theo had declared his loyalty—the actual words had come out of his mouth—but his actions were hinting at something else.

'Theo, set up meets with the Western Alliance commanders,' Byrne ordered. 'We need to get the next phase rolling.'

'Yes, sir. Shall I notify the commander?'

'No. I'm not certain … We don't need to present the options until there's been uniform agreement among the leaders. No need to waste his time.'

No need to let him in on the secret, Byrne thought. Theo's continual reference to the commander rankled. The man was commander in name only. He had little say or understanding in how the real world worked, little comprehension beyond his own losses and little involvement. A new world would be forged without him.

'The queen is dead,' Byrne continued. 'Why are the commanders hesitating? You said you'd be able to align the other leads. If there's a stumble at the final hurdle, if he finds out what's going on, we're all in trouble. You know how he reacts to these things.'

'These things take time,' Theo replied. 'With such a sudden change in the power structure, in such a visible fashion, people are working out whether this is their best option.'

'Best option? I thought they understood what would happen if they had independent thoughts. We are a team. They need to co-operate.'

'Co-operate?'

'Yes, do as they're told.' Byrne walked to Theo and stood directly in front of him, nearly nose to nose. 'You can do that, can't you?

Make it happen?'

'It's complicated.'

'I don't care if it's complicated. You're supposed to be an expert in negotiations. It's your sole purpose. If you can't do that then what good are you to me?'

'I-I-I ...'

'Yes, it's all about you.'

'You can't do this without me,' Theo insisted.

'Is that something you want to put to the test? Because do not, for one second, think I will hesitate to puncture your throat with a corkscrew. You understand me?'

Theo backed away, his hands trembling. 'I-I will not stand for this. You cannot threaten—'

The door opened and a guard marched in, startling the two men.

'Anstrom, you're just in time to witness Theo confirm his loyalty and push on with the plans as agreed,' Byrne said to the guard.

Theo stared at Byrne, then turned and stormed out.

'Don't forget to write,' Byrne called after the retreating man. 'Anstrom, give me an update. Tell me of your progress.'

Anstrom removed his cap and placed it under his arm, his bright eyes focused on Byrne's impassioned face. 'Sir, they're not carrying anything. Completely lacking possessions.'

'Did the boy say where the key is? At least that?'

'No.'

'Keep pushing. I need the key. Get that key.'

Anstrom's chiselled face didn't flinch, as though cast in granite. 'He's a kid.'

'Exactly. He will break. One of them knows something. Is there a link between them? Do they have feelings for each other? Can we use that?'

'They don't seem to. Almost the opposite.'

'What about the daughter? Has she confessed to killing the queen?'

'No.'

'We all saw her. Apply pressure and continue to do so until she confesses. Remind her we have enough evidence. How she lives the rest of her life, or even how long it is, is up to her and her inclination to co-operate.'

Anstrom shook his head. 'A young girl ... it doesn't look good.'

'You're a soldier. Rules don't apply to you,' Byrne reminded. 'If you can't handle it, then find someone who can. There are thousands on this mechCity. We've trained all sorts of individuals with dark thoughts. Find some. Make them do it. Give them rewards.'

'Rewards for torturing a girl?'

'I can see we're coming to a moment of revelation here. You need to decide whose side you're on. Work out where your loyalty sits. I expect you to be loyal.'

'So you've said. Repeatedly.'

'It's important you understand.'

'Speaking of understanding, we have a code of conduct. The PAD covers our actions and we're already too far over the line. If it's discovered what the soldiers are doing here, the council will take action. And I think you'll find yourself quite ... independent, shall we say.'

'You question your leader?'

'To be honest, you are not the actual leader. It's probably wise to remember that, with all due respect.'

'Just do as I say. *Do as I say.*'

'I suggest you calm down, *sir*. The troops don't respond well to threats or bullying.'

'This is it. I put it to you now, will you do as you are ordered?' Byrne demanded.

Anstrom didn't move. His eyes didn't blink. Byrne had 'rescued' Anstrom from the Larrakia when the rig's captain had been drunk. He was a tough soldier who'd never shown a moment's hesitation to be brutal. The list of Anstrom's crimes was extensive, but Byrne had to wonder if he'd reached the limit. Did the man have family?

Byrne couldn't have weakness in the ranks. Disrespect was a

snowball. He wrapped his fingers around the knife tucked into the back of his belt.

'I'll let you know.' Anstrom gave Byrne a salute that bordered on being a rude gesture and left.

[11]

THE MOON HUNG high, shining down on the silent plain, covering everything in a silver-blue glow. The *Hawkesbury*'s engines hummed away, keeping the internal functions operating. Lights from the living quarters twinkled against the dark patchwork metal exterior.

The night guards patrolled in silence around the base of the rig, keeping up an easy pace in the sand, stamping on the sprouting flowers. Cameron watched them from his surveillance point, where he was lying in a clump of tough trees that grew in a shallow dip. The vegetation had grown quickly since the downpour, providing a soft blanket. Beside him, Anthony stifled a sneeze.

Cameron had stolen a screamer to get here and had abandoned it a good hike from the mechCity. Screamers were registered for, at the most, two occupants. Five was going to be a challenge, but there hadn't been much choice.

He watched the guards disappear around the far side of the rig. The secret entrance still looked undiscovered—that is, not welded shut—but at this distance it was hard to tell.

'You two stay here,' Cameron said to his comrades. 'I'm going to have a closer look.' Keeping low, he ran to the side of the mechCity.

Anthony went to sneeze again, closing his eyes and holding his mouth open. The moment passed. 'This is ridiculous. With my hayfever I ain't lying with me nose in the daffs.' He stood, hiding behind one of the trees, and brushed the pollen off his clothes. Cameron had insisted that they dress entirely in black.

'I agree,' Del added. She stood next to him. She'd managed to find an ex-paramilitary uniform that fitted her perfectly, in contrast to Anthony, whose baggy top had sleeves hanging down to his knees.

Anthony moved with a dexterity that belied his size. He'd taken the concept of dressing in black to include a balaclava that left only his eyes—which twinkled with mischief—and mouth exposed.

Moonlight fell through the branches, catching Del's petite features, and her large wide eyes were full of the starlight of dreams. Her dark raven hair glowed almost blue.

'So, what ya doin' after?' Anthony spoke out the side of his mouth, as though each phrase had an ulterior motive, or his mouth was embarrassed by what came out.

'God knows,' Del replied. 'Could be dead.'

'Could be. But there'll probably be a hell of a party after we've saved the day, right?'

She snorted. A moment of awkward silence passed between them.

'Ya want to hang out with me?' Anthony asked.

'No way,' Del replied.

'We could have a milkshake at Mad Clapping Harry's or something.'

'You'll need to be more impressive than that.'

'You're a tough woman.'

'Just one with standards.'

'Ya should take pity on me because of me condition.'

'What's wrong with you?' She wasn't really asking. 'Beyond the obvious mental issues.'

'I've got an illness,' he replied.

'Being young and annoying?'

'I'm not young. I'm the same age as you.'

'Hang on, how do you know my age?'

'Cameron knows it. He knows *everythin'* about you.' Anthony waggled his eyebrows.

Del rolled her eyes. 'What illness have you got?' she asked.

'I'm short for me height.'

'How tall are you?'

'Two metres.'

He didn't even come up to her shoulder.

'You are *not* two metres tall,' Del insisted.

'I am,' Anthony replied. 'Says so on the official documents and everything.'

'… How?'

'People can change their name, right?'

'I guess so.'

'You know, marriage, criminals.'

'Interesting you lump those together.'

'They change them so they ain't prejudiced against, right? So, I've changed me height.'

'But it's physics. Your name is an arbitrary label assigned for the ease of communication. Nothing more than a souvenir. A roadmap to your human history. Conquests or mistakes.'

'Ain't you the romantic one.'

'Shut up. I *am* romantic. It's in my DNA.'

'Is that why ya got 'luv' and 'hat' tattooed on yer fingers?'

'The little finger hurt more than expected.'

'Shh. Cameron's comin' back. Look like you're payin' attention. He likes that.'

Del drove a knuckle into Anthony's arm.

Cameron's footsteps were nothing more than a whisper through the grasses, his large frame appearing menacing against the dark skyline on the lip of the dell.

They greeted him as he slid down the slope.

Cameron came to a halt, staring at Del's face. A moment of

silence passed. Del and Anthony swapped looks.

'Did I just say something out loud?' Cameron asked.

'Nope. Silent as a rock,' Anthony said.

'Although your eyes did go a little funny,' Del said.

'Yeah,' Anthony said. 'Like sultry. Smoulderin'.'

'What are you talking about?' Cameron said. 'It's probably hayfever. All this pollen and everything.'

'I can tell by all the sneezin' yer doin'.'

The patrol reappeared at the far corner of the *Hawkesbury*. The trio watched in silence as the guards ambled along the side, the epic size dwarfing them.

Cameron moved in closer to Del, bumping her shoulder. She gave him a cold stare.

'I'm, er, just blending with the scenery,' he said.

'There's more scenery than just on this spot. You could say the countryside is covered in it.'

'Would ya two lovebirds keep it down?' Anthony whispered.

As the guards disappeared around the corner of the mechCity, Cameron raised his hand and motioned them forward. The trio erupted from the hollow and hustled toward the massive wheels. Heat radiated from the tank tracks, preventing them from resting against the tall hubs.

The behemoth mechCity towered ten stories above them. Del and Anthony hesitated as they stared up at the metal monster. It had been years since they had seen it, but the memories were still fresh. Cameron hissed at them and they continued after the guards, following silently in their footsteps.

At the rear of the rig, Cameron ducked under the base and crawled on his back through the sand until he found the opening. He tapped a pattern on the inside of the open join, testing if it was still accessible. The weld was still rough and cut through his clothing as he dragged himself inside. The crawlspace was tight, and with the others following he needed to keep moving.

Since Cameron's escape and subsequent return to rescue others, he had grown, which now made traversing through the tight passages difficult. What worried him was that it was always easier getting in than out.

The claustrophobia of the close spaces had his heart pounding and sweat streaming down his face. Hand over hand, he pulled himself through the tight tunnels, which were made from a combination of service ducts and poor engineering work, plus the occasional improvement made by escapees in their numerous attempts to flee.

Del, her figure smaller and thinner, called from behind telling him to hurry up. Maybe he was getting too old for this. Next year he'd be twenty, and if that wasn't retirement age then he didn't know what was.

He finally reached a service hatch that could be secured from the inside. Lifting the latch and slowly easing it open a fraction, he peered out. The space was dark and empty as far as he could see. Which, unfortunately, was only in one direction. He pursed his lips and let out a low whistle; in moments the hatch was opened up by unseen hands.

Cameron let out a sigh of relief as the face of a young recruit appeared. He flexed out of the crawlspace, rolled onto the floor and up onto his feet. 'Are you Arni?' he whispered.

The recruit nodded.

'You got the message?'

The recruit nodded again.

'Where are they?'

The recruit leaned in. 'L5A. Cells two and three. You've got fifteen minutes before the guard changeover. That's when you'll find only one person manning the security desk.'

'Keys?'

'New system. Magnetic lock triggered by infrared security harness. You'll need the swipe card for the particular cells.'

'Oh. I hadn't planned on that. Who's on the inside?'

'Dunno,' the recruit replied.

'Great,' Cameron finished. He signalled for the others to follow. 'Let's see how much it's changed.'

The megaCity opened up in front of the team, a vast metal cavern surrounded by balconies supporting buildings. Wide gantries crossed the void and carried dozens of people. The physical scope of it was hard to understand. The interior was as big as a town, but vertical. The inside contacts said the population numbered close to ten thousand these days. Cameron looked around. Ten thousand, and still all this space?

A light breeze floated past. A stack of water bottles was locked behind a glass door, taunting them.

'Come on, we need to be quick,' Cameron said to Del and Anthony. 'No distractions.'

The city didn't sleep. Life carried on at the periphery, the nightshift busily replenishing and preparing for the next day. But the night hours were unpopular, and workers paid little attention to anything beyond their own duties.

The lowest level stank of grime and defeat, a thin film of self-inflicted inadequacy shouldered by the mugs dressed in bright yellow or orange visibility clothing and charged with the continual and efficient operation of the mechCity.

No matter how they filled out the interior with vast shining surfaces, the mining origins of the city could not be hidden, especially in the lower levels. From the roughshod flooring visible through drifts of sand to the ancient, faded branding on the walls, the utilitarian heritage bonded the layers of the city into families, disparate tribes that enjoyed mouthing off at one another. The lower levels comprised those who toiled away in the semi-toxic air, unified by cheap uniforms. And right now, that was going to play into Cameron's plan. Running through each floor was a vertical dagger of unity with the downtrodden recruits.

Hidden behind the walls were the tightly packed cogs and pushrods of the city, the powerhouse keeping it running and liveable, quieter now as the bulk of the inhabitants slept.

Cameron led his team through the narrow alleys between the

mechanisms, where steam rose through the floor and generated a thin mist.

A cleaner wandered by, pushing a large trolley loaded with cleaning products. The team pressed against the wall, waiting for her to pass. Ahead, Cameron spotted half a dozen workers wearing dark glasses and hardhats, milling underneath an elevated spotlight illuminating a large piece of paper held out between them.

Cameron led the others toward the service shafts. A lift large enough for twenty workers was open, its polished steel interior shimmering in the glow cast from the spotlight. He pushed open the door next to the lift and entered the stairwell. He hurried the others through, and they all ran up the steps to the next level, indicated by a large *L2* painted on the wall.

Cameron gave the *L3* sign a rude gesture as they passed it by. This was the old training level. They had perverted him here, twisting his mind into a monster's. The memories sat on him like an immovable pack, and the proximity to the genesis of his abuse inflamed his guilt. It hadn't been him, but when it's your hands doing the hurting, it's hard to proclaim innocence, and so the eternal remorse was a fair cost for the suffering he'd inflicted. Then he could be the exact opposite.

Halfway around the stairs to L4, Cameron caught the sound of footsteps coming down. He peered up through the gap between the stairs and saw a patrol descending at speed. He hurried the team up the rest of the steps to L4 and they pushed through the door, panting heavily as they closed it behind them.

Guards, soldiers and law enforcement. Not the best floor to be diverted onto.

Cameron had rarely visited this level when he was a recruit. But they needed the keys for the jail cells on L5. Most surfaces were coated in black gloss paint. The walls were dotted with posters propounding the benefits of serving in the forces, the main benefits being pride, and the wisdom of the command in leading them to victory. In wars of their own making.

The door behind him rattled. He jammed his shoulder against

it, keeping the patrol at bay, and slammed the lock into place.

'We've been blown,' Cameron said. 'We've got about two minutes before they sound the alarm.'

The team ran through the corridor, Cameron stopping frequently to establish their location. As they neared the centre of the rig, space opened up to reveal a large steel cage. In the middle of the cage, two guards relaxed behind a desk. Behind them sat banks of weapons. The cage door was shut, and presumably locked from the inside.

Cameron recognised the security passes hanging from a hook on the farthest shelving unit. He nudged Anthony. 'You sneak around. I'll distract them, draw them out so you can get the security swipes.'

Anthony nodded and made his way to the far side of the cage.

'Any ideas how to distract them?' Cameron asked Del.

They watched Anthony creep around the far side of the cage, keeping low. The lights were dim, assisting with his concealment.

There was a loud crash behind them. The door to the stairwell smashed open.

Del shrugged. 'Problem solved.'

Shouts. Footsteps. Cameron and Del ducked into a corridor, keeping flat against the wall. The guards ran to the cage. The staff inside jumped to attention. The store sergeant hit a large red button wired to the shelving unit. The siren spun up, its piercing tone ringing out.

Del glanced over at Cameron. 'These prisoners had better be worth it.'

'Every prisoner is worth it.'

Cameron gave her a mirthless smile then returned his attention to the guards. He saw that Anthony was holding his position, huddled behind the cage. Surely he didn't have long before being spotted.

Soldiers emerged from their rooms. The store sergeant opened the cage to the urgent demands from the guards. This was their opportunity.

The door next to Cameron and Del opened and a groggy soldier stuck his head out. Cameron rammed his elbow against the man and forced him back into the room. The barracks was small and tidy, as expected. A poster on the wall showed an old woman dressed in a baggy military uniform pushing a vacuum cleaner with a big red cross through it, and YOUR MOTHER DOESN'T WORK HERE printed underneath.

Cameron unleashed two more blows and the man collapsed. He shook his hand, wringing out the sting.

Del searched the cupboard and pulled out two uniforms.

'Only time for the shirt,' Cameron said. The uniforms were too big, but in the dark they could pass as young soldiers.

They ran out, buttoning up the shirts, joining in with the collecting force. More soldiers were gathering, rubbing eyes and forming up into rows.

'Get the tyke,' Cameron instructed.

Del moved around the side of the cage. Anthony was gone. Her heart leapt and she surreptitiously shrugged at Cameron.

The store guards stood outside the cage, trying to come to terms with information from the patrol. The soldiers were demanding reasons for the emergency. The place tumbled into chaos.

Cameron watched the store guards, waiting until each was involved in the growing argument. The plan should be simple: slip into the cage, grab the swipe cards and get out.

Senior officers in smart uniforms appeared, their expressions determined and annoyed.

'We need to kill the alarm,' Cameron said. 'It's causing too much of a distraction.'

Del nodded. 'I'll take care of it.'

She knelt as though tying a disobedient shoelace and pulled a small knife from inside her boot. Her eyes tracked along the wires from the alarm to the ground and along to the point closest to her. A couple of clever wriggles, and she had moved next to the cables and slashed the blade across the wires. The lights went out, replaced by flickering spotlights as the emergency system took over. Figures became statues, frozen in moments, moving only between blinks.

The soldiers began to disperse, allowing Cameron to slide through the ranks toward the cage opening. The security cards hung unattended, pearl white and tantalisingly close, bouncing gently as the groggy soldiers knocked the metal frame, shaking the shelves.

The store staff were busy steering the soldiers back to their barracks, deliberately not watching. As the entrance approached, Cameron brought his breath under control, slow. Each step was measured, placed not to attract attention, slow. One guard turned, his eyes drifting over Cameron's face before continuing. The man's words, shouted, slow.

At the gate. He reached in. His fingertips brushed over the white ceramic cards, pushing them away. So close. The lights steadied, returning to a subdued glow, radiating blue and catching him with his arm outstretched.

'Oi, soldier, where do you think you're going?'

Cameron dropped his arm and froze. A hand tapped him on the back. He turned.

'Look at you, you're a disgrace,' the quartermaster admonished. 'Unshaven. Ill-fitting uniform. What would your commander say? Get back to your barracks and pull yourself together.'

Cameron kowtowed reflexively, suddenly transported back to his recruit days. The involuntary capitulation to authority that had plagued his training and sent him back through the walls to the past dragged up every single broken moment. Clenching his fists, he closed his eyes, shutting out the red flush dripping over his vision. His head throbbed with the repressed anger. 'I apologise, QM. It's been hard of late.'

'It's hard for all of us with these new commands. Why we're going to war with the *Moonshine* is as much a mystery to me as you. We'll be at each other's throats next.' The quartermaster shook his head and gave Cameron a conciliatory pat on his shoulder.

'Get out of here.'
Cameron saluted and headed to Del, empty-handed.
'That went well,' she said.
'And we've lost Anthony,' he added.
'Why did you bring him? He's so annoying.'
'He's small, can get into small places.'
'What, like you're the fighter, I'm the elf magician and he's the level-one thief?'
'That's one way of looking at it. I like to think we're a team.'
'So you're not looking at us like some kind of bizarre family filling out some hollowness within your soul?'
'I hope they haven't caught the tyke.'
'You know, he isn't some young whippersnapper street urchin. Just a creepy guy who's short.'
The soldiers cursed as they were formally dismissed, stumbling blearily back to their rooms.
Cameron slipped the rope under the shirt and signalled to Del.
'We can't leave him behind,' she said.
'Leave who?' Anthony said.
'Where did you come from?' Cameron said.
Anthony tapped the side of his nose.
'What, can you smell something?' Cameron asked.
'No, it means I have tricks.' Anthony raised his eyebrows.
'Yeah, you're a regular magician. Not an elf, though. Now we've lost the chance to get the cards.'
Anthony smiled, waved his hands and revealed two security cards.
Cameron let down his defences for a moment, and gleeful surprise crossed his face before he regained control and it settled back into its unimpressed-with-anything expression. 'Not bad. I guess it was the distraction I organised that got you in.'
'If ya want,' Anthony replied. 'We'd better get going, right?'
'I was about to say that. *I* give the orders.'
'Go ahead.'
'Er, we'd better get, er, going.'

'Good choice. You're a great leader. The best.' Anthony peered over at Del, giving her a greasy smile. 'Ya like my moves back there?'

She gave him a look of disdain and pushed him away.

They moved off through the dispersing ranks, working their way up to the prison level. Only one guard was on duty, stationed behind a security desk overlooking the corridors stretching out in different directions. The man didn't expect the ferocious punch from Cameron across his jaw or the low jab into his groin from Anthony. The guard carried only a pistol and a retractable truncheon. Cameron checked the pistol's clip, then jammed it back in and tucked the barrel into his belt in the small of his back.

Del double-checked the numbers above the entrances, pointing down the corridor directly in front. The trio ran forward, counting down the doors. The row of cells had Cameron shivering at the recollection of his youth. The secret sanctum was bad enough, but the close walls and ceilings pressed down on him, the discoloured surfaces coming alive and crawling out at him.

'You okay?' Del asked, placing her hand on his back.

Cameron nodded wordlessly as he stopped in front of the cell. He swiped the card over the panel, and the locks pulled back into the ceiling and floor. He kicked open the door and looked in. A boy sat in the corner.

'Are you Arid?' Cameron asked, pointing at the terrified figure.

The boy threw up his hands in front of his face as he huddled into the corner. 'Please, no more,' he cried.

Cameron signalled for the others to jump in while he kept an eye on the corridor. They emerged carrying the boy. His face was black, and he cowered as he was carried.

'Jeez, what have they been doing to him? It's all right. We're here to get you out. Rescue you,' Cameron added, as the words didn't appear to be understood. Maybe taking the uniforms hadn't been a good idea. 'Where's the girl? Frey?'

The stunned boy raised a shaking hand towards the next cell. Cameron switched the cards and moved toward the door. Bullets tore down the corridor, and they all jumped behind the open cell door.

Cameron peered around the edge of the door. 'Great. Guards.'

'Fire back with our laser cannons,' Anthony shouted.

'A brilliant idea, with only two minor issues,' Del replied. 'One, laser cannons don't exist.'

'And two?'

'Laser cannons don't exist. You're the kind of person who needs to be told twice.'

'You're such a buzz kill,' Anthony complained.

Cameron spun around the door on his knees and fired a volley back at the attackers before wheeling back in and pressing himself against the wall.

'Cameron, can we leave Anthony in the cell?' Del asked.

He glanced over at her. 'Leave the little guy alone.'

'For goodness' sake, he's not a little … forget it.'

The air filled with the constant ping of bullets on metal as the barrage continued, the volume of the attack forcing them to stay behind the door.

'Bossman, we gotta make tracks out of here,' Anthony said.

'We really gotta save the kid?'

'No one is left behind. Not them, not you. And not me.'

'It's suicide.'

'Only if we die,' Cameron said. He paused and pointed to the group. 'Nobody die. That's an order.'

The firing ceased. Cameron risked a glimpse around the door. A loud click came from the security desk. 'Come on, everyone back in,' he shouted, pushing the trio into the open cell.

The top half of the door exploded, leaving a semicircular edge in the remaining bottom half. Their ears rang from the blast, and they all struggled with the disorientating effects. Smoke filled the corridor.

Del covered her mouth with her hand. 'We can't stay here, or get Frey. We've just got to go.'

'No!' Cameron shouted.

'We're sitting targets. We'll be dead in minutes if we don't make a break for it now.'

'But the girl …'

'Not this time, Cameron. Cam. *Cam.* Look at me.' She grabbed him and looked into his eyes. 'You can't save everyone.'

He shook his head.

'We've got to go before they fire again,' Anthony said, through his coughs.

Cameron reluctantly led them out into the smoky hall. 'Stay close.'

'Where do we go?' Del asked.

'There's got to be another exit, right?'

Cameron peered out into the corridor. A thick fog covered it from one end to the other. 'We can't get out the way we came in. That only leaves the other way.'

'The one where we don't know if there's an exit? And we can't see?' Del asked.

'That would be the one.'

Del shook her head and pursed her lips.

They felt their way along the wall and shuffled toward the opposite end of the corridor, which took on an eerie atmosphere. Silence. Deserted area. Fog. All they needed were tombstones. Another loud click came from the entrance.

'Down!' Cameron shouted.

They leapt to the floor as another shell sailed over them. It impacted the far wall, blowing a hole in it. Footsteps. They staggered to their feet, charged toward the hole and dived through into the unknown beyond.

The recollection of his escape roared back at Cameron. The horrific chase, a young boy running for his life, terrified of the consequences of being caught; the closing-in tunnels, the horrific things that chased him through the ventilation system. The fear clawed up his back and sunk its talons into his neck.

And they were falling. A steel city wouldn't provide anything soft to land on. This was going to hurt, if not kill. But their descent ended abruptly as they crashed onto the top of the quarter store cage, the metal mesh flexing under the impact and cushioning their fall.

Cameron was impressed. No one had screamed. Not even him.

The impact had shaken the structure, startling the inhabitants, who searched the perimeter of the cage searching for the cause, but never looked up. Above, the four teens held their breath, afraid to move. Two staff took off for the command office, leaving one guarding the store. The teens crept over the roof mesh and quietly jumped down, their rubber-soled shoes absorbing the sound.

Arni was in the distance, watching them, waiting by the service exit—escape and freedom. 'They're here,' he shouted, pointing at them.

Soldiers appeared beside Arni and ran toward them. They were trapped between the cage and the approaching soldiers. Cameron stared at Arni. The betrayal was unfathomable. He shook his fist at him. Shouts from the guards distracted him.

'Where do we go?' Del asked.

Cameron shook his head, and then had an idea. 'I know a way. Follow me,' he said, taking off down a side corridor. He pushed aside the cleaner's cart that was positioned by the wall, and a small hatch was revealed. 'Trash disposal,' he said. 'Sorry.'

More shouts. Soldiers charged toward them; they were carrying long silver cylinders.

'This is bad.' Cameron opened the flap and motioned the other three in. The one thing he didn't want them to do now was rush. The disposal pipe was dangerous, with many sharp edges, and it would be easy for them to take the wrong turn. At least the soldiers wouldn't be able to follow, but what was coming would be worse. 'Go as fast as you can, but be careful. Quick. Quick. They've got pipe cleaners.'

'But we don't know the way,' Del said.

'Down and left when you get to the air-cleaning interchange. It's big and you can't miss it. The wind will give it away.'

"What are pipe cleaners?" Arid asked.

"Mechanical creatures designed to crawl through the drain system and chew out debris. You don't want to be debris, do you? Get going."

The guards approached with the pipe cleaners. Several men were required to hold each one as a technician initiated the device. The blades at the heads spun as the guards prepared to launch the machines.

Cameron squeezed in after the others, letting the flap crash closed behind them, giving them a moment of quiet before the buzz of the cleaners drowned out everything. From the moment he started his descent down the pipe, he knew it was risky. At the top, the pipe was narrow and, from memory, would only get narrower the lower they got.

Between his twisting feet, he watched the others clambering down, banging and groaning as they went. He looked above them and saw the first pipe cleaner pushed into the disposal system. Red lights shone out through the centre of its head, catching the spinning of the blades. Then another came in after it.

Del shouted as she reached the interchange. Cameron also called out, but his lungs were restricted by the narrow confines of the pipe and all he was capable of was a quick grunt. The other two shouted as they caught up with Del, and Cameron redoubled his efforts to squirm after them. His head flushed with relief as his feet touched the base of the interchange. The smell blowing through the large silver box made his eyes water. He could see Arid moving down the tube, presumably with the others in front.

Cameron swung his legs into the left-hand pipe and slid in after them. But only his legs would fit. He glanced up. The pipe cleaners were nearing. He couldn't follow. He'd have to take another pipe, one he'd never been down before. At least he could lead the cleaners away from the others and give them a chance at escape.

Cameron pounded on the wall of the left-hand pipe to attract the attention of the cleaners. He lowered himself into the long tube, which immediately narrowed, dented inward by some external accident. The smell of scum and rotting trash drifted up and took his breath away, making him gag at the stench.

More shouts bounced down the tube, followed by the buzz of the pipe cleaners' blades.

He bent at the waist as the pipe flexed around a corner into a horizontal stretch then back to the vertical. His shoulders ached from the continual wriggling and squirming. And the sides kept closing in. Handholds set at regular intervals jarred against him. Breathing became difficult, forcing shallow breaths.

His feet knocked against something blocking his passage and he discovered the source of the smell. A body had lodged in the pipe. A failed escape attempt. A forgotten child. He frantically scanned the walls for a way around it, but the tunnel was straight and without any exits.

The red glow from the cleaners' lights illuminated a thin line surrounding two handholds. A hatch. He squeezed back up, with the cleaners bearing down on him. He thrust his shoulder against the hatch, which clicked open to reveal a dark alcove. He half fell, half wedged himself in as the machines rattled past. They slowed as the blades bit into the body, the sound of bone and tissue being chewed as they minced the corpse.

Cameron waited until he heard the cleaners pick up the pace as they continued, having pureed the dead body. He slipped back into the tube and worked his way down after them. Blood and bodily remains coated the walls, allowing him to slide down to the point where he was catching up with the cleaners. They made a quick left turn at another interchange and continued along the base of the mechCity in their ongoing search for biomaterial.

Cameron unscrewed four butterfly nuts securing the baseplate, which fell open and was wide enough for him to exit. He nearly cried as his hands touched sand. As he came up on his knees, a heavy blow landed on him from behind. A large hand grabbed his collar and pulled him onto his feet. He saw the rest of the team huddled together nearby.

'What do you think you're doing?' the owner of the hand demanded.

A second guard lounging against the rig laughed and aimed his rifle at the stunned group.

The first guard smacked Cameron across the face, sending him to the ground. He placed his boot on the teen's chest and pushed down.

Someone tapped on the guard's shoulder, and he spun around. A large man in a foreign uniform and his long white hair tied back stood in front of the guard. The guard tried to raise his rifle, but it didn't move. The other man had gripped the barrel and was holding it steady, pointing it away from the teens.

'You have a sword on your back,' the guard noted.

A vicious blow came down on the guard, flattening him. The large man leapt forward, grabbed the other guard and flipped him over his shoulder. The guard landed with a heavy thud. The large man knelt and landed another blow across the man's jaw.

'Nikola!' Arid cried. 'Don't you carry a gun?'

'I've found they can be dangerous,' Nikola replied. 'Now get out of here before they come around.'

[12]

BYRNE EXPLODED. 'KIDS. *Kids.* They were ... sneaking inside in the middle of the night. I had everything I needed and now it's gone. What happened to the external patrol?' He'd been dragged out of the only comfort in his life—his bed—to a freezing command deck after what felt like seven minutes' sleep. He rubbed his eyes, wiping away the drowsiness, and leaned against his desk. Fury burnt through the mental fog.

'They were attacked,' the night guard replied.

'You'd better tell me they had a platoon or something waiting out there.'

'They said there were soldiers, grown men, who assisted outside.'

'About ten? There had better have been ten. And armed with tanks. And frickin' laser cannons.'

'Uh, er, one,' the guard reported.

'*One* is singular. *Soldiers* is plural.'

'I thought it better to ease into the bad news. He had a slightly different accent, meaning he wasn't local.'

'Get the patrol. They'll need to be publicly humiliated. Make up names for them about how stupid they are. Where is Anstrom in this?'

'He's asleep. Most people need to sleep.'

'He's in charge of the prisoners. *I* say when he sleeps. Get him up and prepared for the hunt. Send out the message that Arid is a fugitive wanted in connection with the assassination of Queen Bea of the *Moonshine*.'

'We still have the girl.'

'It's not enough. What is she, anyway?' Byrne slapped his fist on the desk.

The guard shrugged. 'It's something. She's been helpful with some information.'

Byrne hesitated. This was new. 'Really? What?'

'She was around when the Geigers were still talking about the Omen in the *Lady Moonshine*. She'd sat next to the queen for years with no one paying her any attention. She overheard things.'

'Like what, exactly?'

'Like what it was designed to do. How it works.'

Byrne froze on the spot. 'How it *works*?'

'Yes.'

'She knows how it works?' Byrne gave each word its own space, falling into dramatic order to reinforce the importance.

'Yes,' the guard repeated.

'Turn us around and make for the Battery. I'll see to the boy.'

'What about the gas?'

Byrne smiled. 'On the *Moonshine*? We may have just the person to help us with that.'

The sirens wailed and two searchlights swept over the ground in circles. Nikola had disappeared like a ghost in the face of a sceptic, leaving the four teens on their own. They'd put in some distance, running as fast as they could over the sand before their legs gave out.

After several random search patterns, they eventually found the screamer and crammed in. With barely enough room for three adults, it was a squeeze for all four of them. Anthony hotwired the vehicle, sparking the battery to turn on the igniters, and the furnaces roared into life.

Much to Del's annoyance, she was forced into the front seat with Anthony, with his busy hands snaking around her to "adjust" various levers. Cameron and Arid squeezed into the rear.

'Are we sure this is the best combination of body sizes?' Del asked.

'Yes,' Cameron replied. 'I admit it isn't ideal.'

Anthony let out a low chuckle. Del levered herself against the side door, symbolically putting some space between her and Anthony's fetid clothing. His eyes barely scanned over the dashboard.

'Can you drive?' she asked.

'Of course, got me licence and everythin'. Dun't even need P plates.'

'No, I mean can you see out the windscreen? You're really low.'

Anthony glanced over at Del and smiled, then reclined the seat and thrust the yoke forward, forcing her to hold onto the dash. The screamer leapt forward. Del yanked the yoke to the left and the vehicle narrowly missed a boulder. He slipped the screamer into neutral as he readjusted the seat, allowing him a sliver of vision over the dash.

Within an uncomfortable hour they had rumbled into an abandoned town that offered a decrepit post office and a brewery whose ancient brickwork was slowly surrendering to the crawling red dust. The brewery's chimney stood mostly intact, supporting a series of X's painted down one side. Anthony steered around the rear of the building and rolled the screamer to a halt next to a collection of broken-down vehicles that were slowly rusting out.

The sun's rays peeked over the horizon, splashing pink across the dawn. A trapdoor tucked away in an alcove opened, and several 'family' members emerged from the basement. Tumbling out of the screamer like a ribbon of clowns, the crew stretched out their limbs, breathing in fresh air. The rest of the family hurried out to celebrate their return. Through the cheers, the crew made their way down the stairs on shaky legs into the basement.

Arid's vision went dark as the windowless room engulfed them. He scanned the room. A concrete bunker with broken equipment. Brass edges catching the glitter of a solitary globe that hung from the centre of the ceiling. Slogans on the wall. Dilapidated furniture. And a smell that had him rubbing his eyes. He collapsed onto a couch that bottomed out on the floor, placing his exhausted head in his hands.

'We are victorious,' Cameron roared.

'It ain't a total success. We left someone behind,' Arid said.

'Cam, you said no one is ever left behind,' said a lone voice.

'The contract was for one boy. You all heard the Steam Academy soldier. One boy. Job done.'

The crowd went quiet.

Cameron shifted uneasily. 'Yeah, look, I know. We'll get her. I'm sure there are more we can rescue. But today we struck back against those mongrels. That's a good thing. We write the rules of our own destiny. Anarchy!'

Voices crisscrossed in a tapestry of insurrection as exhaustion claimed its price for the night's adventure.

'We were up all night.'

'Yeah, worried sick.'

'No ... partying.'

'We are the future.'

'I'm wasting my youth.'

'Whatever,' Del said, pushing through the crowd. 'I'm having a shower. Start without me. I'll only be a couple of days. Hey, where's Revvy?'

Arid stiffened on hearing the name.

'She's out,' came the answer. 'Wanted to get some fresh air or something.'

'I don't blame her,' someone else called out. 'Did you land in the dunny or something?'

'Only way out was through the trash,' Cameron said. 'It was dangerous, but we made it. Man, have I got some stories to tell you all. Pick a seat and gather round.'

'What is this place?' Arid asked him.

'It's our secret sanctum,' Cameron replied.

'Are we safe?'

'It's secret. And that's the best you'll get out here on the plain. Because of Bea, nowhere is safe.' Cameron kicked over a crate and stood on top of it. He held out his arms wide. 'Mission accomplished.'

'You were meant to get a girl.' The crowd parted to reveal a tall girl. Her face was squeezed into a tight frown.

'That was a bonus extra, Alli. Unfortunately we didn't have time. But we got the assassin.'

Arid sagged. This was going to be awkward.

Cameron gestured to Arid. 'You're a hero.'

'That ain't me,' Arid said. 'I ain't the person y' think I am.'

'Killing the queen, the queen killer, the killer of queens. Bring down the authority. We're not gonna take it. We're not just a brick in the well.'

'Please stop saying that. I *ain't* a hero. I didn't bring down the authority or any of that stuff.'

Alli shoved a finger in Arid's face. 'You don't get it. We had a good future on the *Hawkesbury* before the queen came and captured us all.'

'We *didn't*. It was all horrible. All that training, the pain. At least with her we was just prisoners. We didn't have to prove nuthin'. Know where you are when you's a prisoner.'

'What *are* you talking about?' Alli chipped in. 'In the *Hawkesbury* we had somewhere to rise to.'

'Yeah, for those who were favourite. Otherwise you's worse than a prisoner.'

'Enough,' Arid shouted. 'Look, this is all great, talking about which was worse, but look at it this way. Wherever y' were, adults were making yer life hell. Pushing y' around, telling y' what to do. No reasons. Just because "we" said so. Y' trust them. Y' trust them t' take care of y'. T' keep y' safe. Feed y'. But they don't hang around, do they? They give y' a smack and show that all that trust was for nothing. Trust and love is all we've got, and they break it from us. They say they're preparing us for the real world. They divide us against each other. They hang us out t' dry. Alone. Forgotten. Fending for ourselves. And it sucks. And hurts. Where's the love? They promised it.'

The crowd went quiet.

'Now you sound like someone who's going to bring down the authorities,' Cameron said. 'The queen's dead. Thanks to you.'

'Stop saying that,' Arid cried. 'You need t' understand. I hate t' tell y', but I had nothing t' do with the assassination. And I no longer care.' He stood and walked away from the crowd, leaning against the rough concrete wall. He kicked a loose stone. 'I'm doing my own thing.'

The crowd took off on its own debate as random voices erupted.

'Yeah, right on. We're no muppet to any organ tinder. We dance to our own tune.'

'Who's saying all those stupid lines?'

'Look at the way they treat us, like we don't know nuthin',' Alli continued. 'Just lumps of flesh they think they can order around, and we'll do whatever they say. And what are you going to do? They own everything. They run everything. We don't have a voice. Even if we did, they didn't listen.'

'We make them listen to us,' Cameron replied, bringing the conversation back to the point.

'The only thing that hurts 'em is money. Or lack of it. If we destabilise the economy, disrupt the banking back-ends and inject disparate currency fluctuations, we'll have 'em where we want them,' Alli said.

'And you know how to do that, do you?' Cameron said.

Alli raised herself up to her full and imposing height. 'Can't be hard.'

Cameron shook his head. 'How can you soar like an eagle ...'

Arid couldn't understand the way they thought. They had one

another. They hadn't had to live in a dowser on their own, surviving by the skin of their teeth. They were a gang—similar people, similar pasts—who had grown up together. They didn't know what they had. And their lack of gratitude to each other was hurtful.

He walked away from the argument. They were all useless. After the cell, this closed-in space was the last place he wanted to be. He longed for the open desert he called home, and more importantly the clean air. He made his way up the stairs into the warming day.

Cameron disengaged from the crowd's adulation and followed Arid out. He found him sitting on the edge of a loading bay. 'You all right?' he asked.

'I'm so tired. And I'm a little sad about how everyone is arguing,' Arid replied.

'They're like that. You spend too long with anyone, you end up arguing. But it doesn't mean anything.'

Del appeared from the basement in a fresh set of clothes, drying her hair with a towel as she listened to the conversation.

Cameron sat up straight and smoothed back his hair.

'You guys have a family, but yer at each other's throats,' Arid continued. 'Don't y' realise what y' got?'

Cameron smiled. 'It wasn't a gift. It was something we made.' He wrapped his hand around a fist and shook them both.

Anthony then appeared, scrambling up the steps, his eyes sweeping the area before narrowing when he spotted Del. He sauntered over to the crew.

Arid sat quietly for a moment, his face scrunched in thought. 'How did y' know I was on the *Hawkesbury*?'

'Ah, we had some soldier from over east come and give us a heads up,' Cameron explained, 'the guy who helped us escape.'

'Nikola? With white hair tied back?'

Del smiled. 'Yeah, that was him. He said you might be able to help destroy the Omen.'

'Me? How would I ... *why* would I do that? It's meant t' have the final message from my parents on it.'

'Dunno. Maybe he was making it up. Just another one getting us to do their dirty work.'

'I don't understand why they were like that.'

'Who?' Anthony asked.

'Adults. I got this big ball of anger in me, and I don't know what t' do with it. Where did my parents go? Why did they leave me?'

'You can't trust 'em. Not once. Not ever. You got it, unless you done what Alex done.' Anthony turned to Del. 'You remember Alex?'

'Yeah. Little Miss Popular,' Del replied. 'You can play the game like she did, but you've got your pride.'

'Yeah, ain't gonna roll over 'cause bossman says so, right?'

'Be fair. She fought against it for a long time,' Cameron said.

'Do y' know much about her?' Arid asked.

Cameron nodded but went silent.

Del shrugged. 'For some reason Queenie took a shine to her.'

'That's 'cause she had all the inside info on Byrne and was happy to give it up,' Anthony said. 'It was all about intel.'

'If she hated the queen, why give up the information?' Arid asked.

''Cause she hated him more, what they did to her, the things they made her do. Make you shiver, right?'

'What they made all of us do,' Cameron added.

'You all right?' Del said, as she placed her hand on Cameron's arm.

'Alex had had enough and snapped,' Anthony said. 'Queenie was an easy way out. Ain't like it was the preferred option, just the first, right?'

Arid looked at their faces. Anger. Sadness. 'We've got a common enemy. We should do something about it,' he said.

Del laughed. 'Like what?'

Cameron said, 'You want to hurt them, then make a statement. The Omen seems important. They all want it. Destroy it in front of them. If I was a better strategist, I'd say make them suffer first, give them hope with it, then crush it in front of them all, letting them know you were the one.'

'That sounds a bit extreme,' Del said.

'I don't know,' Arid said. 'What do you think they did to us?'

Arid thought about it. It was hard to soar like an eagle when the whole world seemed to be filled with turkeys, but maybe he could make a statement. All those years of needless lies. But destroying the Omen was a big step. Too big?

Cameron jumped to his feet. 'Ant, go get some supplies. You're our logistics man. We're going to need bigger transport.'

Anthony stopped himself from saluting and ran over to a half-buried outhouse. He kicked open the door and disappeared.

'Del, could you get the maps and a compass? You're navigator.'

'Two hundred scale? We've got good detail covering the tenements,' she said.

'Sounds good. We don't know what piece of junk Ant's going to come back with. We'll need good roads.'

Del hurried down into the sanctum. Cameron loaded ammunition into his rifle, methodically clicking the bullets into place.

In the hustle, Arid felt out of place. They were a slick team and didn't need him.

'And you're our guide,' Cameron said to him.

'Me? It's no good,' Arid said, 'they wouldn't want me coming along. They think I'm a jerk.'

'They don't think you're a jerk,' Cameron replied, a moment of tenderness touching his voice.

Anthony called out to Arid, 'Hey, jerk, you coming or what? I need some hands.'

Arid shook his head. 'Let's do it.' His thoughts rested on the unknown messages on the pendant. But Cameron was leader. It was time to put those childish emotions away. He didn't want to let Cameron down or look weak. 'You get the gas. I'll get the key.

We'll blow it to kingdom come.'

Cameron smiled and patted him on the back. 'We're not the best of people, but our hearts are in the right place. And we're full of enthusiasm, if that means anything.'

And above them, where a section of bricks had fallen from the chimney, Revvy sat concealed from view, her feet dangling as she listened to the plans.

She'd never really been part of the group. They were a bunch of kids tumbling over their hormones in an effort to attract each other's attention. They didn't know what love was, caught up as they were in the shallowness of their own developing emotions. They didn't actually care about anyone else, didn't hold anyone special in their hearts. They certainly wouldn't risk everything to get the one they wanted. That's why they were such children. She didn't belong.

They hadn't made her feel welcome. She'd been offered respect from Byrne, to be treated like an adult among adults. They understood. They'd lived, loved, suffered. Did it matter what side they were on? Ultimately, they were out for themselves. And that's what she needed to keep in mind. Play the game by their rules. If there was a way to ensnare Arid, no matter what the cost, Revvy should do it no matter who suffered along the way.

After Arid and the rest of the team had dispersed in preparation for their incursion, she made her way down and pulled out an e-board from a concealed gap beneath the loading bay.

She picked up a white stone from the ground and pushed off on her board, out toward Tom Price.

[13]

BYRNE NARROWED HIS eyes. 'You're a female cyborg, a'—he searched for the word—'cyborgette? Cyborgnine? Cygirg? We don't see many of them over here.' This one appeared stiffer than the previous cyborgs he'd met.

'I am a cyborg,' she replied. 'My identity label is not relevant to my abilities and is no reason to treat me any differently. I am good.good at performing the same duties.'

'That's not what I meant. I don't doubt your abilities to … what's your name?'

'I am @officalJulia1, the new Iris ambassador.'

'Another one, although I like the title. Might make use of it myself. Look, this is getting ridiculous. What happened to the old one? I can't even remember his name.'

'I had to remove him from his position. He was inefficient and not cooperative.'

'You? Not Iris? That's a first. Have you got some form of confirmation? You're not leading some kind of coup, are you?'

@officialJulia1 rotated her wrist, then pressed a button and was answered with a tinny beep. 'Please connect to Iris.'

'What can I help you with?' a robotic voice replied.

'Please connect to Iri—'
'What would you like me to do?'
'Please connect—'
'Would you like to call @kevinIsCool?'
'No. Connect to—'
'Go ahead, I'm listening.'
'Can you please connect—'
'You were saying?'
'—to Iris.'
'I don't understand you. Would you like me to search the Hive databases for "tyres"?'
'No. Connect a line, connect me—a direct line—to Iris.'
'I don't have an answer for that.'

It was hard for Byrne to tell, but it looked as though the cyborg had shown an emotion. What it was, though, could be one of any number. The cyborg's eye had twitched.

Byrne forfeited. 'Don't worry. I don't have all day. Why are you so interested in the Omen?'

'Iris has calculated that someone is coming who will wield the same power,' the cyborg replied. 'We need to understand the technology.'

'Another weapon?'

'No. They will have the ability within their own hands. To control the flow of electrons with the power of their mind. We need to understand it so we can fight against it.'

'Sounds bad.'

'You need to worry, too. Your world is built on metal. What do you think he can do to you?'

'Does this person have a name?'

'Everyone has a name.'

'Yes, I realise that. I mean, do you know his or her name?'

'No. They will be known as a "tesla", someone who can control electromagnetic waves. Be aware of them and their allies.'

'Such as?'

'The enemy is the Steam Academy. Beware of anything they

tell you. Beware of any dealings. Do not trust them. They are wasteful with resources while we struggle. Their usage of water is criminal.'

'I get the point.' Byrne glanced back to his steam-powered roller. 'Well, not everyone has unlimited access to lithium. The Greenbushes Mining Consortium is *selective* about who they deal with. At the moment. But I hear you have a good contract with them.' He gave the cyborg a brittle smile. 'What if I told you I may have the means to get the Omen started, and the knowledge of how it works?'

'Statistically, although you say that, it is unlikely to be a correct assertion. Iris generates a detailed truth profile of your speech patterns.'

'Say what?'

'Iris calculates that you tell lies 12.4 times a day, with a higher lie-to-word ratio at times of political importance.'

'Rubbish. I'm very honest—quite truthful—only soften harsh statements in times of absolute—other people are worse than me.'

'This is also a lie.'

'Look, there may be times where I get carried away, but with this Omen information, trust me—'

'12.4.'

'*Trust* me on this.'

'If you possess this information—'

'I do.'

'Iris will definitely be interested.interested in discussing a deal. Iris has many.many funds.'

'It's not money I want. I need bodies.'

'We will not surrender the faraday experiments—'

Byrne sighed. 'Talking to you can be quite difficult. I want an army.'

'For this, we ask for the boy. We need to understand the Omen technology for our own survival.'

'I'll even chuck in the girl.'

'I will confer with Iris. We await your call to meet later at a designated point.'

Anthony jumped down from the cab of the truck, landing lightly on the sand. Dust cascaded off the roof of the vehicle when he slammed the door. Great rust holes perforated the sides, exposing the interior and allowing the setting sun to shine through the body. The flatbed was covered in a layer of sand.

'It's not the best truck I've seen,' Cameron said. 'I'm surprised it works.'

'Dun't, but I did some fiddlin' and got it crankin',' Anthony replied. 'Was some of those archaeology people sniffing round it, but I managed to get it out from under their noses without them noticing.'

'Impressive.'

'Nah, not really. The problem with archaeology is that it's too slow. The stuff they're digging up now should've been found heaps earlier.'

'You think archaeologists should be finding stuff buried yesterday?'

'Yeah. Time is money.'

Del went to say something, but Cameron held her back.

'Are we ready?' he asked Arid. 'You get some rest?' Cameron asked Arid.

Arid nodded. 'I got a few hours.'

'Dun't need rest,' Anthony said, unasked. 'Me, I got genes of a god. Goin' to live to two hundred.'

'Is that why you were snoring on the couch?' Del asked.

'It was the dust. Makes breathing difficult. Dusty place, right? Anyway, load up the guns.'

'You asking me?' Del said.

'Please. I got something to talk about with bossman.'

'Sure you do. Is it girl trouble? Because I know you're both experts. I bet it's girl trouble.'

Anthony gave her a flat stare then stomped off to Cameron, who was checking his utility belt, counting the various attachments. 'Oi, bossman.'

Cameron glanced up. 'Yeah?'

'You sure you want to do this? Especially with the kid? We dun't know if we can trust him.'

They looked over at Arid, who was struggling to pull himself up into the cab.

'The Steam Academy guy said he was good,' Cameron said. 'We want to make a statement, so he's the one we need. But I hear you. Keep an eye on him.'

'Okay. I'd better make sure Del's done the gunrack right.'

'She's good.'

Anthony gave him a low chuckle and wagged his finger.

'No, I mean ...'

'I know exactly what you mean,' Anthony replied.

Anthony ambled back to the truck as Del locked the last rifle into place. She stood back and dusted off her hands.

Anthony ran an eye over the work. He took a deep breath and let out a long sigh while shaking his head. 'Look what you done here. You got them in the wrong way round. First bump we hit, they're goin' to go flyin'. Ain't no good at all. Could take out someone's eye. Let's start at the beginnin' and I'll show you. We'll go slow so you can understand ... where'd she go?'

Cameron caught the forlorn expression on Arid's face. The others were occupied with their preparations, buzzing with the anticipation of the raid. Even Del smiled as she approached.

'You all right, Arid?'

'You guys look so organised. Do you really need me? I'm not sure I'll be much help,' Arid said.

'Everyone has something that's useful,' Cameron assured him.

'But I'm a diviner. Not a superspy kind of person.'

'Neither is Anthony,' Del said. 'But he has his uses.'

'You talking about me?' Anthony said as he joined the group. 'You should use my code name.'

Del rolled her eyes.

'You have a code name?' Arid asked.

'Me friends call me Mad Dog.'

'Which is why you've never heard anyone call him Mad Dog,' Del said.

'Come on, Del, give him a break. You know,' Cameron said to Arid, 'when we rescued *Mad Dog* he was a sad, lonely, angry, smelly guy living in a dark and putrid cell. But that's changed now.'

'Yeah?' Arid said.

'He lives *here*.'

'Yeah, yeah. You have a good laugh at me expense.' Anthony stomped around the opposite side of the truck and clambered in.

Del finished strapping her utilities around various parts of her body, clicking the buckles with practised ease. She walked beside Cameron as he made his way to the truck. 'We were lucky last time. You know we can't keep doing this. We're going to get caught.'

'I've got to try,' he said.

'It's not your war.'

'It is. If I do nothing, no one will save them. Not them. Not you.'

Del smiled. 'But that also includes Mad Dog.' She then reached up and grabbed the pole on the side of the truck and pulled herself up to the door.

Cameron shrugged. 'Every choice can't be a good one. At least it's mine. I'm not being told to do it.'

'As long as you want to fight, I'll be beside you.'

'C'mon, lovebirds,' Anthony groaned. 'We've got a long ride in front of us and the light's nearly gone.'

The council meeting concluded with staccato bursts of annoyance and the opening of the buffet. Byrne had given a great speech about unity, stability and the untrustworthiness of the Southern Alliance in the Tom Price council hall to tremendous applause. It was a good, historical venue for an important presentation that would be remembered through the ages. He made sure of that by telling the audience repeatedly. The votes had been counted twice, and Byrne won the nomination as the new regional representative. Without Bea, it had been easy. It was as though they were crying out for a leader. Sheep looking for a shepherd.

Under his guidance, the troops he 'represented' matched any region. Any confrontation, for the first time, would be an even match. Even against the mighty Southwest Consortium, with their endless resources.

But there would be no confrontation, because he would have the Omen. Follow or die. A simple, clean decision for them to make. It was an intoxicating secret that nearly lifted Byrne off the ground.

The heads milled around, firing inane questions at him through mouths half full of dried meat.

There was a nudge against Byrne's hip. Something was slipped into his pocket, the weight dragging. He turned and found no obvious person, but caught the lingering scent of unwashed youth. He paused in mid-reply and pulled out a white stone. Urgent.

'I must leave immediately,' he said, cutting off the conversation. 'I have a date.'

His screamer sat waiting in the car lot next to the hall, with a parking attendant preparing the vehicle for departure. Byrne jumped in and thrust the yoke forward. Within several heartbeats, he was out on the mainstream and heading out of town. Over the rise, a right turn out west, and twenty minutes into the glaring sun.

He checked his watch. Evening fought for dominance over the afternoon, leaving limited time for safe access to the meeting point. He wondered who the girl was and why she wanted to betray the others. He steered down into a gully. Towering rock walls left a narrow blue strip above. He drove deeper, until the track opened into a secluded cul-de-sac with a black entrance to his left.

The isolated hiss of the screamer's door echoed around the alcove, replaced by an eerie silence as it clicked closed. Sand was crushed under each step. Inside the mine entrance stood a bank of floodlights pointing inward, tethered by thick black cables leading to who knew where. Byrne sat in the usual spot, a boulder worn smooth by miners in centuries past. His whole life seemed to be punctuated with endless periods of inactivity in uninviting locations at the mercy of lesser people. Soon it would all be over. They'd all snap to it once he had the weapon.

Soft footsteps approached from outside the mine. He glanced at his watch. She was nearly on time. The place had been well chosen; it showed a devious mind. He'd never actually be able to make out who she was, just a silhouette of another annoying young girl. The bank of lights burst into life, causing him to close his eyes and turn his face away. The hum of the generator powering the lights filled the tunnel.

'What are their plans?' he asked.

'They'll steal gas canisters off the *Moonshine*,' the girl replied.

'Interesting.'

'And they plan to use the Omen against you.'

He smacked his fist into his leg, his fury becoming uncontrollable. 'How on earth will they do that? Do they have the key? It's guarded. By killer cyborgs.'

'I don't know the extent of the plan other than they're on their way now. I have chosen not to be part of it, because of how *he* treated me. Are you sure you can catch him?'

Byrne nodded. 'I'll get Arid just for you. And you can do whatever you want with him. I'll let your imagination run wild.'

'Don't hurt him.'

Byrne smiled. 'I'll do my best and leave the infliction to you.'

The light switched off, leaving him in pitch black. The generator ran down. He rubbed his eyes, waiting for the glare to dissipate.

'Does it get any better?'

The voice surprised him. Of course, there was no need for her to run. She could wait in the dark until he left, and then, if she was clever, follow him and find out all his dark secrets.

'Does what get any better?' he replied.

'Stuff. Life. Love.'

'No one said life was easy.'

'Have you ever been in love?'

Byrne laughed. Then stopped. 'I had a twin. A brother. He was amazing, beat me at everything. Then he wasted away and died. I was there when he took his last breath. The aquifer he'd been drinking from had been polluted. Crappy diviner had given him bad data. What can you do? Now we fight over data, taking the word of deadbeats as gold without any regulation. The two of us used to argue, but he took up every breath and filled me with stars.'

'I'm a diviner.'

'Be a good one. It makes a difference.'

'I love Arid.'

'You're a kid, you don't love him. Love your family. They're the ones who'll love you back.'

He heard her break. The quiet sobs. The hurried steps. Another child out of her depth, completely incapable of understanding what they were doing, blinded by an infantile crush. He sneered. Her fixation with Arid would certainly be her undoing. For all of them. And it was time to end it.

He dashed out after the footsteps.

Outside, it was too dark to search. With the sun below the horizon, he only had minutes before the wildlife emerged and invested their gastronomic interest in him.

Kneeling down, he ran his fingers over the sand, looking for clues. He caught the edge of a track and smiled, standing and tracking his eyes along the shallow markings. There wasn't much in the way of habitable areas in that direction, unless she'd diverted onto another course. In all, she'd served her purpose and wasn't worth pursuing.

He took a few hurried strides to his roller, revved the engine and raced over the dunes to the *Hawkesbury*.

The urgency became unbearable as he waited in the lift to reach the command level. Barking orders at the staff, he soon had plans in motion and two officers in front of him.

'Anstrom, we have work to do, and fast. Maybe you can redeem yourself.'

'Like a voucher?' the guard asked. 'What are the instructions?'

'We're meeting with some old friends.'

The moon, a blood-red orb, rose in front of Revvy as she hurtled along on her electric board. She didn't fear the night. It had taken everything worth treasuring. She slowed the board and coasted to a halt on top of a small hill, the board's big balloon tyres kicking up the sand behind her. Before her, the ground swooped away around a dried-out marsh and then toward the ruins of the town that hid the secret sanctum. The fading light turned various shades of grey and black. Just like life.

The distant clicks of the crawlers echoed through the hills, too far away to be a danger. But there was another sound: footsteps. She wrapped her fingers around the crude blade strapped to her chest.

'Who's there?' she called out.

'Someone who can follow your footprints,' a deep voice replied.

Her heart skipped. Had Byrne followed her? She'd been so careful.

The outline of a man appeared over the hill, running toward her. She pulled out the dagger and turned to face him. 'What do you want?'

'Me? Nothing. I'm making sure no one else is following your tracks.'

'Do you have a name?'

'Captain Nikola Tasman, from the Steam Academy.'

She lowered her blade, still keeping it pointing in his direction, but without the immediate threat. 'You've been here before. I heard them talk about you.'

'Hopefully in a good way.' He gave her a smile.

She didn't feel like being jolly. 'Why are you following me?'

'I was taken with your story. It gave me a smile when little else does. But a young rebellious person can end up in hot water quicker than they realise. Take it from me. I'm just keeping an eye out.'

'I don't need anyone looking out for me.'

'I'm not talking about you.'

Revvy jabbed the knife toward him. 'Good. I can look after myself.'

'Have a seat. Let's talk.'

'I have nothing to say to you.'

'Then listen. I have to ask you, what are you doing talking to Byrne?'

'You wouldn't understand.'

'Try me. I've seen some things. Been in trouble enough times.'

Revvy sat down and stared over the fading landscape. Her body slouched forward, letting her gaze drift over the desolate land. She let out a long and forlorn sigh. 'This is all so dull. Life used to be exciting. You'd discover something and you'd feel alive, every part of you tingling. Where has that gone? Now, everything is crap. Boring. Grey.'

'It's still there,' Nikola said. 'It changes. You get older, you discover responsibility. Looking out for others can be as rewarding as looking out for yourself. The world is still full of colours, but subtle ones, ones you can only see as you mature.'

'Where's the fun in that? It's all so dull. Adults get to do whatever.'

'I hate to tell you this, but it's not how it looks. I grew up in a military school, trained to fight. When you're a fighter, you're potentially going to die every time you go out to do your job. The last day we knew we were safe was graduation. Times got wild approaching that day. Lots of rules broken. Lots of mistakes made. Lots of hearts broken. Lots of regrets. But that's it. They're personal scars, with the only consequence to the individual's pride or heart. You cross that line into adulthood and suddenly the consequences are a lot more serious. You can still play with the fire, but you know you will get burnt at some point.'

'I kissed him once. Arid. He wasn't the first, but there was something about it. I wanted that moment to last forever. For there to be nothing else in the world, just us together with pounding hearts.'

'You know there will be other people to kiss.'

'I don't want that kind of reputation.'

'Somewhere between the extremes lies reality. I don't know what you've got against him, but you'll only hurt yourself if you don't let it go. The choice is yours.'

'Choice?' Revvy scoffed. 'Where has choice gotten any of us? A bunch of abandoned kids living in a hole in the ground. If this is all I have, I don't add up to much.'

'We aren't defined by things,' Nikola replied. 'A clear sky with a perfect sunset. A moment of peace. The company of a pretty girl. If this is all I have, then it's more than enough. Life is about breathing. I lost someone who just got up and disappeared the day after graduation. I miss her every day. But life goes on. We surf the day on hope and the things we can change in our life; the hope that we can succeed if we take destiny into our own hands. When we sit in dark times, the good has to shine. It can be found in the most unexpected places, and that can be enough to give us all hope. I'm not sure what choices Arid will make in this battle, or even if he knows what his role is. Bad choices on either our or his part may claim him, and your chance for repentance will be gone. You can do one of two things.'

Revvy stared down at her interlaced fingers in her lap.

'Can you tell me where they've gone?' Nikola asked.

'Out to the *Moonshine* to get gas canisters.' Revvy paused. 'I told that to Byrne, too.'

Nikola went quiet for a while. A wind picked up and fluttered the errant strands of his hair. 'The way I see it, today is a day when you can decide to change something. I need a guide. How about it?'

[14]

THE TRUCK'S ONLY working headlight exposed a minimal expanse of the terrain ahead. The quartet bounced on the bench seat as the vehicle struggled over the bumps. Cameron clamped his hand over his rifle, pressing it against the seat.

'At your sanctum, was everyone from the *Hawkesbury*?' Arid asked Cameron.

'No. From all over the place,' he replied. 'We've been breaking kids free for a few years.'

'Not we, you,' Del said.

'Only at the start.'

'Not every rig can treat them badly,' Arid said.

'Lot of orphans in this game. Nothin' wrong with givin' them a family, right?' Anthony said.

'The problem we've got is that people go back,' Cameron said.

'Why?' Arid asked.

'Don't like it without adults around.'

'Even if they're being treated badly?'

'If your world becomes hurt, you eventually don't notice, rationalise it away.'

'What about you, Arid?' Del asked.

'I thought my parents used t' be diviners, cutting it hard out on the plain, but it turns out they weren't that nice. More lies. They built the Omen. Then they ran away. One day they made a mistake and the crawlers got them.'

'Ow,' Anthony said.

Cameron sat for a while in silence before speaking. 'If they were diviners, and they were smart enough to build the Omen, how would they make such a simple mistake? I mean, you only need to be told one story about the crawlers and you remember it. Forever. It's a brutal way to go.'

'Thanks,' said Arid. 'I still remember the screams.'

'Sorry, I wasn't thinking.' Cameron tapped his fingers on the window ledge, staring out the window. The warm air blew his hair back, and he thought back to things he'd heard in the *Hawkesbury*.

'I guess it's hard to get yer head around the fact that things were different before ya was born,' Anthony offered. 'This is the only life we know. You appearing in people's lives changes it, changes them. We all have a glimpse of the light of life, but are blinkered when it comes to what happens before and after. Do we make a difference when we get here? Do we make a difference when we go? Our existence changes everything, but is it for the best?'

The others stared at him. He glanced back. 'What?'

'Look,' Del said, pointing ahead.

On the horizon sat the dark shape of the *Lady Moonshine*, glowing a deep red from the fire venting from the stacks.

Anthony hit the brakes on the truck and it shuddered to a stop, causing the others to slap their hands on the dash to keep from flying through the windscreen. Even at this distance and shrouded by the night sky, the mechRig was imposing against the horizon. Its stabilisers had been deployed, meaning the rig was drilling. The earth hummed with drill vibrations.

Cameron lifted his binoculars and watched a couple of guards patrol the perimeter of the *Moonshine*. 'You've got this memory of it being this agile fighting machine, then when you see it again it looks too big to be useful at anything.'

'Ain't as big as the *Hawkesbury*,' Anthony said.

'Yeah, but you think that's going to be big. You *expect* it to be big. And it is. A great, big hunk of metal that dominates the skyline.' Cameron lowered his binoculars. 'Okay, we break in, get the canisters and roll them down here.'

'No trash this time, Cam,' Del warned. 'This is my only other black outfit. If this gets ruined, how can I be all angsty?'

'Ain't you getting a bit old for that?'

'I'm a teenage girl, I've got years of it left inside.'

'I think colour would suit you,' Cameron added. 'You'd look … nice.'

'*Nice*? Do you even know me? Colours? Do I even know you?'

'Um, what if they fire at us?' Arid asked.

'They won't. One, we'll fire back,' Cameron said, tapping the gun on the seat between them. 'Two, those canisters hold gas at a pressure of over 110 psi. They are bombs and will literally kill you if they're shot and you're close. If you're next to it, it'll smear you over the ground like jam. The damage is felt for dozens of metres. The guards won't fire.'

Arid wondered if it was worth bringing up what might happen if the cylinders crashed into the truck. Also, if they were being fired at, wouldn't the guards be farther away from the explosion, meaning they'd survive?

Anthony patted Arid on his shoulder. 'Dun't worry, gas is valuable.'

'Del, how long was the rotation?' Cameron asked.

She glanced at her watch. 'Eight minutes.'

'The *Moonshine* is pretty tight, security-wise. Arid, how did you get out?'

'Frey blew a hole in the wall on the rear,' he replied.

'It might've taken them a while to fix it. Let's check it.'

They made their way around the base of the mechRig. Looking up at the second level, they saw that the hole had been patched. The service entrance below it was shut, locked and well made. No chance of entry. They examined the patch on the hole again: multiple dark shades.

'There's something unusual about the repair work,' Cameron observed. 'Del, have you got your blade or something that could pry it open? Doesn't look like heavy-duty steel.'

Del buckled her work belt around her waist.

They watched the guards disappear around the corner of the *Moonshine*.

'Up there,' Arid whispered, pointing to a piece of dark metal set against the rig's yellow body.

Del aimed a crossbow suction grapple upwards and fired, the bolt trailing a black nylon rope behind it. The grapple hit the body, securing to the metal as the mechanism activated. She gave the rope a tug then climbed, quickly scaling up hand over hand until she was level with the repaired wall.

As they watched her climb effortlessly up the rope, Anthony gave Cameron a nudge. 'I can see why ya sent her up first.'

Cameron elbowed him and gave him a stern look.

Del hung for a few moments, examining the exterior. It was a grating with darkness beyond. She pulled out a ratchet and unbolted it. Sliding it open, she leaned into the hole and crawled inside. Once in, she waved for the others to follow.

Anthony went second. He climbed the distance in seconds. Cameron, third, was heavier than the team members and took longer.

Arid heard the voices of the guards. He peered around the corner of the rig. They were already halfway along the side. Cameron wasn't in yet, but Arid had to move.

Deep breath. One hand on the rope. The other hand higher. Jump. Scramble. Arid's limbs thrashed as he clumsily flailed his way upwards. When his head banged into Cameron's feet, he realised he'd been a little too successful. Too much energy. Too little skill.

'What are you doing?' Cameron whispered.

'They're coming,' Arid replied. 'Please be quick. My arms are really hurting.'

'The rope won't take the weight.'

The knots helped, but this was a new activity for Arid, and his muscles burnt. The thick strands cut into his skin.

The guards approached along the side of the rig, their torches sweeping over the ground like deranged pupils as they walked. The guards turned the corner and stopped, noticing the footmarks in the sand.

Arid desperately struggled up the final knots on the rope, his arms searing. Cameron grabbed his hands and he was pulled in. Del reeled in the rope just as the guards turned their attention to the rig. They shone their lights upwards. Cameron slid the metal back into place as Del pulled in the last of the rope.

The guards saw nothing but the mismatched metal grating. Shrugging, they continued their way around the rig.

The team let out a combined sigh of relief.

Arid took in the room. No real memories of it. Racks of equipment. Stairs up. And the walkway out over the storage deck ending with its assortment of gear, repair rooms and vehicles. Maybe even his dowser was down there, being worked on as the queen had promised.

'Where to?' Cameron asked.

'I'll go for the key, since I know what it looks like,' Arid replied. 'You get the gas. It's down on the lower level.'

'We know where it is. We were prisoners for two years,' Del said.

Arid made his way to the stairs.

Cameron's team moved into the heart of the rig. A light flashed up ahead.

As Arid crept through the *Moonshine*'s subframe, the familiarity of it struck him again. How could he know this place? Looking at it was alien, as was the inside of any rig, but if he closed his eyes he was sure he knew every inch of it. After every step, around every corner: déjà vu.

Where would the key be? Somewhere safe. The queen seemed taken with it. But now she was dead, so would someone else move it? Or take it? Maybe someone close to her. The stretched-out Suzie lady seemed a bit intense, but she could be the kind of person to keep a memento. She'd be quartered on the upper decks.

Arid crept past a security patrol wandering the passageways between the cells and sleeping quarters. The only other sound apart from the hum of the drill was the hush of the air ventilation. The trick was to be a cat, stealthy like a lethal predator, unseen, soft-footed and precise. Ducking around a corner, he slipped past the guards as they complained to each other.

Stairs. Up. Stop. Hide.

It was the medical level. A foyer with exits to the left and right. A large counter presented a barrier. Stern receptionists hovered behind it. The night staff milled around the desk, talking quietly about the duty rota.

The next level up was the officers' quarters. He could see the stairs. On the other side of the counter. He shook his head. A broken bolt lay to his side. It had weight in his hand. It bounced across the floor, clattering to a stop in the middle of the left passageway.

The group turned to check out the sound.

Arid scurried across on his hands and knees, concealed by the counter. Some of the staff examined the bolt, and others searched where he'd been hiding. *Now.* He ran for the stairs. No raised voices. No shouts of 'Stop!'.

Foot on the first step. A couple more and he'd be around the turn in the staircase and free.

Two steps. Three. Four.

Darkness.

Arm wrapped around him.

Lifted.

He landed heavily on his feet. Rope around his wrists. Rough hands pushed him in an oscillating direction of ahead, blind steps stumbling quickly in anticipation of unknown obstacles. The hood was removed. Arid blinked out the brightness, adjusting his eyes to the new surroundings. A solitary light shone in his face. He raised his tied hands for shade.

Nikola smiled at Arid and indicated the gloom in front of him. Out of which stepped the queen.

'Everyone said y' were dead,' Arid said.

'It was an expensive illusion,' Queen Bea replied. 'But vital.'

'Do y' know the misery it caused me?'

'Yes. And I thank you for it.'

'I didn't volunteer for it. Well, not all of it. Not the bad stuff.'

She nodded. 'You have been integral to the reveal of the assassin. To win, we have to take risks. Without you, we wouldn't have known it was Ella.'

'You didn't know it was her?'

'No. It was a masterful deception.'

'But do you know who sent her?'

Bea shook her head.

Arid thought it odd that she didn't say 'no'. She'd always responded directly before.

'We need to prove the link,' she said. 'We need Ella to say who her trainer is.'

'But she could name anyone.'

'That's why we need her to show us.'

'How do we do that?'

'We maintain the fiction. You need to run. We'll spread the appropriate misinformation. But you must keep me as a secret. She must continue to believe I'm dead.'

'You do know yer other daughter, Frey, is in a jail cell on the *Hawkesbury*. She thinks yer dead.'

'My heart is heavy with that knowledge.'

'That's a weird way of saying yer sorry. Unless, of course, yer not. How can y' treat her like that?' Arid asked.

'We're doing what we can to assist in her release,' the queen replied. 'But negotiations are tricky.'

'Just attack the *Hawkesbury*. You have the firepower to bring it down.'

'It's not that simple. That's why your continued assistance is so important.'

'I've had enough of this. Y' can sort out yer own problems.'

'We need you.'

'No.'

'I can return your key. It will give you the opportunity to listen to your parents' final message to you. Would you like that?'

'Yer asking a lot for something I have a diminishing interest in.'

'Then why did you return?'

Arid paused. 'I' see if my dowser had been fixed. I wanted t' be free of all this.'

'Sorry. Not yet. But we can offer you a screamer. Please. Do not underestimate your importance.'

Arid stared at the queen. Could he trust her? Of course not. She was ruthless and focused and a complete mystery. Her use of 'sorry' was as nothing more than a five-letter word. She seemed impassive, and impervious to any kind of inscrutable examination.

He glanced over at Nikola, who gave him a friendly smile. There was clearly a reason she was queen and he wasn't.

Arid sighed. If the queen was going to be ruthless and focused, it was better if she was focused on him being alive. 'Okay. But y' owe me.'

She handed over the pendant. 'Run.'

'Someone's coming,' Cameron hissed. 'Over the side.'

Del and Anthony swung over the handrails to the right and grasped the base of the walkway, threading their fingers through the grating and hanging from the underside of the floor. Cameron followed on the left side. They held their breath as the guard slowly ambled along, peering over the side and casting his torch over the collection of military and service vehicles. The deck gently vibrated as the rig's drill buried itself in the ground.

The guard trod on Del's finger. She winced and retracted her fingers, leaving her hanging by one hand. Screwing up her face, she stifled a cry and shook her hand. Cameron motioned to the coiled rope on her belt.

She grabbed the grating with both hands and rested while her muscles cooled from the excess strain. Then she unclipped the rope and attached it to the side of the walkway, letting the coils unwind to the floor below. She shimmied down, and Anthony reached out and followed behind her.

Cameron clutched at the rope, but couldn't grab a solid hold as it hung tantalisingly out of reach, eventually knocking it farther away. Sweat rolled down his face. His fingers slipped and he fell. The rope swung on its slow arc back, and he grabbed it and held it against his chest, quickly wrapping it around his arm to slow his fall. The suction cup gave out and he fell the rest of the way—to be caught by the other two and lowered to the ground.

'I planned that,' he said quietly.

Del coiled in the rope and gave him a disbelieving look.

'Are we clear?' Cameron said.

'Clear,' Anthony whispered. 'If we're done saving ya, can we get the gas and leave this hellhole?'

'Okay, if they're drilling for gas, the compressors will be nearby. Come on.'

The ten-centimetre drill bit churned away toward the rear of the rig. During Cameron's time as a prisoner on the *Moonshine*, the guards had tried to push his head against the drill when he'd been difficult. He wasn't totally sure that life here was worse than being a recruit on the *Hawkesbury*. At least here, you knew you were the enemy.

The pipes ran alongside the drill and curved away to the compressor pumps. Several canisters occupied a steel cage. A dozen powered trolleys sat to the side. The cylinders towered two metres in height and were as wide as two people.

'How many of these do we need?' Del asked.

'I can't see how we're going to get more than three out of here,' Cameron replied. 'One trolley each.'

'Is that going to be enough?'

'It's what we're going to get. Grab a trolley.'

As Del placed her hands on the trolley handles, she paused. 'How do we get them out without anyone seeing?'

'A good question. And one I have zero ideas about,' Cameron replied.

'Do we open the service gate and roll them out?'

'We need a diversion.'

'Well done,' Del said, 'that's an idea that could work. Anyone got a tiger or something we can release?'

'No need to be like that,' Cameron said.

'How 'bout we set some kind of neuro-elastic diffuser to knock them out?' Anthony suggested.

'There are only two minor drawbacks to that,' Del said. 'One, we have no neuro-elastic diffusers. And ... say it.'

'Yeah, yeah. We have no neuro-elastic diffusers.'

'Maybe we should've been more prepared,' Cameron said.

'That's the story of your life.' Anthony looked above them. 'Wait, the drill is powered by a steam motor on the next level, right?'

'Yeah,' Del said.

'Puncture the engine. Steam everywhere. Covers our escape. We're all heroes. Girls all round.'

'I like your thinking,' Cameron replied.

'Yeah, if you like moronic thinking,' Del said. 'Gives you a laugh, I guess.'

'Whatever. Let's go,' Anthony chanted.

Cameron ran to the stairs and sprinted up. He turned and ran to the next level. A guard patrolled by, causing him to duck behind an ammunition store. He charged onward. The engine's pressure gauges indicated the drill was running just below the red line. He grabbed the revolution limiter and twisted it all the way clockwise, winding up the speed; the pressure rose as the drill spun faster.

Anthony searched for a bar, picked up a long piece of steel and prised the lock off the canister cage. Del wheeled the first trolley around to the cage opening, fastening the clamps on either side of the canister. The hydraulics hissed as they took the weight. She engaged the motors and the lifter rolled back with the canister. A quick turn to face the service platform. Power on. The trolley steadily rolled forward.

She looked up at Cameron, who had already disappeared into the smoke and mist pouring from the engine. Time would tell if it worked. When the air cleared, he was gone.

Steam billowed out of the drill engine and spread out along the walkway. The cam mechanism skipped and threw the piston, as the metal shrieked, causing the engine to spin out of control. Clouds tumbled out from the motor. Shouts followed, and running footsteps.

Anthony followed Del's lead, quickly clamping the lifter to a gas cylinder.

Del pulled open the grating across the service platform then moved in the trolley with impressive grace. Anthony wasn't far behind, but Cameron was still to load his. He wrenched the trolley, skipping the wheels as he forced it to circle. The clamps fastened into place and he manoeuvred it toward the exit. Cameron checked the end; Anthony and Del were in and waiting for him.

The sound of the shouts changed from panic to organisation. Then more footsteps coming down.

Cameron pushed the trolley toward the service platform. The others signalled for him to hurry up. Over his shoulder, the guards ran after him. The trolley refused to move faster than the motors allowed. Shots rang out over his head. There was a command to stop, and a more urgent voice commanding the guards to stop firing at the *highly flammable cylinders*.

As soon as Cameron moved his canister onto the platform, Del rammed the grating closed. The guards crashed into it, rattling the metal. The holes were too small for the guards to reach through and they watched helplessly as the team descended, giving them a bright wave.

The platform lowered for what felt to the team like three weeks, and then clicked into place at the base of the *Lady Moonshine*. The service door opened. The coast was clear. Del jammed the service door shut with a steel bar.

Cameron laughed as the team rolled the cylinders through the service exit and onto the sand. The wheels sank and came to a halt, tipping forward and threatening to topple over. Del and Anthony took the weight, and all three of them lowered one of the cylinders onto its side. They repeated the action with the remaining two, then rotated and pushed them down the hill toward the truck.

The patrol guards appeared as the teens gained some distance from the rig. One guard went to fire, but the other guard forced the rifle upwards and the shot discharged harmlessly into the night sky.

The guards came charging after the team, catching up and leaping at them. Del went down and her cylinder rolled away. Cameron swung at one guard, knocking him to the ground. Anthony jumped at the other guard, pulling him off Del. Del turned and pounded a few punches into his stomach and then knocked him out with a right hook.

Keeping up the momentum, the team pushed the giant canisters down the slight gradient, to where the service truck was waiting.

The truck's window was wound down and Byrne leaned out, resting his gun on the window ledge. 'Load 'em up, boys.'

'How the hell—' Cameron began.

Anstrom stood behind on the top of a military roller, machine gun in hand.

'Where's your mate?' Byrne asked.

'He ain't out yet,' Anthony said.

'I can wait.' Byrne pulled down the remote for the flatbed. 'We can work until he turns up.'

The side of the service unit lowered to the ground. Byrne jumped out of the cab, keeping an eye on the three youths. 'What are you waiting for? Push them on.'

The team put their backs against the cylinders one by one, forcing their feet into the sand, and rolled the cylinders onto the service unit's platform. Byrne then indicated for them to jump on and hit the remote button. The platform rose to the level of the flatbed, and the team rolled the canisters onto the flatbed and secured them in place.

Byrne stared up at the *Moonshine*'s silhouette as the cargo was secured. 'How long is your friend going to be?' he asked Cameron.

'I don't know. He may have been captured.'

'Better not have, otherwise you're going to have to go in and get him.'

'Oh, man, ya got no idea,' Anthony complained. 'Ya ain't pushing us around.'

'I've got the gun.'

'One gun ain't going to be much help.'

'Calm down, Ant,' Del said.

Shouts then came from the service entrance of the *Moonshine*, light spilling out into the night and over the sound. Black figures ran out, silhouetted against the yellow light. Shouts were followed by shots.

'Jeez,' Cameron shouted as bullets whizzed past them. 'Byrne, we need to move it. They got us spotted.'

Byrne swung into the cab and planted his foot and the truck surged forward, the cylinders knocking together from the rough start.

'Don't just sit there, fire back,' Byrne said. 'We've got to get out of here before they send out attack screamers. Anstrom, I'll see you back at base.'

Anstrom discharge a couple of quick bursts.

The viewing room was dark, occasionally lit by the flashes of gunfire.

'Will the boy buy it?' Suzie asked. 'Are they going to be resilient enough?'

'I think together they'll find a way,' the queen replied.

'They're just kids.'

The room remained dark, allowing Bea to watch events unravel on the plain. The chase. The defence. At this distance, it was a dance.

'They're more than they seem,' Bea said. 'You know, you look at kids all living together. They have their differences, but they *are* together. They argue, but then ten minutes later they're the best of friends. We hold grudges for generations, poisoning our own families with an ideology and a call to arms they don't even understand. Yet they buy into it with more passion and belief than we do, and we created it. We create the problem to empower ourselves, grinding up respect and trust in favour of greed and victory.'

'Those are harsh words. Do you need to lie down?'

'I'm more awake than ever.' The queen traced the line of fire against the glass, drawing rings around the fighting groups. 'Where does it go wrong? People like Byrne will label them naive or lacking real understanding of the dangers of the world. But maybe we make the 'real' world so we can be horrible to each other through philosophies of division. Maybe we all struggle to come to terms with life and what it's dealt us. The thrill of a new day rising is replaced with the monotony of survival. Or we lash out at the pain caused by being ostracised, spurned or different. We're born from love, unless there was too much drinking, and the pain breaks us day by day. Then suddenly you wake up, and you're old and full of hate and anger at the difficulties life has smeared over you, and your existence becomes built on fear. Fear of change. Fear of missing out. Fear of being left behind. Fear that life hasn't turned out like you were hoping. Fear that you're not as great as you think you are. And the one thing they can't see is that it was their fault. The fear kept them caged. They never tried, or reached out, because they were afraid of failure or ridicule.'

'You are talking about Byrne?'

'Yes and no.'

There was a knock at the door. Suzie opened it slightly, only allowing a sliver of light into the room. A muted voice sent a volley of hushed words at her. She nodded and closed the door.

'Byrne has caught them,' she reported.

The queen nodded. 'I was hoping it wouldn't come to this. And that's where age gets you.'

'What do you want to do with Byrne? The gas is valuable.'

'Pull up the drill. Call back the guards, and let's rattle some cages.'

[15]

As soon as Arid entered the secret sanctum, with the pendant pressing into his palm, he knew something was wrong. Squeezing past the soldiers and getting back had taken hours. The basement was quiet. The teens sat around in small groups looking glum. Several packs were stored in the corner.

'Where's Cameron?' Arid asked.

'Caught. Someone ratted him out to Byrne,' a girl responded. It was Alli, less of a cheerleader in the despondency.

'Y' don't have the gas canisters?'

'You know, that's the least of our troubles. They know where we're based. They're sending soldiers after us. We have to leave and disappear forever.'

'Who ratted him out?'

'Dunno. Someone who knew about the mission, obviously. And since you were the one who suggested Cameron go there, and you're the only one to return, it don't look too good for you,' Alli said.

'But I have the key,' Arid replied. 'We can still do something.'

'Without Cam? No way. It's over, man. We're through. We need a leader.'

'Y' don't need a leader. That's what this whole action is about. Y' can decide what t' do for yerself.'

'Why should we do this?'

'It's what Cameron would have wanted.'

'No, it ain't. He wanted to eat heaps and meet girls,' a boy shouted.

'The guy I met wasn't like that. He wanted t' make a difference.'

'That's not the Cam we knew,' Alli said.

'But we have to do something, otherwise they'll win,' Arid said.

The group collected their packs and loaded up.

'What are you talking about?' Alli said. 'They've already won. They always have. We lived under an illusion that we were worth something, we could do something, but they always block us. Always shut us down. Never listen. What do we know, they say.'

Arid scanned the line of teens. 'Where's Revvy?'

Alli shrugged. 'If she's got any sense, she's already far away from here. Came with the news. Tears and everything. Then she took off. Like we should. Thanks for leaving us homeless.'

And with that, they all marched out, loaded up with packs stuffed with their meagre possessions, a ragged line of refugees forced into hiding. And there was no space for him.

An abandoned building. An abandoned boy.

The earth started to shake as a rig approached. Probably a Collins Class, Arid thought. Small and deadly. No need to make a scene when killing a bunch of kids.

Arid hadn't known what to do with the pendant when the queen lowered it over his head. He'd been through so much in the last few days, and it didn't even feel the same now. Was it important anymore? Should he clutch it to his chest like a long-lost heirloom? Or should he be all casual, as if it never was that valuable anyway? It represented his parents, but he didn't know who they were anymore. Strangers from across time. Their part in his life was over. They really shouldn't have a hold over him from beyond the grave.

He tucked the pendant under his shirt. It was something he'd have to think about later.

Queen Bea had said he would need to run. The obvious place would be back to the Omen. So he needed to go the opposite way. An idea struck him, making him laugh out loud. Genius. It would get them all back. The question was, how to make contact?

Arid wondered who was approaching.

Byrne had placed a new, bigger desk in his office on the command deck. The mechCity rolled on toward its new destination. Its slow speed was infuriating. He sat with his elbows on the desktop, his fingers intertwined under his chin, and watched the view out the panoramic window crawl by. The horizon, as unchanging as it was, gave him a chance to think, to plan, even to fantasise. Everything was nearly aligned.

Theo knocked and entered, clasping his hands in front of his stomach. Byrne glared at the man as he made his way across the room. He continued to stare as the dignitary positioned himself on the opposite side of the desk.

'You come here with a better attitude?' Byrne asked.

Theo glanced around the room. 'Are you sure this place is secure?'

'Certainly.'

'You seem distracted.'

Byrne shook his head as he let his eyes drift over the desk. 'Just some interesting news. Tell me the good news about the negotiations.'

'Good news, indeed. I've spoken with the southwest division. They're willing to join us. They're mineral rich; they'll be good partners. But this is a one-time-only offer. They see an opportunity for security that will be mutually beneficial.'

'Partners? I don't want *equals* or invested parties,' Byrne replied. He smashed his fist on the desk.

'Can we look at the bigger picture, other than just … the gratification of your identity?'

'I want a better deal.'

'We all want a better deal, but don't confuse deals with demands. We're trying to generate a strong network where everyone can benefit, built on negotiation.'

'Would it help if I turned up to … enable agreement?'

'Force of personality is not as influential as it once was. We live in different times.'

Byrne sighed. He knew it was a lie. If Bea had offered, they'd all jump at it. 'And what about the others?'

'There is some hesitation,' Theo replied. 'Shifting alliances are making the leaders conservative with their decisions. They want to see how things play out before ripping up the old agreements and working out new offers.'

Byrne laughed and slapped his hand on the desktop. 'I've come up with my own offer.'

Theo paused. 'What better offer do you have?'

'I know where the key is.'

'Key to what?'

'The Geiger weapon,' Byrne said with a smile.

'You don't know if it even works. Don't forget the PAD. Let's not burn a good proposal over reckless ambition.'

'PAD. Ha! We will offer them *nothing*. They must agree to defer overall and complete control to us otherwise I am not interested.'

'They will not accept that. You would throw away this agreement, this moment for peace? This is not how negotiations go. It's a good deal.'

'It's a stupid deal, when the alternative is complete power. With the weapon, they will bow to me whether they want to or not.'

'You're being reckless. There are better ways of going forward.'

Byrne shook his head. 'You are so weak, like a sick dog. You go deal with them. When I turn up with the weapon, all deals will be off anyway. Then you need to decide where your loyalties really lie.'

Theo sat, stunned by the response.

'Get out!' Byrne shouted. He repeated the words until Theo

finally rose and exited the room.

Byrne calmed, taking a sip of chilled water. He waited for his heartbeat to return to normal, breathing heavily, then said, 'Come.'

A door behind him opened, and Alex stepped out, dressed in her usual cloak.

'Where is he?' Byrne said.

'I don't know,' she replied.

'You're meant to be a ruthless killer. A top agent.'

'I don't know.' She emphasised the statement.

'Well, find him,' he shouted.

Alex stood firm, staring back at him. 'If I do this, it can only end one way.'

'I don't care. I want that key. I want that weapon.'

'I want you to understand that what happens next relies on your definite decision about sending me out *at all costs* and all that may entail. Or reveal.'

The two remained fixed on each other until Byrne broke away and returned his gaze to the horizon.

'Just do it,' he muttered.

If nothing else, Arid had picked up a few tips from Cameron about sneaking into a rig. The intricate but poorly made service ducts were a constant between the mechs, especially those that had been caught in combat. They were big. And there were only so many trained metalworkers and welders, and only so much metal. Like water, it was a resource worth warring over.

Arid crept forward. He could hear the voice. It sounded calm and matter of fact. The kind of voice you could do business with. He let out a long breath and slowly opened the door. The voice hesitated.

Most of the room was in darkness, with the only light spilling weakly from a lamp on one end of a desk. The lamp had a bulbous brass base with a green glass shade. A man sat behind the ancient wooden desk. He held a black banana to his ear, a long curly cord connecting it to a small black box. He had neat hair, mousey brown in colour and longer than the other leaders', with a fringe sweeping over his forehead. He had a trimmed beard. And, as usual, was wearing a colourful short-sleeved shirt.

'I'll call you back,' the man said into the receiver. He replaced the handset in its cradle on top of the box. Interlacing his fingers, his head tilting to the side, he turned to smile at Arid. The pose seemed comical.

'I do believe I've seen your weary body traverse the cheerless avenues,' Hunter said. 'Welcome to the *Rankin*.'

'And I've seen y' talking to interesting people. Y' look like a reasonable man.'

'Looks can be deceiving, even in the mirror.' Hunter brushed his fringe to the side above his eyes. 'You're either brave or desperate to enter my wonderland. I should let you know, perchance you come with ill intention, that I have a large gun fastened under my seat that has the capacity to soil my walls with your insides.'

'I've got something for sale that y' might want.' Arid handed over the pendant, dangling on its chain.

Hunter extended his hand and Arid lowered the key. Hunter held it under the lamp, feeling it between his thumb and forefinger and then weighing it in his palm. He placed the key on the desk and pulled open a drawer.

Arid gasped as Hunter pulled out a large screwdriver and smashed it onto the surface of the key. 'Hey, wait. What are y' doing?'

Hunter lifted up the key and displayed the interior. It was empty. A case with no contents. 'Nice try, flower, but it's a fake.'

'What? It can't be. They promised—'

'Who? You shouldn't go believing people who want you to do things.'

'They didn't want … or tell me t' see y—'

'Sure about that? Come hither for investigation.'

Arid slowly approached. He looked into the man's eyes. They didn't seem to be attached to his brain; they seemed almost independent. His mouth certainly had no direct control from his brain.

'You're young,' the man continued. 'Young like a blossoming flower. Naive about how things work. You only see the surface, and you believe what you see. The quicker you learn life is more complex than you can realise, the quicker you'll become a survivor. You may even benefit, gaining a few trinkets on the way. But there are costs that you cannot possibly understand. Although you may be learning.' Hunter brushed the remains of the fake key into a bin at his feet. 'It gives me no pleasure in doing this. Well, some pleasure. But that's the kind of guy I am.'

'Doing what?' Arid asked.

Guards burst into the room and grabbed him by the arms and legs.

'I'm sorry, kiddo, you're not the person I'm interested in,' Hunter called out as the guards dragged Arid away.

'Commander, your instructions,' said a guard who had remained behind.

Hunter sat still, once more back in the pose of interlaced fingers and staring straight ahead. 'The boy turning up is unexpected. I'm not sure things are playing out correctly. Throw him into incarceration until I can make a decision, or until life brings a surprise solution.'

'Is it safe keeping him here? What if the others find out?'

Hunter clicked his fingers. 'A good point well made. Tell the helmsman—woman, person, whatever—to make way to the *Hawkesbury*.'

'Stealing gas is a huge crime. They will come after us,' Anstrom said. The command deck on the *Hawkesbury* heaved with staff. The mechCity's engines were at full power.

'As if I care,' Byrne replied.

'They are a powerful foe. You have all but declared war on them.'

Byrne went quiet. 'You're right. We need to cripple the *Moonshine*.'

Anstrom shook his head. 'It's a ferocious opponent, with an exceptional battle team. They're built for combat. We are not. We will struggle.'

Byrne shrugged his indifference. 'Either way, we can't have it roaming around and getting in the way of our plans.'

'This game of yours is getting very dangerous. Some might call it reckless. Are you sure you want this to happen?'

'We need to appear weak.'

'You *are* weak,' Anstrom said.

'Only on the outside.'

'Where it matters.'

'Stop worrying, I'm sure it'll turn out fine.'

A science officer spoke up. 'Our sensors show that the *Moonshine* has stopped drilling.'

'So?' Byrne said.

'Abandoning the well is a significant action. I would suggest they're expecting an attack.'

'Just as well I have a secret weapon.'

On the *Moonshine*'s command deck, Suzie stared out into the night desert. Nikola stood next to her. The queen's chair remained empty. The massive outline of the approaching *Hawkesbury* could not be ignored. No matter at what distance, its size was undeniable. Suzie's eyes darted over to the young girl joining them. She'd already had a conversation with Nikola about Revvy, and although he seemed trustworthy, she still had her doubts about the girl.

'Have they sent any communications?' Suzie called out.

'No,' replied one of the command staff.

'They're going to stop, aren't they?' another asked.

'I hardly think they're going to smash into us,' Suzie said, following up with a less than convincing laugh. 'Even if they did, what would they achieve? A cracked frame? We have weapons.'

The command crew shifted quietly, attending to their

responsibilities, but continually checking on the path of the *Hawkesbury*, which was becoming a greater looming presence.

'Maybe ready those weapons,' Suzie suggested.

Nikola squinted. 'Is that a big black object moving in this direction?'

Suzie's hand swept over the controls. 'We're not detecting anything on the sonar.'

'Something is moving out there, approaching us. Does your sonar pick up flying objects?'

'No. What flies?'

A scorching line of fire scythed through the night, reflecting off black wings dozens of metres across. The *Moonshine*'s command crew instinctively ducked away, shielding themselves against the ferocious light.

'What the heck is that?' Suzie cried.

Fire lanced down from the dark creature, leaving a trail along the ground and up the face of the *Moonshine*. The heat could be felt through the glass. The intense light washed out the chamber's contents in a sea of white.

'That's a cyborg dragon,' Nikola replied.

'Could you say that again?'

'It's a flying weapon created by the cyborgs. We've been seeing them for a few years at the Steam Academy. I think the fact that it's working with Byrne is enough of a clue as to where his allegiances lie.'

'I've never seen anything so horrific,' Suzie said.

'Welcome to the war on terra firma.'

As their eyes adjusted back to normal Revvy shouted and pointed through the window. 'The *Hawkesbury* is getting really close.'

The rig looked close enough to touch.

'They'll stop,' Suzie said, in a deteriorating tone. 'Can we prepare anything quickly?'

'Preparing the main thruster will take three minutes if everyone's at their posts,' the deck officer replied.

'Ready them now.'

The officer pulled on a lever on the wall, slamming the handle down between two points. A siren wound up, ringing through the subframe of the *Moonshine*.

'They're not stopping, they're not stopping,' Revvy shouted.

'Everyone, grab something bolted down,' Nikola shouted.

With the unstoppable force of an iceberg, and at deceptive speed, the *Hawkesbury* crashed into the *Lady Moonshine*. The force knocked everyone to the floor as the rig jolted under the impact. Dials exploded, showering steam and glass across the room. The steam hung suspended in the room like a fog.

'Anyone badly injured?' Nikola asked.

There were muffled responses.

A communications tube set across a series of downpipes wailed. The comms officer pulled it free of its cradle and listened intently. 'Frame on level two cracked,' she reported. 'Still holding, but can't take much more pressure.'

'If they get through the subframe, the gas will blow,' another officer called out.

'Haven't they extracted the drill?' Nikola asked.

'The drill hole hasn't been sealed,' the officer replied. 'It will leak gas until it's plugged. The whole rig could be filling up.'

Another fireball blossomed toward them in a straight line that boiled the ground and blasted over the command level. The panoramic windscreen cracked, a long line lancing from one side to the other. The glass shattered, sending strands through the chamber like glass bullets, embedding into the backs of seats and ricocheting off the metal command equipment.

'Suzie, we need a decision,' Nikola said. 'You know the *Moonshine* best.' But Suzie was missing. 'Where is she?'

'Sitting behind the command chair,' Revvy said.

Nikola spun and knelt next to the trembling woman.

'I didn't do anything,' she shrieked. She held her shaking hands in front of her face, her eyes unfocused and her face as white as a sheet.

'What is the defence protocol?' Nikola asked.

Suzie continued to cower as tearing metal echoed through the rig. The *Lady Moonshine* was being pushed sideways, with the walls of the structure visibly twisting. Bolts snapped and twanged across the room. Finally the movement stopped as the *Hawkesbury* lost its momentum. The cyborg dragon circled in front of them, preparing for another approach.

'We're trapped,' Revvy said.

'I need her here,' Suzie cried.

'The queen is dead, you idiot. She's not coming,' Revvy shouted.

Nikola snapped his fingers as his eyes lit up. 'Suzie, how do the venting stacks work?'

She sat shivering, unable to provide an answer, her face stuck between fear and a search for unseen people.

'She's useless,' Revvy shouted. 'Things would be different if I was running the rig.' She raised her hand and slapped Suzie's face. 'Hey, we're talking to you.' No response. The girl turned to Nikola. 'How is this woman in command?'

'She's not a warrior. She's not trained for this,' one officer said. 'She's a political aide.'

'And you?' Nikola asked.

'Science officer,' the woman replied. 'Calculus or death.' She flashed Nikola a nervous smile.

'How do the vent stacks work?'

'You're kidding, You want me to explain thermodynamic exchange?'

'Okay, how about this: can the leaking gas be routed into the stacks and vented out the top?'

'Er, maybe. But the discharge points will need to be cleared, and the intakes in the storage level will need to be rotated.'

'Do it. I'll head up. Make sure it's done by the time I get up there. Is there any way to communicate?'

The science officer pointed to the comms tube. 'There's a command point up there.'

An animalistic screech echoed in through the open windscreen.

'I'd better go before the dragon comes back,' Nikola said.

'I'm coming with you,' Revvy said.

'It's okay. I can handle this.'

'No, I'm coming.'

'To do what, exactly?' Nikola asked.

'Help. What am I going to do down here? Get barbecued?'

'I can't promise to look after you.'

'No one does.'

'You are a defiant one. You can be on the comms tube. Let's go.'

'I'll do what's best for me,' she stated.

The pair hustled out of the command level, instinctively keeping their heads down. Black smoke hung in the air. Breathing became hard. After turning around several corners, they found the ladder leading to the observation deck. One side had broken free.

Nikola quickly and deftly clambered up the swinging ladder. The hatch had buckled under the impact. He slammed his palm into the hatch, flipping it open. Cool air rushed in. He pulled himself out onto the observation deck. Revvy followed.

The shadow of the *Hawkesbury* towered over them, its imposing size blotting out the horizon. But at this height, the rig's patchwork skin revealed it to be a victim of the desperate era it survived in.

'I'm surprised it didn't fall to pieces when it hit,' Nikola said.

A deep groan, the screech of tearing metal, and the *Hawkesbury* pulled away from the *Moonshine*. Smoke billowed up from between the two rigs, forming a dark curtain. The *Moonshine* lay dormant, with a fissure ripped down its side, exposing the rig's internals.

The dragon roared as it circled and approached again.

'Is this one of those moments where the enemy strikes, and if it's successful we all die horribly?' Revvy asked.

Nikola gave her a flat look and pointed to the comms tube. He examined the approach line of the dragon and tested the alignment of the venting stacks. 'Are they ready?' he asked.

Revvy listened intently to the tube. 'They've had to abandon the command deck. The science officer is the last one there. She's about to go. She's issued the order, but can't say if it's complete.'

'Revvy, get *down*,' Nikola shouted.

She turned. The dragon was nearly on them, its dead mechanical eyes glaring at them. The creature opened its mouth, revealing flaming pilot jets on either side. The air reeked of fuel, sharp in the nose and abrasive in the throat. Fire erupted and rolled toward them.

Revvy froze, staring at the horrific creature. Nikola grabbed her and dragged her behind a stack as the flames rolled over them.

The venting stacks vibrated and then shook, increasing in intensity. Fire spiralled out of the tubes as the dragon sailed over them, lifted and blasted by the wall of flame. It struggled to control its flight through the upwards currents.

The science officer appeared. 'You still alive?'

The metal pinked as it cooled. Nikola and Revvy stepped out from behind the stack. The *Hawkesbury* was a diminishing figure as it gained momentum. The rig's motley exterior reclaimed its ominous outline as it melted into the dark.

'Can't we chase after them?' Nikola said.

'Not until everything is fixed,' the officer replied.

'They have everything they need to start the Omen.'

'And we can't stop them,' Revvy said. 'Makes you wonder about whose side you want to be on.'

It had been hours since the horrific crash. Frey had sat terrified for the entire time since. Every loud noise or unexpected vibration trampled her senses under a spectre of inevitable ruin. The door to the cell opened without warning, smashing into the wall in one wide swing. Frey raised her dirtied hands, tied together, in defence and lurched into the corner, the whites of her eyes catching the light.

The guards appeared. Due to Frey's age, there was only a certain kind of guard that would carry out Byrne's orders: those that enjoyed domination, and were small-minded and mean. Yet they always seemed to find power. Maybe there was a need for people like that, even on the side of good. Frey saw the thrill in their eyes, and how it drove them on to be more violent, more ambitious. There wasn't much left they could do to her.

But she had kept the secret, stayed true to the plan. She had surrendered the information she knew she was allowed to, and in a believable way.

Today, the guards were different. They didn't attack, instead just standing at attention and waiting. Was it over?

A new man appeared. Randy. Although vile, his familiarity felt almost friendly.

He squatted in front of Frey, giving her a lopsided smile. He reached for her hair, moving the thick curls to the side. 'New orders from the boss. Today it's over for you.'

Her eyes opened wide and she gasped.

Randy gave her a pat. 'Up you get, princess.'

He led her out of the cell. Arid's old cell had been patched with secondhand metal sheets covered in garish and mismatched colours. The contrast looked out of place in such a severe location. It made Frey smile in her delirium. They made their way to the level's exit and descended to the lowest. Randy collected a bottle of water from a vending machine, ripped off the top and handed it to her. She poured it down her throat, some spilling out of her mouth in the rush. She closed her eyes as a delirium swept over her.

A service entrance opened up and a ladder descended to the ground. Looking out, all she could see was desert. The bright sunlight didn't help. She closed her eyes against the glare as the guards led her ahead.

In the light, Frey's injuries became apparent. Bruises and dried blood coated the side of her face. Her body ached. Her mind was exhausted. The wind picked up, blowing sand into her eyes. As she squinted, she could make out the ruins of an old town, hardly anything but derelict and decaying buildings being consumed by the marching sands.

'Where are we going?' she asked. 'Am I being taken on a ride back to the *Moonshine*? Is it here? Is there a prisoner swap?'

'Uh-uh,' Randy said, waving his index finger. 'No talking.'

The small team trekked for ten minutes into the ruins. She could see the *Rankin* positioned next to a small collection of decaying architecture. They entered an old courtyard that was surrounded by broken-down buildings. In the centre was a long, thin metal pole. Red stained the ground around its base. The far wall was showered with small divots.

As soon as Frey saw the pole and the blood, she shrieked.

Randy laughed. 'Hope is a dangerous thing for a girl like you.'

'Wait, no. I've told you everything.'

'In that case there's no need to keep you around.'

'No, *please*.'

'Where is the key?'

Frey lowered her head. Tears rolled down her face.

'Tie her up,' Randy ordered.

The guards forced Frey against the pole and lashed her hands behind the steel bar. The wind buffeted her, rippling her dress against her body, forcing her hair down over her face.

Randy touched his communicator. 'Ready to go,' he said. 'Is the widecast link up? Good. Let the world see.'

The guards formed a loose line, standing to a vague form of attention.

'And we are live,' Randy continued. 'Dear viewers, today we offer to you the execution of the assassin who murdered Queen Bea, commander of the *Lady Moonshine*. Betrayed by a ward she had taken on out of the goodness of her heart. A reminder of how all those who betray the command are treated. There is no forgiveness, and no one is above the law. Let this be a lesson.'

The cameraman shifted uneasily, putting the focus on the young girl. He made Frey the attention of the shot, blurring the background.

Randy moved to the side of the firing line and turned to face the squad. 'Soldiers, raise arms.'

The guards lifted their rifles, sighting along the barrels.

'Ready.'

The courtyard went silent. The wind died.

'Aim.'

In a final desperate move, Frey thrashed against the ropes. The pendant ripped from the pocket on the inside of her dress and bounced onto the outside of her clothing.

'Wait, wait, wait,' Randy shouted. He raised his hand and indicated for the guards to lower their weapons.

He stepped up to her, examining the object. He picked it up and twisted it in his fingers.

'You know the reasons. And you know what I've tried to do and where I started from. But now we need to put those things aside. You must take care of this. Keep it a secret.'

Bea hands Frey a small box.

Frey opens it. Her eyes go wide. Inside is Arid's pendant. 'You used to talk about this all the time. Isn't this really important to you?'

'Frey, you are important. Don't forget it. Ever. Now, there are a few things I need you to do,' Mama-Bea says. 'Our survival depends on your protecting this at all costs. Don't ever let it be in the hands of anyone else.'

'This.' Randy yanked the chain and the necklace broke. 'Why, you little minx. You had it all the time.'

He stepped away and turned his back to her, grinning as he stared at the key in his hand. 'Aim,' he shouted.

And she cried.

Frey closed her eyes and the world dropped dead. Gunfire rang out through the courtyard.

[16]

'YES, HE'S HERE,' Hunter says. He offers Alex a seat, but she refuses and paces around the man.

'I don't understand why you're doing this,' she says. 'Is it some kind of betrayal?'

'Of whom? Are we not on the same side? He seems to mean more to you than to me. Surely this is a wonderful gift. I would expect it to remove any doubt of betrayal.'

'I don't trust you.'

Alex is surprised when a large silver handgun is placed against the side of her head. She has her twin pistols strapped to each leg, but she knows Hunter's strengths.

He says, 'You're learning. But if we cannot trust the leadership team, who then?'

'Where is he?' Alex keeps her eyes trained on Hunter's trigger finger. It's steady. There is no doubt.

'That would be no fun. The challenge is to find him. And to make it interesting, I might release him. A real cat-and-mouse adventure. Imagine the embarrassment if he escapes and I turn up without the prisoner I boasted about arresting. And why? Because of you. Tears to ice, my friend. Because of you.'

'All things considered, I'd prefer to think without a gun to my head.'

'Ask and you shall receive,' he says, stepping back and slipping the handgun into the back of his belt. *'Flee, my child, like the wind. And one more thing: don't ever come back.'*

Alex stares at him for a moment, then turns and runs out.

Hunter claps his hands and summons a guard. *'As times are uncertain and we should not be imprudent, I shall find this confrontation to be the highest form of parsimonious entertainment. Bring me blooded wine and a small glass to relish in the activities. And my theatre spectacles.'*

The cell door opened. Arid waited, but no one entered. He stood and slowly approached the door, creeping along the wall. Still no security. He peered out. The corridor was empty. Momentarily. Running footsteps. Bullets roared past him. Ella approached, guns drawn. More shots forced Arid back into the cell. He couldn't stay here. He jumped out and ran. The corridor was short. He cornered. Stairs. Up left, or down right? Shots ricocheted off the handrail to his right. Up.

Arid took the steps two at a time. Up halfway, turn, up second half. His legs burnt. A metal wall ran down the centre of the rig. Two doors. Two choices. Left or right. He chose left.

The corridor opened into sleeping quarters on his left. The area was empty, with freshly made beds. He charged past and into a meeting area. The roof opened up into a double-height void. The wrecking-beam gyro sat exposed, attached to the ceiling.

A window from the command deck looked down into the area, and the opposing one. Hunter was up there. In front of him, several soldiers stood behind a large bench. Behind them were racks of equipment. A pistol lay on the bench.

Arid grabbed it before any of the soldiers could drop their coffee and reach it. 'Hands up.'

The quartermaster raised his hands.

'How do I get out?' Arid asked.

'The way you came in,' the quartermaster replied.

Arid's eyes scanned the area. A service platform. A down button. 'Is there an exit on the next deck?'

'The rescue alcove. But it's a big drop.'

Shots from his right. Arid turned and faced the barrels of two pistols.

Alex climbs the stairs, spins at the halfway point. Left or right? Left. No, right. She forces open the door. Medical bay. Several medical staff organising supplies. She weaves through the array of small rooms, pushing past the staff, and bursts out into the mess. A dozen soldiers are eating.

'Where is he?' she shouts.

'Who?' says a nearby soldier.

'The boy.'

'Not here.'

'Where is he?'

'Is that him?' the soldier says, pointing through a window set in the long metal wall dividing the rig at the quarter store.

Arid points a gun at the QM, who raises his hands.

Alex spins and aims both pistols at Arid. Is the glass bulletproof? She unloads both guns at him, drawing the boy's attention.

The bullets track along the glass, leaving imprints in the oversized window. It holds. Arid hits the down button. They stand on either side, breathing heavily and staring at each other. The service platform slowly rises from the lower deck. Alex catches the movement. She curls her fist and smashes it against the window. Her eyes dart from side to side, searching for a way through. A soldier leaps from his seat and throws her to the ground.

Arid flinched as the bullets sprayed across the glass. He panicked and squeezed the trigger. The shot had the soldiers diving for cover behind the bench. Was it bad to apologise? Arid watched a soldier leap and tackle Ella to the ground. The two fought as the platform arrived.

Hunter tipped back his glass and emptied the dark red liquid within. He held a small set of brass binoculars secured on a stick. He laughed with the occasional brief applause as the action played out before him.

As Arid steps onto the platform, Alex breaks free, firing shots over the soldiers' heads. She glares at him and then sprints off back to the medical rooms. Down the stairs. Jumping the first stretch in one go. Turn, down in two. The deck is crowded with equipment towering up from the engine deck below. The long walkway appears empty. Steam drifts through the deck. Then she sees him at the far end.

The Rankin *judders. The gears slip into neutral. The rig stops.*

She fires, narrowly missing Arid. The bullet punctures the boiler, and steam billows out across the walkway. She charges ahead through the clouds. He is gone. Running footsteps. He passes underneath on the lower walkway. She holds onto the railing and leaps over, swinging her feet high, and lands heavily in a crouch on the grating.

Arid glances over his shoulder at her, terror filling his eyes.

Down, three at a time. Stumbled at the base. Up. The walkway extended over the engines of the *Rankin*, great pistons driving huge cogs, slowly turning. Arid ducked around the great machinery as more shots clanged off the metal. Light was visible ahead. He ran forward as fast as he could as Alex's footsteps closed in on him.

The *Rankin*'s rescue deck was open, similar to the *Moonshine*'s. He hoped it wasn't too high. He jumped blindly and sailed out into open air. They were in the middle of an old ruined town, long deserted. Below him were the remains of a building.

Alex follows Arid, firing rapidly, both guns blazing as they drop onto the derelict building, which is nothing more than an eroded stone box covered in sand. Below them, a small group of people forms an arc around a person tied to a long metal pole. Arid lands, rolls forward and over the side of the building. He grabs the edge of the stonework and hangs for a moment before dropping.

Randy's heart blossomed through his shirt, a crimson carnation. More shots. Fewer guards. The remaining men ran.

Arid landed and rolled, picking up Randy's pistol, and fired back at Alex, on his back in the sand with the gun in both hands. She dived for cover behind a stone column. Randy's hand lay open. Arid's pendant. Relief flushed through him as he crawled over and picked it up. Home. His past. He slipped the necklace over his head.

He rose and moved toward Frey. Keeping the gun trained on the stone column with one hand, he pulled the rope with his other and Frey fell to the ground.

'Frey, are you all right?' Arid said.

There was no response. Then she moaned and rolled onto her back, breathing heavily. 'I'm not dead, so that's good, isn't it?'

'Depends what happens next.'

Ella stepped out, aiming both pistols at him.

Arid centred his sight on her. Deadlock.

'So, here we all are again, happy families,' she said. 'Two against one, you're going to lose.'

'Y' know when we were like eight and we'd say "I wish y' were dead" t' someone. And our concept of death was just a big sleep that we'd wake up from.'

'Yeah, sort of. My life was different to yours.'

'I just mention it as we stand here, pointing guns at each other. And I know yer an assassin, but do y' know we don't wake up? It just feels like a final kind of situation, and I don't think any of us wants t 'be dead.'

'I'm not the one who's going to die.' Ella's eyes dart over to

Frey as her sister moved, rising onto her knees. 'Mother gave you the key?'

'It was meant to be a secret,' Frey replied.

'I'm the favourite,' Ella said. 'Me. Not you. She didn't even want you. You were a burden put on her by Stephanna. She chose me. She *chose* me.'

'Er, didn't y' try to kill her?' Arid asked.

'I don't *try* anything,' Ella replied. 'I succeed.'

'Oh, yeah. That's right, she's dead.'

Frey and Alex looked directly at Arid. An awkward silence descended on them. He shifted uneasily on his feet.

Hesitantly, Frey asked, 'Is she still alive?' her voice lifting with hope.

'No. No. She's dead. I killed her,' Ella cried.

It was another of those moments where truth and its power were assessed. 'I'm sorry, y' failed,' Arid said.

'You're sorry?' Frey said. 'Are you still entranced by her, although she has a gun pointed at you?'

'What, *no, o*f course not. We're going t', er, hand her over t' the authorities.'

'And which ones would those be? Byrne? He's now the authority. We're alone.'

The wind picked up, blustering dirt and debris into the air. A piece of paper was caught in an eddy and spiralled upwards.

'She's not dead,' Ella muttered. 'I killed her. Mother is not dead. No, no, no. I killed her.'

'Are y' all right, y' know, in the head?' Arid asked.

Ella shook her head, as though dislodging a difficult thought. In a quick movement, she moved in behind Frey, grabbing her sister around the neck and placing a gun against her head. 'I'm done playing. Hand over the key,' Ella demanded.

Arid sighed, lowered his gun, and held out the pendant. Ella shuffled over and grabbed it. Before he let it go, he said, 'No one gets hurt. Right?'

The ghost of a half-smile lifts the side of Alex's mouth. A joke only she is privy to. 'If you want.'

Arid releases the key and she snatches it away. Noises from the Rankin. *Her eyes dart over to the warcraft. She backs away as a gate starts to lift. Her chest heaves as she struggles for breath. Her hand shakes. She calms her nerves as she places both hands on the grip, closes her eyes, and squeezes the trigger. The lone shot is amplified in the courtyard.*

The echoes die away. Silence replaces the moment. Alex drops the gun and stares at her trembling hand. She screams.

Frey grabs her stomach, staggers backward. She collapses as blood oozes from the wound.

Shouts from the Rankin.

Alex turns and runs.

Arid knelt next to Frey.

'Why did you give it to her?' she asked.

'T' save you,' he replied.

'Do you know what I've had to endure? You made it all for nothing. That was stupid.'

'I know.'

Ella was gone. Soldiers emerged from the *Rankin*.

'If only we had a tiger t' worry about,' Arid said.

'Go, you idiot. Run.'

Too late. The soldiers had surrounded them.

[17]

BYRNE HADN'T EXPECTED leadership to be so quiet. There were delegates everywhere, volunteering to carry out tasks yet seemingly incapable of doing so. He missed the day-to-day bustle of hands-on confrontation. The management structure hadn't changed, but perception had. Now everyone bowed and said, 'Yes, sir.' He still had to, annoyingly, supply the reports to his boss, because that was the one issue left: his suspicions about the commander.

Alex burst in through the door, startling Byrne from his thoughts. She held the key aloft as she strode across the command deck and smacked it down on the table in front of him.

'You said the queen was dead,' she said.

Byrne picked up the key between his fingers. He smiled, feeling its weight, watching the hypnotic pattern of the lights. 'What was that?' His eyes remained riveted to the key.

'You said the queen, my mother, was dead. You said it was a successful hit.'

'What are you saying?'

'Are you terminally stupid, deaf or rude? The boy says she is alive.'

'Are you saying Queen Bea is still alive?' Byrne asked.

'Hallelujah!' she cried.

'That's not possible. No one has seen or heard anything.'

'Could it be that she's hiding while recovering? I know I sank the blade in to the hilt. Do you know how hard that was, after living with her for all that time?'

Byrne raised his eyes to Alex. 'Where is Arid?'

'You have the key. You don't need him.'

'Idiot. The Omen is useless without him, and with her still around we'll need the weapon more than ever. I said get him.'

She sighed. 'That may not be possible.'

'Where is he?'

'The *Rankin*.'

Byrne went quiet. 'How did you let that happen?' he then asked.

'They outnumbered me,' she replied.

'They normally do. Why was it a problem this time?'

'I made an assessment. I had the key. Soldiers were coming. He would have slowed me down and I'd have lost the key.'

Damn. She had a point. But Arid was a vital bargaining chip with the cyborgs. The situation was getting tricky.

'Just do your job,' he sneered.

'A job implies payment or reward.'

'We shall see whether your actions offer any value. Then we may talk about reward.'

'Be careful, I might take what I see fit without your involvement.'

'You need to remember your origins, and who did what to and for you.'

Alex glared at Byrne, not releasing her intense stare.

Byrne then turned and waved her toward the door. 'By the way, speaking of origins, Cameron and some of his friends are downstairs. Just like old times, right?'

Alex hesitated. 'What are you going to do with them?'

'I'm not sure whether to celebrate or execute them. After all, they were caught, in a way, helping us. But it's hard to forgive the past. Do you have a suggestion or request?'

'No.' Her response was sharp and without emotion. He could see her struggle with the news.

'Funny, isn't it?' he said. 'After everything, we end up back where we started. Just like a happy family.'

Alex's face turned to granite.

A red cube at the centre of Byrne's desk flashed. Byrne picked up a handset and tapped the cube three times. '*Hunter*, yes. We were just talking about you.' He reclined in the seat and winked to Alex. 'I hear you have the Geiger boy with you.' The response went on for a long time. He hung the receiver up without saying a word.

'And?' Alex prompted.

'He won't hand him over.'

'That puts a crimp in your plan. Odd, though.'

'Why?'

'Hunter didn't really seem interested in Arid. Was happy for him to die. But he doesn't want you to have him. Says something about your authority.'

'It says nothing. Hunter is a game player. You know that best of all. He's not a tactical genius. Get him.'

'Who?'

'Arid Geiger!'

'You're kidding me. Off a fortified Collins class? They'll be waiting for me. I'm not welcome there. If Hunter doesn't want to give him up, we can't fight. How will it look if one of your agents is seen interfering with an ally?'

'Just do it,' Byrne shouted. 'He's playing us. Testing. You need to show him who's boss. This is the moment.'

'You know what you're asking. I do this, I'll be an enemy of the state. I'm paying a high price. I shot my sister.'

'And stabbed your mother. You're probably not in the will.' Byrne gave Alex a brief smile before his face dissolved into a mask of anger. 'Maybe you can go back and finish the job properly. Like you've been trained to do.'

'Do you even know where Hunter is going?'

The cyborg comms cube buzzed.

'Maybe there's a way you can lure him out so I can attack him,' Alex continued.

The comms unit continued to buzz. Byrne sat on the corner of the desk and watched the cube. 'Ah, maybe I have an idea.'

He picked up the handset and tapped the black cube three times. A short, aggressive tone, oscillating between a piercing screech and distorted rumble, had him pulling the handset away from his ear.

'Is this @JuliaOfficial1? It is? That's a surprise. You've been leader for more than a few hours. Congratulations. Regarding your interest. Yes, the boy. He's on board the *Rankin*. I'll send you the comms number. The commander will, we believe, be willing to make a deal. A meeting point? I would suggest …'

Alex wrote down a name and handed to Byrne. He relayed the name. The call ended.

'What have you organised?' she asked.

Byrne tapped the red cube absentmindedly. 'Hear me out on this. Cyborgs want Arid and will pay a lot for him. I want Arid, but he's with Hunter. Hunter doesn't want Arid, but would probably sell or trade him. We get Hunter to hand over Arid to the cyborgs and then steal him away from the cyborgs. Simple.'

'Is this your specific order? You're fully aware of what you're instructing?'

It was a risk. It was a challenge to the entire command structure, tearing it down in a fit of anger. But maybe that was needed. Generations of complacent leaders who felt they were owed the positions rather than earned. Burn them all. People would respect that. Even so, the words stuck in Byrne's throat.

He nodded.

'I need you to send a message,' Alex said. 'Widecast. Let the world know that Arid and Frey are being handed over to the cyborgs, where they will be assassinated. Let's see what hero turns up.'

'Is that all?'

'Now give me something fast, and a reel of explosives.'

'The quartermaster will sort you out. You don't have much time.'

'None of us does,' Alex said, striding toward the exit.

Byrne positioned himself behind his desk. 'What shall I do with Cameron and company?' he said.

Alex hesitated at the door, staring out into the passageway. Byrne remained seated, his hands resting on the desk as he leaned forward.

She closed her eyes. 'Do whatever. They mean nothing. Not now.'

Del and Anthony sat quietly in the cell. After the tears and moments of hysteria, Anthony calmed down. Del held him and offered soothing words.

The door opened. Cameron tumbled head over heels as the guards threw him in. He crashed against the wall in a heap.

Del rushed to his side, rolling him onto his back. 'Help me get him up,' she said to Anthony.

They lifted Cameron onto the bed. His face was covered in black and blue patches.

'What have they done to you?' Del asked.

Cameron groaned.

There was a laugh from the door. Two guards were still there.

'A bit of special attention,' one of them said.

'Just like we're going to give you,' said the other. He pulled his belt free, forming it into a loop and whacking it into his palm.

'You're not touching her,' Anthony shouted. He launched forward, his arms an uncontrolled windmill.

He didn't stand a chance. The first guard smacked him down, sending him sprawling on the spot with a sickening thud. Anthony tried to raise himself onto his knees, blood streaming down his face, but was met with a kick to the side of his head that spun him into the wall as a dead weight. Out cold.

'Just you and us now,' the first guard said to Del. 'You want the same, or are you going to be nice?'

Del backed into the corner, with the guards' vicious faces looming over her. Her hands scrabbled behind her, searching for anything that could be thrown or stabbed.

'Are you one of those who looks forward to a bit of rough play?'

'Don't just stand there,' she replied.

The two guards looked at each other, hesitating, but sharing a dark smile.

'A bit eager, are we?' the second guard said.

'I wasn't talking to you.'

The heads of the guards cracked together, and they collapsed. Nikola stepped over them, wiping his hands on his top.

'Do you ever actually use the sword?' Revvy asked Nikola as she followed him inside.

'Only when I have to,' he replied.

'I'd hate to be around in that situation. Aren't you meant to say something funny? Some snappy putdown.'

'Me? No.'

'What's the point of winning if you can't … it doesn't matter.'

'Where's Arid?' Nikola asked Del.

'They didn't get him,' she replied.

'So, Byrne has Arid, key, gas and instructions?' Revvy said.

'Yep.' Del nodded in a determined but defeated way.

'And we have …'

'Determination and fraternity,' Nikola said.

'Great,' said Revvy. 'I'll make a flag. It'll be useful against guns. Let's get out of here.'

Nikola extended his hand and pulled Del to her feet, nearly lifting her into the air. 'Help the small guy,' he said to Revvy, indicating Anthony, who was moving slowly in the corner.

She groaned. 'Do I have to?'

'Can you carry Cameron? Come on, we're a team, we don't have much time.' Nikola lifted Cameron over his shoulder in one easy movement.

Revvy led the way back to the service corridors they had crept in through.

'It's good to see you, Revvy,' Del said. 'I was always concerned about whose side you were on, but you've come through when we needed you.'

Revvy snorted. 'You know, honesty isn't always the best policy.'

'I'm saying thanks, that's all.'

'Well, don't get too caught up in your appreciation. I'm only here because I thought Arid was here.'

The walls closed in, forcing them into single file.

Cameron's weight slowed Nikola down, allowing him to take in the condition of the *Hawkesbury*. The flooring creaked under his increased bulk. 'This place is a dump. Can't any of you build anything properly?' he said.

'You get used to it. And this isn't exactly the main entrance,' Revvy said.

The narrow passage had Nikola ducking and weaving through random pipes. Everything he touched left a coating of soot. 'Any longer in here and I'll get accused of racism. You lived in these conditions?'

'As I said, you get used to it.'

'I don't think my lungs will.'

Cameron stirred, the constant knocking against the confines of the passage waking him. Nikola placed him on his feet, resting him against the wall.

'Where are we?' the boy whispered as his eyes regained focus.

Nikola went to speak, but stopped to look around. 'I know we passed through quickly on the way in, but I don't recognise this area.'

'It's a shortcut,' Revvy said. 'Quick.' She pushed ahead and the others followed.

The passage ended and opened up into an open space.

'We're here,' Revvy said, louder than expected.

'Where?' Del asked.

'I wasn't talking to you,' Revvy said, parroting Del, with each nasty word dripping with disdain.

Movement to the sides. Hustling of feet. Rustling of uniforms. Clicking of guns.

Nikola sighed. 'Why? I thought we had a connection.'

Revvy laughed in his face. 'I looked into the mirror. What I saw was weak. And weakness will never win.'

Lights flickered on, revealing them flanked by rows of guards on each side.

'Guards!' Revvy screamed. 'Prisoners escaping.'

The response was swift—from Nikola. He snapped his hands around the grip of his sword and pulled it free of his back. Before the closest guard could move, Nikola had slashed the edge of his blade across the man's forearm. Nikola spun around, grabbing the man from behind and using him as a shield as the others fired. He spun again, spearing the next.

Running feet. A shout. A scream. Another two guards fell.

Nikola smashed the sword's pommel in a wide underarm swing, up into the jaw of the remaining guard, who was lifted off the ground and slammed flat onto his back.

Cameron, Del and Anthony stood wide-eyed and terrified in the centre of the still and bloodied bodies.

Nikola lowered his blade at Revvy, backing her against the wall. Stepping in toward her, he glared into her eyes. 'You really want to make an enemy of me?'

'I thought you said we had a connection,' she whimpered.

'Yeah, sorry. I needed a way in. Consider it a life lesson. You use people, sometimes they'll use you right back.'

'Don't tell me this was about Arid,' Del said.

Revvy shrugged. 'I trap you all, I trap him. Except the fool wasn't here.'

'You need to let it go,' Nikola warned. 'Your obsession will destroy you.'

She glared at him, and then turned and fled.

'Del, lead the way,' Nikola ordered. 'We need to be quick.

Everything is falling apart.'

A siren wound up, echoing throughout the floor. Del took off down a corridor to the team's left and signalled for the others to follow. The passage twisted several times before emerging into a workshop.

Del slammed to a halt and raised her arm to stop the others. The area was filled with mechanical repair equipment. Several guards sat at one end of the workshop, talking amongst themselves.

Nikola grabbed Del and pushed her out into the workshop, pointing to the exit on the opposite side. 'Don't think about it, just go,' he commanded.

He quickly outpaced her and reached the other side without being noticed. Del arrived, panting heavily. Cameron followed, with Anthony closing in behind. As Anthony neared the exit, he stumbled, falling against a collection of long rods. They clattered and bounced against the wall. The noise attracted the attention of the workers, who paused in their tasks and looked up. Cameron grabbed Anthony by his collar and hauled him the final metres to the exit.

The team ignored the shouts of 'Stop!' as they scuttled out into another service corridor, doubling their pace to keep ahead of the pursuing guards.

Nikola dodged down narrower passages that were tangled with the results of poor maintenance. It was going to slow the soldiers chasing them. He spotted a recessed duct shielded by a fallen sheet of metal, and signalled for the others to enter. After Cameron had filed in, Nikola squeezed in next to them and pulled the sheet over the entrance.

The soldiers ran past.

Nikola waited until their footsteps had dwindled and the ambient noises of the mechCity had returned. 'I think we might've passed an exit point,' he said. 'Double back. When we're out of here, Cam, Del and … the other one, follow Byrne. Stop him getting to the Omen. I'll track the *Rankin* and get Arid.' He forced open the sheet and they ran back along the passage.

Del stopped and pointed down a side corridor. An exit sign shone above a solid door that was crossed by two solid bars forming an X. Rounded corners. External exit.

'Final dash, peeps. Heads down and go for it,' Nikola said.

Their feet clattered along the metal passage, which rose as they approached the door. A matter of metres. The door release was tantalisingly close.

The barrel of a gun appeared in front of them, causing Nikola to pull up. The others crashed into him.

Anstrom stepped out. There was a pause as the guard ran his sights over the assembled crew. 'You're a soldier,' he said to Nikola. 'Who are you?'

'Nikola Tasman.' The Steam Academy soldier remained calm, keeping his voice even.

'Commander?'

'Maybe one day,' Nikola replied.

'I know your name,' Anstrom said. 'The stories are legendary.'

Nikola shrugged. 'People like to exaggerate.'

Anstrom shifted uneasily. 'You're meant to be one of the good guys.'

The corridor went silent. They all watched Anstrom's face. Footsteps behind. Quiet, but getting louder.

'What does that make me?' Anstrom said.

'A man doing his job,' Nikola replied.

'The job defines the man.'

Voices getting louder. Shouts. Commands.

'Why are you here?' Anstrom asked Nikola.

'Byrne shouldn't have a weapon like the Omen, and we have to stop him,' Nikola explained. 'These kids are important in the scheme of things. And they're *kids*.'

Anstrom began to sweat. *Kids*. The word stung, causing him to flinch. 'I told Byrne he was going too hard on them. We have the PAD.' The end of the gun was shaking. 'But it's my job. I have a family. What else am I going to do?'

'I can't tell you how to live your life. You have to look in the mirror and see if you can stomach what looks back.'

'I hand you over to Byrne, I get promoted. I no longer need to do this.'

The approaching troops could only be seconds away. Once here, there would be no way out. Game over.

Anstrom holstered his gun. 'But who would I be to profit from doing something wrong. I have a family. I have to show honour in the face of adversity. Go.'

Nikola sighed. The others sagged. As he ushered them down the hall, Nikola instructed them as they went. 'Cam, go get Byrne. I'll get Arid. If we can stop the two from meeting, we'll avoid disaster.' He nodded to Anstrom.

Nikola's Steam Academy badge buzzed. The face dissolved to be replaced by a blank screen. Text displayed on it.

'Okay. Not good news. Hunter is going to hand Arid over to the cyborgs. Is the *Rankin* far away?'

'No. You can catch it easily. You'll find an e-board in the store locker by the exit.'

'Thank you. I hope we can meet again on friendlier terms.'

'You were never here.'

Hunter and the *Rankin* approached Yandarai Gap. The call from the cyborgs had been a surprise, as was the request for Arid. Still, cash was cash, and it all helped add to the war effort. The hills on either side of the pass were solid rock, the fading light reflecting off the decorative strata. The *Rankin* couldn't squeeze through.

Then the helmsman—woman, person, whatever—reported sighting the cyborgs on the far side. Waiting on electric motorcycles, their headlights spread a crisscross pattern over the sand.

'Get a roller,' Hunter shouted. 'Ship the boy off.'

His second in command appeared. 'I thought you weren't going to hand him over.'

'Not to Byrne. Anyone else with cash is welcome to the little troublemaker. The cyborgs want him, they can have him.'

It has been a busy few hours. The Rankin *eases to a stop. Alex watches a roller emerge from the rear of the mechRig. It picks up pace as it drives around the rig and into the pass, then slows as it approaches the narrow point. She glances over at the cyborgs. They are still on the designated spot. They are following their instructions to the letter, true to form. Her thumb brushes over the top of the detonation button. Timing will be everything.*

Nikola—the hero arrives—charges out from behind a rockfall on the far side, riding a large e-board with four balloon wheels. He jumps off and runs in front of the roller, raising his hands. 'It's a trap,' he shouts.

Alex smiles and presses the detonation button. The explosives she'd buried earlier erupt in a long line, the blasts rolling through the pass in a wave. Nikola leaps to the side, but the force flings him against the rocks. The roller is thrown into the air and crashes down on its side.

Alex runs down the slope, her legs taking long, manic strides. She grips the hatch handle and prepares to wrench it open. Arid bursts out, blood flowing down his head. He runs toward the cyborgs. But he is limping. Alex tears after him, throwing her arms around his waist and dragging him to the ground.

Nikola is unconscious against the rocks, blood coating his face. The roller lies in ruins. The cyborgs dismount, hefting their weapons.

Should she check for her sister? No. She'd shot her. It could be awkward. Alex's body is exhausted.

Arid struggles, trying to twist free. She pulls his head back and places the machine gun against his temple. 'I am so tired of chasing you,' she says. 'It's over.'

Alex drags him up as the cyborgs begin firing. Bright bolts of blue light erupt from their weapons, throwing channels of sand into the air as the powerballs shoot over the land.

Alex wheels around and fires back. Most of the bullets are melted in the electromagnetic wall, but some make it through, impacting against the cyborgs' armour. One goes down. Another wave approaches her, and she is forced behind a collection of boulders. She fires blindly over the rocks. Her shredder sits on the other side of the pass, hidden in a cave. There is no choice.

She grabs Arid, hefts him over her shoulder and charges across the pass. The world erupts around her as she runs. She dives into the cave, collapsing.

The cyborgs mount and ride toward the cave. As they near, the shredder screams out, leaping over them and burning away over the sands.

Hunter watched from the command deck. 'By the fires of Zeus, I wasn't expecting that. Well, I was. But it smacked of desperation.'

The second in command leaned in. 'What shall we do with the princess?'

'Is Frey stable?'

'Yes. Patched and recovering well.'

'Let's get her home to her mother. A deal is a deal.'

'And the girl?' he said, indicating Alex battling in the pass.

'Let it play out. Best to inform everyone that she tried to assassinate me and about her involvement with Byrne.'

[18]

'Move it,' Ella said, pushing Arid in the back.

Even as a killer, Ella still looked stunning to him. The moonlight caught her features and made them glow. Arid had to wonder how such a person had become so hateful. What had Byrne done to her to turn her into an assassin?

Ella switched on a torch and shone it into the mine. The light didn't reach the walls or ceiling, illuminating only the patch of earth in front of them. She pushed him forward.

'What do I call you?' he asked.

'My name is Alex.'

'Like Alexandra?' He noticed her wince when he said the name.

'Call me what you want. You won't be alive long enough for me to care.'

The Battery was empty, and the power was out. Word on the ground said trouble was coming. The key to the Omen weapon was on its way. No one knew what it would do, but being close was a bad idea.

Except for …

Byrne ran his hands around the curved surface, his fingers picking out the imperfections in the metal.

Alex pushed Arid into the chamber. It was empty, apart from Byrne. The furnace fires lay dormant. The gas canisters stood in the centre of the chamber, with a pipe connecting them to the turbine intake on the Omen.

Byrne didn't face them, keeping his attention on the weapon. 'No one knows how this works,' he said to Arid. 'It's been sitting here for years. Your parents disappeared and took the only key with them. I have it now.' He stretched his arm out to the side and dangled the pendant. 'But it appears to need identification to activate the Omen. The queen's daughter mentioned something, which took me a while to understand. Sometimes something is so obvious you can't see it.'

He spun and approached Arid casually. 'There is something about *you* that is central to the weapon starting, something you know or have.'

'But I literally have nothing,' Arid said, pulling his pockets inside out. 'Everything I had was destroyed when the *Rankin* crushed my rig.'

'You are lying.'

'Lying?' Arid laughed. 'Why? Prove it.'

'I really don't have to listen to this,' Alex said. 'You are leader, Byrne. And I've got the kid and the key for you. You've got the weapon of doom, or whatever you want to call it. You have everything you wanted. My responsibility to you is over. I've had enough and I'm not doing it anymore. I quit.'

'You failed with the queen,' Byrne said.

'You're not holding that over me. The result has been the same. Deal with it. Everyone got what they wanted except me.' Alex wheeled around and strode toward the exit. A gunshot had her stopping and sighing in exasperation. 'Oh, come on. After everything?'

She turned. Byrne was pointing a pistol at her.

Arid was tense. The canisters were close. If there was a leak, a spark from a pistol flint meant they'd all be part of the walls.

Byrne indicated with the gun for Alex to return. She bowed

her head and rejoined them. He lowered his gun, and Arid let out a sigh.

'There is nothing on the outside other than wires and pipes, except for this black panel,' Byrne explained. 'The cyborgs tell me it's an identification unit. I've touched it. Others have touched it. Nothing has happened. It's up to you, and you'd better hope that something happens for you.'

'I am the key?' Arid whispered.

He stepped forward and placed his hand on the panel. A light scanned over his fingers. An outline appeared, flickering between his hand the size it was now and a smaller version; his hand as a boy. It seemed so small. And the memory of his parents came back. They were always playing some kind of hand game. He traced the shape in an ingrained pattern over the surface.

The cylinder groaned and unlocked. The two halves separated, revealing a small control area, and an empty interior. It was a shape Arid recognised, but in this case in a magnitude of scale different.

'Shouldn't there be something in here?' Byrne said, as he examined the interior.

'I know what it is,' Arid replied.

'Tell me.'

'It's a metal disrupter. It'll fire a beam between the two halves that does something t' the electron structure in the metal and makes it disintegrate. I had smaller versions of it on my rig. Don't ask me how it actually works.'

'So it disrupts the integrity of steel.' Byrne traced his fingers over the curved metal surface. 'In a world of steel, this is a kingmaker.'

The screen flashed green.

A voice said, 'Authorised.'

It was the voice of Arid's mother. A slot opened above the screen, revealing a small rectangular hole. Arid looked at the pendant hanging from Byrne's hand.

His. Mother's. Voice. Arid hadn't heard it for years. Tears welled in his eyes.

But this was a horrific weapon his parents had built, and it showed they had been two kinds of people, before and after him.

This was a weapon in two halves.

Tragedy is a barrier. Life is two halves. You choose which side of it you're going to be on. The past or future. Old or new. Everyone gets the choice.

Energy flowed from one semicircle to the other, like the past to the present. It wouldn't work without both. Just like time. Or plans becoming history. You needed a *before* prior to an *after*. Without it, the after was just stuff happening without any context. Were we better people or worse? You might not like it, but your past was your anchor; you could loath it, argue about it, but you couldn't ignore it.

And there was his name on the display: ADVANCED RAPID ISOTOPE DISARRAY.

He stepped back.

Byrne dashed in and placed the key in the small chamber. It clicked perfectly. Nothing happened. He pulled it out and put it back in. Still nothing.

'Hey, evil genius, how do you get it out?' Alex shouted.

'What?' Byrne muttered.

'You can't use it here. What are you going to do, bring the enemy down here? It's obviously meant to be mobile.'

Byrne looked at Arid. 'I think she's right,' he said. 'I'll get the cyborgs to drag it out. What matters is that now it's mine. Now shut up.' He tried the key a few more times with the same lack of result. He wheeled around to glare at Arid. 'Did you do something?'

'Me? No. It ID'd me, that's all.'

'ID. It must need you.' Byrne held out the key. 'You put it in.'

'I'm not going t' be doing it any different t' you.'

'Just do it.'

Arid held out his hand. After several false starts, Byrne handed over the key. Arid stood fixed to the spot.

'I'm waiting,' Byrne said.

'I'm thinking,' Arid replied.

'Say that again?'

The boy clenched his fist around the key.

'You forget I have a gun,' Byrne reminded him.

'There are canisters of gas here. If there's a leak and y' fire the gun, we all die.'

Byrne laughed. 'I'd be able to smell a leak.'

'Not natural gas. Y' need me. Y' kill me, it'll never work.'

Byrne lowered his gun and fiddled with the grip. 'Look, kid, I don't want to kill you. There's been enough death. We fight needless, endless wars over reasons that don't even mean anything anymore. We lose family. We lose friends. None of it is right. We stand here now with another opportunity. I lost my brother. He meant everything to me, and I'd give everything to hear his voice once more. What about your parents, don't you want to know what they said? See what they were like?'

It was true. Burning deep within Arid was the desire to hear their voices once again.

Urgency crept into Byrne's voice. 'With one simple action, you can have that, and you will also allow me to bring peace to the region. See the amazing *weapons* your parents created? Your name should be revered across the land, not hushed by the lowlifes and deadbeats. This is the pinnacle of the brilliant Geiger family. Their creations will be revealed for everyone to see. And the world will bow to your family name.'

Arid had seen hints of what they'd created, and it had been amazing. He stepped forward.

But would that be learning from the past? They left it behind for a reason. They ran away from it. They had run, for reasons unknown.

But the answer could be revealed if he unlocked the thing.

But if unlocked, a horrible weapon would be unleashed.

'This is ridiculous,' Alex said. She pulled out her pistol and aimed it at Arid. 'Do it. I don't want to die of old age down here.'

Byrne sighed and raised his weapon. 'And there I was thinking we were making progress.'

Arid stood rooted to the spot. Alex and Byrne both had their weapons aimed at him, tracking his every movement.

Making progress. Tragedy is a barrier. We move from one side to the other and define ourselves as better people. The queen had said the same thing. We progress. Byrne lived in the world that wanted them before their barrier. But Arid didn't want that, and they were his parents. *I want to think of them as good. I don't want my illusions shattered.*

'I loved my parents,' he began, 'but I've moved on, had t' move on. There's no point going back. Maybe some things are better left unsaid.'

'No, that's not the way to think about it,' Byrne replied. 'You tell him, Alex. You'd love to know what your parents thought of you, how much they cared before we got rid—the queen killed them.'

Alex's eyes darted over to Byrne. 'Say that again.'

'You, when your parents were killed.'

'By the queen.'

'What? Oh yes. The queen,' Byrne responded in a distracted way.

'Say the sentence in full.'

'When your parents were killed by the queen.' Byrne shook his head. 'Don't give me grief. We had to sacrifice so much to make you.'

'You said it was the queen who killed my parents. You made me watch it.'

Byrne sighed. 'What does it matter? She's an evil cow. You've seen it. You know how she treats people.'

'But if she didn't kill my parents ... She took me in. There was no guilt, or malice. She *cared* for me.'

'Did she? Don't be a fool. She was using you, trying to get to me. Remember how it played out. Remember our plan.'

'But it was all built on the fact that she killed my parents.' Alex swung her weapon around and levelled it at Byrne. 'Tell me who did do it.'

'You are a child. You'll believe whatever I tell you. You'll believe the most ridiculous fantasies.' Byrne laughed. 'There may not even be a war at the Belt. The Colaman in his red-and-white suit who rewards children who do what they're told. And there is no cavalry. I am the power. Reality is what I say it is.'

'It was you.'

'Grow up. You're an assassin, the finest fighting machine in the west. Don't get drawn into a bog of self-pity.'

'Look what it did to my life. I did this for you. You tell me now.'

'You did it for yourself. Revenge. To reclaim your guilt.'

'No, I didn't. I did it because you told me, and I was too young to understand. You made me into this.'

'You were a command project. The tendrils that created you stretch into many interesting places. Ones you don't want to know about.'

'I don't care,' Alex insisted. 'Tell me who killed my parents.'

Arid stared into Alex's face.

'You made me live your lies,' she continued, her cool facade fracturing, 'do things I never would have done. Twisted me.'

'Grow up,' Byrne replied. 'This is war. Sacrifices must be made.'

'These canisters are super-high pressure. At fifty feet, the explosion will disorientate you. At twenty feet, it will puncture your internal organs.' Alex positioned the barrel of her pistol against the cylinder and placed her index finger on the trigger. 'At zero feet, it will obliterate everything. There will be nothing but blood.'

'You wouldn't dare.'

'It's over.' Alex spun around.

'Ella, *no*,' Arid cried.

She fired a bullet into the closest gas cylinder. The moment hung in time. She and Arid looked into each other's eyes, and he felt his heart crushed as sadness and relief resonated on her face. *I have lost, but I will lose no more.*

Arid ran. In the blink of an eye, the canister erupted.

Fire billowed out in a ball that expanded to engulf the Omen. Alex's burning image remained for a moment before evaporating in the flames. The other cylinders exploded, shaking the chamber. Fragments of the ceiling cracked and fell. The turbine burst into life, providing power to the Omen. Electricity crawled over its surface. And for a flash, an image of Arid's smiling parents was projected into the cavern, hanging in the smoke and fire. They were replaced by a word: HADRON.

Arid and Byrne were blasted across the chamber. The ceiling caved in, crushing the Omen and filling the room with a cocktail of electricity and debris. Byrne was up and running in moments.

Arid shook his head, fighting against the dizziness, coming to terms with what he'd seen. The roof of the mine cracked, the sound shaking the walls. A piece broke free and crashed down next to him. And he was off.

Byrne charged out of the mine entrance as it caved in behind him. A tumbling ball of dust and debris rolled out. Arid burst through just before the mine collapsed completely, leaving the outline of his body in the cloud.

Nikola stood leaning against a nearby barricade, resting his elbow on his sword. He was still covered in blood, but managed a brief smile.

Byrne pulled Arid in front of him and levelled the gun against his head. 'Back off or I'll kill him,' he shouted.

Nikola looked around. 'I'm not doing anything.'

'Don't try anything. I mean it.'

Nikola shrugged. 'I'm out of my jurisdiction. There's nothing legal I can do to stop you.' He peered over his shoulder. 'I reckon you've got about five minutes before the Feds get here.'

'What do you mean "legal"?' Byrne asked.

'I wasn't talking to you.'

Cameron smashed his fist across Byrne's jaw. The man twirled and crashed into the dirt. Then Anthony kicked him in the groin.

[19]

IT HAD TAKEN several days for the information to be gathered, collated and understood. Queen Bea and Frey stood out the front of the Tom Price civic hall. Both were wearing the military uniform of the *Lady Moonshine*. The council waited inside. It was going to be an epic confrontation, unlike any seen for decades.

'You okay, Mama-Bea?' Frey asked.

'Hopefully this visit will end better than the last,' the queen replied. She hesitated at the base of the steps.

'Do you have to go?'

'The game is in play. If we stop, we lose.'

'Do you need to win everything?'

'Unfortunately, yes,' the queen said. 'Believe me, there are days when I wish I could stay in bed and pull the covers over my head. But duty calls. It always calls. If I don't answer, people will die.'

'Someone else can answer.'

'If it t'were so simple. Maybe you could take over for me one day.'

'But I couldn't even escape from the *Hawkesbury*.'

'You're a teenager, Frey, not a world-conquering titan. You don't even know your mind yet let alone your skills. Have faith.

Your time will come, and you *will* be a world-conquering titan and I will burst with pride. Anyway, let the endgame commence.'

Queen Bea straightened her clothes, smoothed back her hair and strode up the stairs. The doors swung open and she entered the council hall to rousing cheers, the auditorium standing as one. She smiled and waved.

From the front of the crowd, Theo approached the queen, clapping and smiling. He nodded as he greeted her. 'It is a pleasure and a relief to see you alive. If there is anything I can do for you, please call me. I will chair the meet today so as to not tax your injuries. Let me know when you are ready.'

The queen spotted Nikola to her left and veered toward him. 'Do you go everywhere with that sword?'

'Yes,' Nikola replied.

'How do you sleep at night?'

'Carefully.'

'Indeed, don't we all these days. It is comforting to see you here. Thank you for keeping the train on the rails. I feel safe with you around.'

'I'll do what I can to help, but this is where I have to step back into the shadows. You need to be seen to solve your own problems. The last thing we all need is a rift between east and west from some misunderstood action, or an allegation of interference.'

'Understood.' The queen smiled. 'If only they knew.'

'I've learned plenty from you. You are recovering, both of you?'

The queen looked back at Frey. 'Better than new.'

Nikola nodded his respect and disappeared into the crowd, or as much as a towering warrior with a sword strapped to his back could. Within several steps, some of the older leaders who had become widows had beset him.

Meanwhile, Queen Bea found herself being crowded by a dozen wellwishers with repetitive questions. It quickly became tiresome. She signalled to Theo, who clapped his hands together to draw the attention of the assembly. The hubbub died down and the members took their seats.

'Bring forth the defendant,' Theo cried. 'Let him stand before the assembly. And, *please*, no booing this time. We are adults, even if politicians.'

Two guards hustled Byrne into the hall. His eyes were dark, and he walked with a limp. His appearance caused a stir in the audience, with a wave of whispers rolling across the talking heads. He stood in the centre of the oratory square; a space cleared among the quadrangle of assembled seating.

'Is there a representative for the defendant?' Theo glanced around. No one came forward. 'Fine. I will read through the charges.'

He quickly scanned the list and then cleared his throat. 'Mathias Byrne, as a senior officer on the *Hawkesbury* megaCity, you must be held to the highest possible standards. Although this is not a court of justice, there will be recommendations issued to the federal police for action. If warranted. Sorry, innocent until proven guilty and all that.' Theo let out a small laugh. 'Does the accused have a recognised voice to argue on his behalf?'

'I will answer for myself,' Byrne replied.

'As you wish. The assembly recognises your senior authority. This is still an informal gathering. You can interject if you feel you need to. We shall get underway.'

Theo turned to address the gathered crowd, and continued. 'Mathias Byrne, you are accused of, ten days ago on the third of August, the attempted assassination of a council head, being Queen Bea, commander of the *Lady Moonshine* megaRig, by a trained asset with the intent of attempting to destabilise the Western Alliance. This accusation is supported by witness statements. You are accused of breaking the Peace Alliance Declaration 157 and commissioning the repair and initiation of the Omen. You instructed the personnel of the *Hawkesbury* to be in breach of the PAD. You are accused of colluding with the cyborg enemy—'

'They are not the enemy,' Byrne interrupted.

'—at several times with specific dates within the two weeks, regarding the commissioning of the Omen in breach of PAD 157. You are also accused, on the first of August, of inciting fellow senior officers to break the Western Alliance. And finally, you are accused of attempting to start the Omen for your own political gain in breach of PAD 157. There is accompanying evidence, and testimonies, with each of the accusations. These are the charges laid out before me. These are traitorous acts that carry the severest penalties.'

The room went silent.

'What have you to say for yourself, and how do you plead?' Theo asked. He took his place in an ornate high-backed chair to one side of the oratory square.

Byrne cleared his throat. The assembled leaders focused their attention on him. Silence fell over the room. Once he was certain he had their attention, he began.

'I am innocent.'

'Furthermore ...' Byrne paused as the crowd exploded in a series of shouts suspended over a deep rumbling of dissent. 'Furthermore, I will show you that the opposite is true, that I am the victim of a ruthless plan to tarnish my name while tracking down a traitor. I was not the one destabilising the Western Alliance; it was Queen Bea and Hunter in an unholy coalition. They were framing me to look like the traitor.'

The onlookers erupted with outrage. Theo stood and motioned for them to calm.

Byrne continued. 'I had for some time suspected that we had a mole within the hierarchy of the Western Alliance. Our security was being breached. The enemy, I mean false alliances, knew our tactics before we engaged with them. So I set a series of tests to send out specific information to see which of it ended up with the enemy. To see where the line of collusion went. And, boy, did it go some places.'

His voice became hoarse in the dry air, forcing him to raise the volume.

'I will not address all of these charges against me because they will be redundant and irrelevant as I reveal to you the plot behind the plot. Some of these will expose a particular pattern of behaviour, and you shall see without doubt that I am merely a victim in this complex process.'

He gestured to a security guard, who handed him a glass. He took a sip of water.

'But first I shall address some of the minor allegations. In regard to the so-called asset, it was true that Alex was trained onboard the *Hawkesbury*, but she was stolen away from us by Queen Bea. It was a mistake, as they didn't know her history. Alex had always been mentally unstable since the tragic death of her parents. I can only deduce that when Arid Geiger turned up, it provoked some psychotic episode based on jealousy. The boy was a son of fond friends and was in a position to expect favour.

'Alex went rogue, not only attacking the queen, but also beginning a vendetta to track down the boy wherever he was to be found, a case in point being the surprise raid on the *Rankin*. She stabbed her adoptive mother, shot her sibling, and hunted a boy with close connections to the queen. At the time of her demise, she was clearly mentally unstable and delusional, as can be attested to by Arid Geiger, who was there and the object of her rage. I was able to interject and stop Alex's reign of terror before her major targets were assassinated. These are facts no one can refute.'

Arid squirmed in his seat. Nothing Byrne had said was incorrect as an outcome, but the information behind it was all messed up. He glanced at Queen Bea and Hunter. Both sat with impassive expressions on their faces. Not frowning. Not upset. Just listening. He didn't get it. Byrne had accused them of the worst crime and they just sat there.

'With regard to the cyborgs, we have long dealt with them,' Byrne continued. 'They have been the backbone of our maintenance operations, and have always been reliable and trustworthy. It comes as much a shock to me to learn that their endeavours have been to revive the Omen project. Perhaps this is through a renegade sect. Who knows, but they are not part of the PAD 157, and have no restrictions on their interactions with the old technology. We might not like this fact, but we cannot ignore it. For this, I cannot be held accountable. If anything, the commander of the region should have been keeping an eye on this kind of operation in particular.

'I went to the *Lady Moonshine* with the assistance of Cameron, Del and Anthony to collect gas. As I had doubts about the *Moonshine*'s alliance with the cyborgs, due to a link I shall reveal later, I wanted to make sure we removed their ability to provide any excess LNG to the cyborgs. We took several canisters, which I seized with the express purpose of destroying the Omen. An act I completed successfully. These are facts no one can refute.'

Byrne paused for another drink. Intrigue had silenced the crowd.

'As you see, my results have been in line with the expectations and responsibilities of my position. I have secured the west in the face of a threat from a terrorist, from the nefarious activities of the east, and brought safety to the region. These are my duties, and I have gladly and totally completed them. But for all these dangerous responsibilities, which I completely accept as my duties, I have been plotted against, demeaned, imprisoned. This shall be the most surprising revelation of all, and all I can say at this stage is hold onto your hats because the ride is about to get wild.'

Arid glanced around at the assembly. They were staring intently at Byrne. He was one of them, and, Arid felt, they were yearning for a way for Byrne to explain himself. Byrne resumed his testimony.

'I mentioned at the beginning that there was a mole. There are only a few possible individuals who have the contacts and authority to travel the countryside without prior approval. I needed to send out fake information to see who disseminated what. Only then could I know who the mole was, no matter how senior they were. Some ended up being killed. As is the way of war or life in such a hostile environment, unfortunate but often the result. But one managed to evade most of the traps.

'It all started to come together while tracking down a particularly notorious pirate. It had led me to Marble Bar, where I was also able to catch up with our own Theo'—Byrne gestured to the old man—'where we uncovered an unwitting spy network at the heart of the operations where Randy was the linchpin. While at Marble Bar, I saw one individual, and although I had forgotten I had sent out the tests it all fell into place. The revelation was a shock and needed to be confirmed. The individual is known to like cash, so I immediately put out some specific new information.

'I tracked the individual to Tom Price, where I saw them interact with another individual who is known to be from a hostile enemy in the east, and who has also been colluding with Queen Bea. Of this there is a witness other than myself, who I will call shortly. I saw this individual again interacting with known enemies, continually undermining the political work of the *Hawkesbury*. The question remains, why was he doing this? For an answer, we need to look at the man himself. His past, who he is. How he escaped. How he evaded the guards and soldiers and got out.'

Byrne paused for dramatic effect. 'And that individual was Commander Hunter,' he said.

And the audience gasped.

'You are charging your own commander with these crimes?' Theo interjected.

Byrne nodded. 'For a decade, our interactions with Queen Bea have been tense and terse. We fight for the same water leases. Our own commander, Hunter, once lived under her protection. I had suspicions about how he had escaped so easily. I believe Hunter was caught and turned by the *Moonshine*, becoming their man on the inside. These coincidences, instances of him turning up at the exact time that there was a *Moonshine* representative nearby, literally fill pages. Hunter caught Arid Geiger. Why didn't he hand him over to me for questioning? That is my responsibility. So I say spy, murderer, betrayer of the people. Are we ready?'

The audience went quiet and visibly leaned in toward the speaker.

'I call a witness,' Byrne called out. 'Arid Geiger.'

Arid's eyes went wide. The assembly gasped and various strains of disapproval crawled through the crowd. Did he have to go? Could he make a break for the door? Before he had a chance to decide, a heavyset lady in a *Hawkesbury* uniform appeared next to him. She grabbed him by the collar and dragged him to the square in front of the assembly. Thankfully, he was stationed on the opposite side to Byrne.

'Please, be calm,' Byrne said to the crowd. 'I'm sure you're aware of the name, but Arid is not his parents. Judge him on his own merits.'

Arid stood in the dock and looked up nervously at the rows of stern faces. In the centre of them he noticed Nikola, sitting still, leaning forward and staring intently at the queen.

Theo stood and cleared his throat. 'Please raise your hand and honour your faith or personal integrity.'

Arid swallowed nervously. A bead of sweat trickled down his temple. 'I will tell the truth.'

Byrne started. 'We met at the Battery. Did you meet a Captain Nikola Tasman there?'

'Er, yes.'

'With the cyborgs.'

'Sort of. They had captured us—'

'Capture. Cyborgs. We have never heard of this action from them before.'

'Yes, but Nikola—'

'The Battery was where I rescued you and from there I took you to Marble Bar, correct?'

'Sort of. But I'd like t' clarify about Nik—'

'When we were at Marble Bar, did we see Commander Hunter there?'

'I guess so.'

'He was walking somewhere. Where to?'

'Er, Mad Clapping Harry's Cafe, I think.'

'And what a fine establishment that is. And one,' Byrne said, turning back to the audience, 'where there is the only payWave point in the town, in fact, for some considerable distance. And I believe one of the evidence submissions was a receipt from the cyborgs for a large sum of money on that day. As you are no doubt thinking, this is not just a coincidence. And this is where we move on to Tom Price. There was a meeting conducted between Captain Tasman and Hunter. Arid, you brought these men together?'

'Yes.'

'Who asked to meet who?'

'Er, Hunter asked t' meet the captain.'

'And what did they talk about?'

'I literally have no idea. It all seemed like gibberish.'

'Such as a code?'

'I don't know. Maybe.'

'Why would Captain Tasman wish to meet with Hunter? Especially as he had been dealing with Bea. They are enemies, we're expected to believe.'

'Dunno.'

'Did they ask you to leave?'

'Yeah.'

'Why would they ask you to leave if they were speaking in code? Unless they knew you had a connection to the queen. You're just a boy with no understanding of the political world around him.'

'Hey!'

'It might be a hard truth, but you have not grown up in it. Nor have you grown up.'

There were a few titters from the audience. Arid gave them a frown.

'Then, at the Omen,' Byrne began.

Finally, thought Arid. Now we can set the record straight.

'Did Alex try to kill us both?'

'Not technically—' Arid started.

'Did she not aim a gun at the canisters while in a fit of rage and threaten to fire?'

'Er, I ... sort of.'

'That would be a yes. And did she not seem dangerously upset?'

'I believe she was upset at you.'

'All of us. She didn't seem too happy with you. And did I not, through the use of clever rhetoric, get her to destroy the Omen, burying it forever in the depths of the Battery?'

'Er, I'm not sure that I would say—'

'Was the Omen not destroyed?' Byrne demanded, interrupting the sentence.

Arid was quiet for some time before responding with a slow, 'Yes.'

Byrne clapped his hands together. 'Thank you for your honesty. You can go.'

Arid's mouth fell open. He looked desperately at Theo, the queen, even Nikola. The academy warrior was the only one who moved, offering him a small shrug.

Byrne continued. 'Hunter was the one who trained Alex. He was the one who worked with the cyborgs and paid them. He was the one who leaked information about the *Hawkesbury*'s movements, handing us continual defeats while he sat by playing in the *Rankin*. And when I got close to discovering all this, Queen Bea set about undermining my authority with rumour, speculation and disgraceful acts. Her actions are the ones that need to be investigated. She is the real villain here.'

Theo stood. 'I think we need a point of clarification here. Hunter only lived under the queen's protection as a prisoner. We are aware of his escape and what it cost. And it has taken nearly two decades for a modicum of peace to exist between the two of them. They even had a minor skirmish recently. General communications are handled through third parties.'

'How did he escape from the *Moonshine*?' Byrne asked. 'Are the guards that useless? I think not, although three teenagers were able to steal the gas canisters from under their noses. I was chasing a mole, someone who is intent on bringing down the entire Western Alliance. And on discovering this, Queen Bea has turned everything on its head, retroactively fitting actions to plans. She is *the* only one in a unique position to protect Hunter. Her connections from the east have obvious and questionable ties to local felons. Let us not forget she was a friend of the Geigers, the creators of the Omen.

'And so I show you, hiding in plain sight, an evil plan and a person who is a liar, manipulator, someone who wants to bring you all down, and make you bow to her might.'

Then Queen Bea took the stage. She looked over at her friends based in the gallery and gave them a wink. A quiet room. A sip of water. She clutched her stab wound, wincing. Breathe.

'I may not be as dramatic as Byrne has been, but I hope to demonstrate through plain evidence and dull facts that there is no plot behind the plot, save one. And that is Byrne's manipulation of many individuals, like a skilled juggler or plate spinner, to his own ends. I shall correct some of the allegations made, based on fact and detailed research.'

She paused for a moment.

'We have endured continual attacks from Byrne. His agenda has been personal more than political. He is a man who would vanquish enemies. And when you crave power, everyone who does not bow to you is an enemy.'

'It shows strength,' Byrne called out.

'To imprison your own people?'

'You mean rivals, usurpers, criminals.'

Theo stood and said, 'Let's calm down. Interjection does not mean argument.'

Bea continued. 'He claims this information has been fabricated to match life. But it is, in fact, the opposite. You will find that this evidence, sadly and uninterestingly, reflects reality. His story has been well crafted. His plan has been intricate, but I have looked beneath the obvious and looked for the weaknesses, the human frailties that affect us all. The mind is not stronger than the heart. Those emotions tied to the heart will override the sharpest of minds. Who of us, when in love, has not done the most ridiculous of things? Who, when faced with tragedy, has not changed? So, what weaknesses did I find?'

Bea let the moment linger, casting her eyes over the audience and resting them on her team. 'I call as *my* witness ... Arid Geiger,' she said.

Y' got t' be kidding me. Arid lowered his head. Today was going to be a bad day.

The guard again appeared next to him. He waved her away. 'Yeah, yeah. I know the way.'

'Please raise your hand and honour your faith or personal integrity,' Theo repeated.

'Yeah, I'll tell the truth if y' let me.'

'Hopefully the full truth this time,' Bea said, as she gave him a cursory smile. 'Let's dive straight in. Did you see Byrne at Marble Bar?'

'Er, yes. He was our lift—'

'Just answer the questions. No more than that. Did he meet with anyone there?'

'Yes.'

'Do you know who they were?'

'Frey said it was Theo and Randy.'

'Did Byrne meet with anyone else?'

'Er, he got attacked by Captain Jozee.'

'Hopefully he didn't lose. Anyone else?'

'No one else attacked him.'

'I mean, did Byrne meet with anyone else?'

'I don't know about meeting, but I heard him say 'Hunter' then he chased after, er, Hunter,' he said, indicating the man in the audience.

'And when was this?'

'Just as we were sort of leaving.'

'So it wasn't the main reason he was there?'

'No, he was sort of surprised by it.'

'What happened then?'

'Er, they disappeared down the road.'

'Did Hunter head off to Mad Clapping Harry's?'

'No.'

'So, as far as you are aware, Byrne could have been the one who went to Harry's.'

'I guess so. Wait. I saw him with something. A small black card with blue circles on it.'

'Do you know what kind of card it was?'

'No.'

'Are you sure?' Bea pressed.

'That's what I said,' Arid replied.

Bea reached into a pocket and pulled out a black card with blue rings at one end. 'Did it look like this?'

'Yeah.'

'It's a payWave card. You saw Byrne with a payWave card?'

'I guess so.'

'But I suppose we cannot conclude that he was seen with a rare payWave card in one of the few places a point is located on the day it was used. It could be a coincidence.' Bea raised her eyebrows to the assembly. 'Moving on to Tom Price, did you see him there?'

'Of course' Arid confirmed. 'It was the big meet—'

'And what did you see?'

'I overheard a meeting he had with'—he glanced over at Byrne—'Randy.'

The movement from Byrne in response was nearly imperceptible. A narrowing of the eyes. A slight twitch.

'And what did they discuss?' Bea asked.

'They were organising where t' get enough gas t' power the Omen,' Arid replied.

'To power it?'

'That's what I said.'

'Not destroy it?'

'No.'

'Were any promises made?'

'No. Only threats. He said that if y' don't help, yer the enemy, and when he was leader he wouldn't forget who his friends or enemies were. Then Byrne punched Randy in the face. Or something like that. There was blood.'

'Finally, we shall discuss Alex.'

It seemed wrong to Arid let the last memory of Alex be of the twisted and abused character. 'Ella.'

'If you wish. She—Ella—took you to the Omen?'

'Yes.'

'Why?'

'She said Byrne wanted me t' start up the Omen. She said she'd done those things and now she was finished. She wasn't some assassin; she was a broken person. She never had a chance.'

Bea nodded. 'We don't need any more. Thank you, Arid.'

His emotions erupted. The look in Ella's eyes as she detonated the canisters still haunted him. The thought process was alien. He looked out at the assembled leaders.

'No, it's not enough,' Arid said. 'I must say this. I don't think she was bad. She'd been tortured by Byrne t' be something she wasn't. She'd been twisted by lies. Trained by deceit. It wasn't her fault who she was. Look, I'm not a hero. I have no superpowers, or incredible bravery, or a giant sword. All I can do is tell the truth, and she deserves a better memory.'

'I'd say that is the biggest hero of all,' Bea agreed. 'You can go.'

Arid stood for a moment, his feelings tumbling inside. Had he said enough? Bea had changed; her shoulders had lifted, like in some kind of relief. As he turned to return to his seat, she commenced her conclusion.

'On the *Lady Moonshine*, we do not wish to interfere with the politics of other factions, but this is clearly a manoeuvre from Byrne to usurp his own commander and blame it on us. We know he was dealing with known pirates. We have a record of a funds transfer to the cyborgs for Omen services. We have witnesses seeing him meet with other megaRig leaders and behave in a threatening manner. We have the cultivation of a terrorist asset that was placed within my crew for one and only one task. And we have the eradication of that asset to remove the link back to him. And to tie all this together, we have one single person who was there for all of it. The pieces are there. Taken individually, these actions could be innocent, but when added together they provide a complete picture of his intent.

'But let us argue that it is all mere coincidence. How do we find our proof? At the heart of all this is the desire for power and greed, and the blindness they create. And that is where we find the ultimate proof. Where the failings of man are gathered.'

Bea paused, looked down at her feet and took a deep breath. 'It's time to be frank and honest. Hunter and I have a difficult relationship. It may never heal. But we operate in a world where trade is vital to survival. We have agreed to communicate with each other on trade via independent third parties. Captain Tasman is one of those third parties. Byrne wishes to see an alternative truth in this interaction. His desire for a world where he is king and everyone is out to get him has tainted his perception of reality. Byrne did not go to these places to spy, to check how his plan played out, but rather to pursue his own agenda and undermine those around him who were strongest. I don't mix with these people because the *Moonshine* takes all my time, but the information about rival megaRigs' political structures are relayed to me.

'Hunter's first officer, Major Maria Tyson: killed. His second in command, Major Danny Latter: jailed. And Hunter is implicated in this. Threatening behaviour to other megaRig leaders. What a coincidence. Beyond his actions, we have the intent of a man who will stop at nothing to achieve ultimate power. Greed.'

'Stop these lies,' Byrne shouted. 'Yes, I did these things, I was in these places, but the data about what was done there has been changed to create this story. I am trying to protect the west, bring it together.'

The crowd bristled. They weren't buying it.

Byrne's expression soured. 'Once you bow to me, you will all be much safer. I, and I only, am the one who can bring peace. I have the best intentions here: your safety, your prosperity. How can you fools not see that?'

Theo stood, waving his hands at the rising dissent from the assembly. 'Do we need to vote on progressing the accusations to the federal police?'

'Stop this,' Byrne shouted. 'You'll be sorry. The truth will come out.'

The guards dragged him away, his threats ringing out.

Theo continued once the ruckus had died down. 'And I believe I can speak for the majority here and declare Queen Bea as the rightful commander in chief of the Western Alliance.'

Bea laughed. 'I don't know about rightful, but I will take the mantle for now. Until someone better comes along.'

The councillors behind Arid stood and clapped.

'It's amazing that Hunter doesn't strike her dead for what she did to his family,' one said.

The other replied, 'Politics is a complex and long game. Who knows what his intent is?'

Bea scanned the audience. She saw Nikola nod to her as he made his way to the exit. He'd seen the outcome, been the independent witness, and could relay what had happened to the command in the east.

Then she saw Theo sitting with a glum expression, but he brightened as they made eye contact. He jumped over to her.

'I was behind you all the way,' he said, swinging his fist in a small playful arc. 'Just playing devil's advocate.'

Bea gave him a stern look. 'You're meant to say that before your statement, otherwise you look like a jerk.' Theo's face fell. She stroked his face with a soothing hand. Her eyes were ice. 'I'm sure we can sort it out. Don't let me detain you.'

Arid stood and watched the assembly dissolve.

Frey moved next to him. 'You all right?' she asked.

'This is not how I expected the whole thing to go down,' Arid replied. His mood soured. The process felt flawed. Something inside of him felt he'd been manipulated. What he'd said wasn't what had been heard.

'Politics is a complex game.'

'But they are evil. I expected so much more. They were no better than the pirates. I lost everything and they only made things worse.'

'You can't expect them to solve all your problems. You have to understand that they're people, not gods.' She paused and then added quietly, 'Except for Nikola. They were once like you and me. Now, they're still like you and me, only bigger.'

Then the screaming started.

[20]

THEO'S FACE REMAINED smiling, but his eyes changed, opening wide at a disturbance behind the queen. Shouting came from the foyer first. Then sharp bursts of automatic fire. More shouting in an elevated and urgent tone. Screaming.

The attack was so brazen, no one knew how to respond. Two masked attackers with machine guns appeared and fired into the roof. Shells sprayed across the floor. People dove for cover.

Another man charged through, pushing aside the guards, and ran up to throw his arm around the queen. Dragging her backward.

Bea's face morphed into disbelief as she tipped backward. She twisted, but the man rolled with her movements, keeping her off balance.

One of the masked attackers pulled out a canister, ripped off the attached ring and threw it across the floor. Smoke billowed out as it bounced, engulfing the room and obscuring the entrance. When it cleared, the queen was gone.

'Someone has kidnapped the queen!' came a shout.

'Where can he go?'

Arid waited quietly for the audience to move out. He'd learned a few things about hiding in plain sight over recent days. He watched the crowd cram together as they hurried out the narrow doorway. No one paid him any attention as he squeezed out, including the two cleaners with odd-fitting uniforms and hats pulled down low over their faces.

He watched the cleaners emerge from the cleaning closet and track along the wall. They walked briskly and mixed in with the crowd, one dragging the other. Arid's feet followed without him thinking, and he ducked out of view when the front one turned and looked back.

It was Byrne.

Outside, the two figures turned left and followed the pavement to the edge of the building and into the carpark. Byrne tried several roller hatches before he found one that opened. There was a brief moment of defiance from the queen before he whacked her across the temple with his gun.

The diplo-roller raced out of the carpark, the queen staring out the window at Arid as it passed by. He chased after the vehicle, but it was gone in a puff of steam. He turned back to the carpark.

'You need a hand?' Cameron gave him a wave from the door of the carpark.

'Do you know how t' hotwire one of these things?'

Cameron laughed. He searched through the remaining rollers until he spotted an appropriate one, kicked the hatch, slipped inside and pulled open the dash. 'Override the ignition. Easy.'

He pushed the start button and the igniters burst into flame. The heat exchangers bubbled as the intense fire boiled the water. Cameron stepped back and motioned for Arid to get inside. 'All yours. And it'll be quicker than that piece of junk Byrne is in.'

Frey came running up. 'Arid, they've got Mama-Bea.'

'I know,' he replied. 'I'm trying t' do something about it. You go tell the others he's in a diplo-roller, and that I'm chasing.'

'Be careful,' she said.

'I will.'

'She's more than a queen, she's my mother.'

'Oh, I thought you meant me.'

'That, too. Good luck.'

Frey quickly hugged him, which took him by surprise. Cameron slammed down the hatch and Arid sped away.

Byrne planted his foot on the accelerator and shifted up a gear. The furnace screamed as the steam exploded into the engine. The roller raced through the countryside, putting some distance between it and the town. Ahead was a small former battlefield, the location of a brief and ancient battle between two unknown factions.

Out of nowhere a roller with Arid at the controls pulled alongside. Byrne drove with one hand while the other kept his TEER trained on the queen. Byrne wrenched down on the right side of the steering wheel, and his roller smashed into Arid's. Metal screamed as the two vehicles tore into each other.

Byrne broke free. His roller rocked to the side and spun off, with him fighting the controls. A dinocroc lay sleeping and he crashed into it, tearing strips of flesh from its side. The creature reared up on its hind legs and howled. Its body thrashed, then it took off after the roller, limping badly. Byrne veered out of the creature's path and back toward Arid. The croc tried to turn after Byrne's roller, but the injury limited its movement, which ended as the creature twisted and fell as it charged forward, tumbling and coming to a rest. It thumped its tail into the ground.

Byrne pulled up alongside Arid and swerved several times. Each time, Arid steered away. 'Open the window,' Byrne screamed.

Bea cranked down the pane and hot air streamed in. Byrne aimed the TEER, steadying his hand as the roller bumped over the rough terrain. He fired.

Arid stamped on the brakes, and his roller veered to the side. But it was too late. The controls went haywire as the electrical beam from Byrne's TEER phased through the vehicle, with the dials spiking out to maximum and sparks flying out. The roller lurched from side to side, its steering circuits corrupted by the blast. It hit a hill and launched into the air, then crunched down into the soil. The axle on his roller bent, causing his vehicle to veer into Byrne's. The two smashed together. Sparks flew from both.

Byrne lost control of his roller and ploughed into the wreckage of an ancient sweeper. The front of the roller crumpled in as it bent around the leading edge of the other vehicle.

Arid's roller then dangerously tumbled before coming to rest on its side.

Byrne and Queen Bea pulled themselves out of the vehicle's remains, both covered in blood. Byrne checked the TEER; it was dead. He threw it away, pulled out a pistol from his belt and pushed it into the queen's back. 'Move it,' he ordered.

'To where?' she replied. 'We're now in the middle of nowhere.'

'I need height. See where we actually are.'

'You can go, I'll stay here.'

'Don't get smart with me.' He pulled her backward roughly, forcing her up the side of the sweeper.

Arid's hatch was jammed shut. Boiling water dripped down onto his head. He could hear a faint hiss. The ignition canisters were leaking. If there was a flame or spark anywhere in the cabin it would blow, and he would be pasted against the glass. He could even suffocate if he wasn't out quickly.

He kicked up, slamming his boot into the door. Fragments of debris rained over him each time he planted his foot into the metal. Stars rolled across his vision. After several more kicks, the hatch opened upwards: an egg cracking open. Light streamed in, catching the dust suspended in the air. Every part of him ached. Hands on either side of the opening. Lift. Clean air filled his lungs. The engine continued to tick over, spluttering in neutral with a steady stream of steam venting from the exhaust. He leapt out, landing heavily on the sand as the leaking water spread out and turned it to slush.

Byrne's roller had severe denting on all surfaces and sat still, smoke and steam coiling up from the ruptured furnace. It was dead. Arid saw Byrne drag Bea on top of the sweeper, then scan the horizon for any other approaching vehicles.

Arid looked up from the ground. Being so much lower than Byrne put him in a weak position. An old drilling rig sat to his left. He climbed the structure and checked the motor. It looked to be in working order. He fired up its diesel engine and the rig's drill hammered into the ground. It spun and pounded away, setting up a consistent beat. Arid swung off the side of the frame, holding on with one hand, and whistled.

Byrne spun, dragging the queen around in front of him, and stuck his pistol against her shoulder. They scrabbled on the roof, fighting for grip on the smooth and sandy surface.

Arid and Byrne stared at each other across the expanse. The silence was punctuated by deep thuds that vibrated the ground.

'Mathias, it's over,' Arid said.

Byrne wiped the sand from his eyes and blinked, a mixture of grit and blood. 'Only for you and Queenie.'

'People are coming. Let the queen go and give yerself up.'

'You're a kid. You don't tell me what to do. Get out of my face.'

Dust rose on the horizon. The various colours of the approaching vehicles took shape, forming in a line.

'What on earth is that noise?' Byrne said.

'It's the dinocroc smashing its tail into the ground,' Arid replied. 'It does that when it's angry.'

'Thanks for the biology lesson. Now, give me your roller.'

'Really? I don't think mine's in working condition, either.'

Byrne shifted uneasily on the roof of the sweeper. His options were limited. 'You're a smart kid, you can get it going.'

'Why would I do that?'

'We could work great together and reshape the land. You and

me. Remember, I wasn't the one who turned you in. I didn't accuse you of anything. When you said you were innocent, I was the one who believed you. Look at what your life has become, what you lost, and ask yourself what they did for you.'

'Don't listen to him, Arid,' Bea called out.

'Shut up,' Byrne screamed, shaking her violently.

'I'll admit it's been eye-opening,' Arid replied.

'You see. I knew you would see sense.'

Arid thought about the confrontation. Does the action define the person, or the intent? If bad people do good, does that make them good? Or does it make people complicated? People need to be allowed to change. His parents, the queen, they'd all changed. Although they had done bad, they had understood that it was wrong and had walked away. Faced with tragedy, they'd had a change of heart. Most people needed a reason to change. Your actions after the choice defined who you were.

A caterpillar dies. A butterfly is born. But they are not the same thing.

'No. Yer words are lies,' Arid answered. 'Yer desire for power is without bounds or conscience. You are, and will always be, who y' are.'

Byrne shouted in rage. 'You think the queen is so innocent? Remember what she did to your parents. You're a fool if you let that memory go.'

'We're all allowed t' change. Sometimes we're forced t' change, but we can't be afraid of it. The bravest thing I've done is let go of the past. And the strongest I've been is when I realised I needed help. That didn't weaken me, it defined me, and I'm better for it.'

The approaching vehicles were getting closer, with the *Moonshine* prominent among them. They were moving fast. Arid wondered how the *Moonshine* would be able to stop.

Byrne tightened his grip around Bea's throat and quickly fired a shot at Arid before bringing the gun back to his prisoner's head. Arid leapt for cover, landing on a piece of metal sticking out of the ground. He cried out in pain and clamped his hand on the injury.

'You're not so clever once you're outside metal,' Byrne shouted.

'Or y' missed what I've actually done.'

Byrne hesitated, glancing around at the surroundings. Vehicles were stopping at a distance and watching the confrontation. But the *Moonshine* wasn't stopping; it was pounding straight ahead.

'You're bluffing.'

'Look behind you,' Arid said.

Behind Byrne, swarming over the ground in an undulating carpet of legs, charged a sea of stick crawlers, their clicking finally audible over the humming of the vehicles.

Arid jumped back into his roller and slammed the hatch closed. The crawlers tumbled over each other, forming a wave out of their sheer numbers. The clicking became a racket that rose like the sound of a saw as they crested up to eye level.

The *Moonshine* thundered onto the scene. Byrne snapped his head back in time to see the rig's rescue claw clip around the queen. But the crawlers were already on them. Byrne leapt for safety.

As soon as the claw's tips touched, Bea was wrenched away, her limbs flapping like a rag doll's. A crawler leapt after her, piercing her leg with its claw. It stabbed its other pincer into her leg rapidly as she was reeled toward the *Moonshine*.

Byrne landed heavily on the ground. Struggling to his feet, he dashed toward the remains of the screamer. The wave of crawlers hit him, mowing him down like a harvester. The screaming lingered.

Greyson shifted his weight and readied, judging the speed of the claw's cable as the motors spun in. Bea sailed in through the recoil point and landed in his heavy arms, and he spun her away and into the rubber wall. The crawler was snatched away by another guard, blood spraying out of the queen's leg. The crawler turned in the guard's hands and stabbed into his chest, coating Greyson with more blood. The pain made the guard howl as he pushed the creature away. It scuttled around, ready to attack its next victim.

Greyson stamped his foot on the giant insect until it crunched, and its legs stopped flailing.

The queen's impact had left an imprint in the soft material of the wall, her arms outspread. She collapsed as Frey ran toward her. Medical staff closed in and helped the queen to sit. They prepared a stretcher and placed a clamp around her leg.

Bea wrapped her arms around Frey and pulled her close. 'Good work. Don't let me forget that you're my favourite.'

'And you're mine.'

'I'd like to say that today has been a really horrible day.' Bea smiled as she hugged Frey even tighter. 'Greyson, bring in Arid. There is much to discuss.'

The guards were rough with him again. Arid didn't understand why. Didn't he just save the queen? And the day? And everything? But they'd pushed him around and made fun of him and shoved him back in another small, dark room. As if he hadn't been in enough.

But this time, no jail cell. Arid was back in the class-B room.

But it was still four walls and no sky. Just a different kind of cell. And the door was locked. He did enjoy the bed, though. And the cold water was dispensed as easily as turning the tap.

Greyson knocked on the door. 'The queen will see you now.'

'What if I don't want t' see her?'

'Then you're a braver man than me. Come on.'

Medics were still attending to Bea as Arid entered the command level. She sat in her command chair, reading a thick document with pen in hand. She wore a large pair of glasses. Both legs were bound in thick bandages. A set of crutches rested against her chair. She fended off the occasional intrusion from a doctor. As Arid entered, she handed the document to Suzie and ordered everyone to leave.

'Please sit, as I cannot stand,' Bea requested. She removed her glasses and placed them in a small container.

'I prefer t' stand.'

'Of course.' She moved a pile of paper from in front of her to the side. 'You are a hero. Well done. You were everything we hoped you could be.'

And she continued to say nice things. But it was just a wash of lies, because it's what was needed for everyone to believe in her. It was one of those moments where Arid could finally sit back and accept something good, or open his mouth and ruin everything.

'Y' lied t' me,' he said finally. Then he lowered his head. One of these days he'd get it right.

Bea sighed and patted the seat next to her. Arid stood defiant for a few moments, but eventually capitulated and lifted himself onto the wide ceremonial chair. She turned on the seat, folding her leg under her knee, which caused her to wince, and rested the side of her head against the back of the chair. That simple move knocked years off her, Arid thought, adding a vulnerability that he assumed rarely appeared. Even when being attacked by a mutant monster with a gun held to her head.

'I'll explain,' she began. 'We live in complex times. Our survival is at risk from people who have greed and power as their goals. I know this to be true, because I was once one of them. But things change. We play a smarter game. Pieces are in play to protect our safety. As such, I have people placed in various teams to monitor the situation and alert us to danger. Hunter is our inside man. If he is discovered, then our tactical advantage is lost. We must protect him at all costs. He must be seen as honest and trustworthy. Byrne was onto him, collecting evidence against him. And he was getting close.'

'But how do y' know that if y' were being watched?' Arid said. 'Unless y' had someone inside telling y' that your inside man was being—'

Bea patted his leg. 'Better let that thought go.'

Arid nodded and sighed.

'Understand this, Byrne *was* tracking Hunter. But also setting up his own meetings as cover. He was a resilient man. Not overly cunning. But determined. Hunter was at these places to hand over info to our contacts. But with Byrne breathing down our necks, we needed a new piece in play. Something that undermined his actions and could relay them from our point of view.'

'What?'

'We were switching the evidence around to show that Hunter was following Byrne, who was colluding with the enemy and planning to seize power of all the megaRigs.'

Arid scratched his head. 'That seems awfully complicated.'

'Anyone who thinks politics is simple is a fool,' Bea replied. 'War without death is a complicated game, especially with people like Byrne, who is happy to deal that card. It really was the only way. Even then, there were no guarantees. We had to trust that you would be the person we hoped you were.'

'We're meant t' be the good guys. We won by lying.'

'In the end, we won. There were minimal casualties. That's what good guys are meant to do. Overcome adversity.'

'Not at all costs.'

'I can tell you, the cost of losing would have been a lot higher. It really would have been at all costs. Now, we'll be safer together.'

'Yer forming a treaty?'

'Yes.'

'But y' said y' didn't want one.'

'Obviously not with Hunter. We can't let the illusion break. And I certainly didn't want one under Byrne. With me in control'—she cocked her head to one side—'things will be different. We have the illusion of competition with Hunter, and we will continue to spar. People will have a sense of purpose. Exciting times are ahead.'

'But people will die. They don't know y' have some phoney war. They think it's real.' Arid shook his head. 'Yer just a bunch of intertwined snakes. In one breath you say y' won't form any treaty, then in the next y' do exactly that.'

'There are differences, and I don't expect you to understand.

But we got to the right ending.'

'I'm not even sure if I'm on the right side. You endangered everyone, yourself—*me*.'

Bea's eyes remained dark; her face impassive. 'Sorry.'

'But you're not,' Arid insisted.

She shrugged in a not-unsympathetic way. 'It's complicated. Wars and disasters have devastated us. We live like this now. I spoke with Nikola, and they have cities in the east that are continually attacked. The cost has been immense. We are mobile. We don't fight like we used to. But it has come at a cost. We can't simply say build a wall and expect all the problems to disappear. Walls aren't that hard to get over, under or through, for the determined. We wrap ourselves in cities of metal, yet the greatest battles are fought with the least protection. The truth rips down the barricades. To face the truth, you can only stand alone.'

'Everything he said was true. Y' set him up.'

'Yes. Sort of.'

'Y' hoodwinked the council, using me.'

'Yes. Sort of.'

'I'll tell them.'

'Go ahead. The truth doesn't matter to them. Only stability and strength. Civilisation relies on progress and security. Progress can never be too far in advance. We need a long goal, which only we know. For them, we offer a tomorrow slightly better than today. And they will be happy.'

'So that's what all this was about?'

'Yes.' She paused and smiled. 'Sort of. We knew there was a potential assassin, but no idea who. You were able to draw Alex out, which was helpful but it revealed a deeper problem. We have a spy. And that is far worse.'

'A spy is worse than an assassin?'

Bea nodded. 'I'm the only victim for an assassin, but a spy is disastrous for my entire population. Which is now quite vast.'

'So, do y' know who the spy is?' Arid asked.

The queen simply smiled.

Arid had been made an offer. A home. He could have his own class-B room, access to everywhere in the mech, and even a career path, whatever that was. It sounded like a way of crashing slowly, emotionally and physically. But the bed was soft. He closed his eyes and drifted off into sleep.

He woke to another knock on the door. Did anyone get sleep around here? It was Frey.

'There's a party up on the viewing deck,' she said.

He rubbed his eyes. 'What?'

'We're celebrating. Mama-Bea is the leader of the entire Western Alliance. You have to come.'

'Do I?'

'Always.'

'Yeah, all right. I'll be right along,' he said, rubbing his eyes again. 'Are y' going?'

'I don't know. I've got a few things to do before I can party.'

Arid smirked. 'Yer not much of a warrior princess.'

'The first part is the important bit. I looked into the mirror and decided who I wanted to be.' Frey gave him a casual salute that bordered on offensive.

He sat back on the bed.

The world was complicated. People said one thing and did something else. Two weeks ago, things seemed so much simpler. You drilled for water. You sold the data. And he had a new word in his life, which obviously meant everything, but with no context or understanding it was incomprehensible. *Hadron*. He suddenly felt out of his depth.

Some time later, Arid walked the decks, clearing his thoughts. He'd stared into his mirror for some time. As Frey had said, you need to face your reflection and work out who you want to be. The mirror doesn't lie.

Who did he want to be? Who the hell was he?

Nearly the all of the *Moonshine*'s occupants were celebrating on the upper decks, drinking, being loud, watching the fireworks. It was time to make a decision. And the decision was … to go.

Now was the time. If he could get his dowser working just enough for it to move, even if it had a limp, he could be gone. A soft bed was nice, but not as nice as your own. On the *Moonshine*, they'd want to make a big thing out of him being a hero; he'd be pretending to be someone he wasn't, like the queen. She knew who she was, so she knew it was pretend. But he had to think about everything he'd learned. If he knew where he fitted in, maybe that would help.

Was he part of Cameron's group? Was he to be a hero? Arid didn't know. Maybe it was okay to belong to none of these groups, to be his own gang. A gang of one. A me party. At least there would be no leadership challenges.

He made his way down to the lower deck. It really was deserted. The next floor was the quarter store. His dowser was there. This was his last chance to turn back. No. He opened the hatch and lowered himself down the stairs, keeping as quiet as he could.

The corridor seemed longer than possible. In the confines of the lowest levels of the *Moonshine*, the shiny black walls disappeared to an infinity point in the dim lighting. The illusion was broken when a guard appeared with a torch, wandered to the end and turned the corner. Arid's heart thumped in his chest.

The queen's offer had been good, but four walls were still a prison when you couldn't steer them. He needed the open spaces of the desert to think about things, to think about who he was and, more importantly, who he wanted to be.

The damage to his dowser from the confrontation with the *Hawkesbury* was still being repaired. A temporary wall had been erected around the reparation work, blocking off the vehicle maintenance area. There was no lock. The door hushed open. Glancing around, Arid saw that he was still alone. Step, step, step. Door closed. Breathe.

Sweepers and rollers lined either side of the large room. He couldn't see his dowser among the collection. He became even more nervous when he couldn't find it. Had they got rid of it? A maintenance section had been marked out at the far end. He held his breath. Had they been working on it?

The maintenance section contained two partly disassembled rollers. Tools lined the wall. And at the back, something sat behind the other vehicles under a black sheet. Arid pulled the sheet free and smiled as he revealed his dowser, looking in pretty good condition.

He ran his hand over the remote-control pad sitting on the bench. It lit up as he brushed his hand over the display. The dowser's suspension engaged, and the cabin rose. He pushed forward on the display and the dowser stepped forward. It was better than he could have hoped for.

He hurried to the rear and pulled the lever to the service exit. The wall lowered, making a shallow ramp down to the outside. Warm and clean air tumbled in. Outside, the night sky was bright with a blanket of stars. Out on the plain he could breathe again.

He turned and spotted a silhouette approaching. The figure emerged into the moonlight. It was Frey, with her hands behind her back. Her wild hair had been tied back, making her look older, a changed person. Falling directly in line with her mother. Probably following in her footsteps.

'What do you think you're doing?' she asked.

'I'm getting out,' he answered. 'I don't belong here.'

'Nobody belongs anywhere, that's why we live in rigs. And we could really use a good diviner.'

Arid lowered his head. 'I can't stay. I thought about it, but I'd be living a lie. Everything I thought I knew about my family is a lie, and I'll never find out if I don't look. I don't even know who I am.'

'In a way we all lie to ourselves, creating versions to fit in. Your past doesn't need to define you.'

'But it can give me a clue to what I could be.'

'Go out and invent who you want to be. Every day is a new chance of being better,' Frey said. 'But do it here. You're among friends.'

Arid laughed. 'No one can like me until *I* like me.'

'I didn't want it to come to this. You can't go.'

'Try and stop me.'

She brought her hand in front of her. Her palms were wrapped around the grip of a TEER-2. She aimed it at him.

'You'd shoot me?'

'Of course. Now that I know I can pull the trigger. You can't go.' She lowered the gun. 'Not without me.'

He sagged with relief. 'But y' could be a spy.'

She shrugged. 'Let's find out together.'

Arid smiled. 'That would be good.'

[EPILOGUE]

Before (Eight years ago)...

Byrne stared out the window over the childcare compound. The parents were lined up along the compound wall, waiting to collect their prized miniatures. The queen's latest victory over him burnt. He couldn't believe she was such a strategic mastermind; even after everything he'd studied, luck always fell her way. If war was chess, she was playing cheat, with the rule sheet thrown away. It was time to turn the tables and even up the chances. He needed a long-term plan.

'Hunter, just a thought,' he said. 'I think we have a leak.'

'Pray, no,' his comrade replied. 'We should do something about it, post haste.'

'Yes, I agree.'

'If you have a name, I could get rid of them for you.'

'No, then she'll just get another one. I'll think about it.'

Of course, Byrne had been thinking about it for some time and had several plans already playing out. But none struck at the heart of his problems.

He continued. 'I'm thinking that if you could go down and get the children to look out for their parents for a moment, I'm going to make a little display. Tell them it's a surprise from Queen Bea.'

'As you command,' Hunter replied.

'Thank you, Commander.'

After Hunter had left, Byrne opened a concealed cupboard. His contact stood inside. 'Sorry about the hiding hole, but you understand you can't be seen here. Especially in a *Moonshine* uniform.'

The contact nodded. 'I didn't have time to change. What's your plan?'

'Your information has been helpful, but I need more, something that will hurt. Bea needs to be betrayed.'

'I only want her to want me.'

'She doesn't suspect you poisoned her partner?'

'No. Stephanna didn't love her. Not like I do.'

'Maybe we keep that narrative in your head. Are you sure Hunter escaped and wasn't let go?'

'After what she did to his family? They hated each other. He wasn't let go. So, what is your plan?'

Byrne looked out over the nursery, where the adults were queuing to pick up their children. 'Angry orphans.'

Alexandra picked up the simple stick doll, barely more than two pieces of wood wrapped in worn cloth. She twirled it in her fingers, humming to herself. The sound started as a faint hiss.

Hunter approached her. He knelt down next to the young girl. 'Hello, Alexandra,' he said. 'Can I call you Alex? Queen Bea has a surprise for you.'

The hiss became a wave of noise. Then screams. They both looked up at what was happening. A team of soldiers ran in with flamethrowers and torched the parents. The burning bodies writhed on the floor.

Hunter's words faltered as the horror sank in. 'Queen Bea has a surprise for you.'

After…

As the roof crumbled in on the Omen and Byrne and Arid fled the chamber, a concealed panel opened. @redFive stepped out.

His eyes scanned the area, looking for the target. A red outline formed around a lump on the floor. He strode towards it, the ground shaking under each step.

There wasn't much left of Alex. Most of her face. Parts of her body.

His scan revealed no life signs.

The comms unit on his arm beeped.

'Yes, Iris?'

Collect the body. It is required for the faraday project.

'It is dead', @redFive replied.

Only for now. Bring it to me.

'You want me to carry it?'

Carry? Kerry. A good choice for a name. Bring Kerry to me.

DEGRADE [291]

WELCOME TO THE EVOLUTION!

ON SALE NOW!

Book 1
The chart-topping novel that spawned the explosive multi-award winning series!

Book 3
Prepare to accelerate as our heroes go head-to-head against new enemies. Includes zombies!

Book 2
Follow the multi-award winning best-seller into new territory as dark secrets arise. Friends and enemies are not what they seem...

Book 4

The award-winning epic conclusion to the Tesla Evolution. Our hero must face his darkest moments to survive.

VISIT MARK-MYWORDS.CO TO
CHECK OUT ALL THE TITLES
FROM MARK LINGANE

FREE YOUR IMAGINATION!

Printed by Libri Plureos GmbH in Hamburg, Germany